Praise for
Dharma Kelleher

THE SHEA STEVENS THRILLER SERIES

"Kelleher keeps the reader guessing until the very end."
—Book Reviews to Ponder

"Gritty, dangerous, and hard to put down"
—Pure Textuality

"The pacing is excellent and fast-moving and the prose is tight and a pleasure to read. The protagonist is just as cool!"
—Son of Spade

"Her first book in the series, Iron Goddess, *set a high bar but* Snitch *jumps it with ease. This is money well spent. Fire up that bike and get ready for a hot trip down a highway with no speed limit."*
—Steve Shadow, author of *Savage Little Flea*

"Shea Stevens is just about the most interesting and sympathetic criminal you'll meet."
—Paula Berinstein, author of the Amanda Lester detective series

CHASER

CHASER

A JINX BALLOU NOVEL

DHARMA KELLEHER

Dark
Pariah
Press

Dark Pariah Press, Phoenix, Arizona, USA

This is a work of fiction. Names, characters, businesses,
places, events and incidents are either the products of the
author's imagination or used in a fictitious manner. Any
resemblance to actual persons, living or dead, or actual
events is purely coincidental.

Cover design by Damonza.com

Paperback ISBN: 978-0-9791730-3-5

Publisher's Cataloging-in-Publication Data
provided by Five Rainbows Cataloging Services

Names: Kelleher, Dharma, author.
Title: Chaser : a Jinx Ballou novel / Dharma Kelleher.
Description: Phoenix : Dark Pariah Press, 2018. | Series: Jinx
    Ballou bounty hunter, bk. 1.
Identifiers: LCCN 2017919477 | ISBN 978-0-9791730-3-5
    (pbk.) | ISBN 978-0-9791730-1-1 (ebook)
Subjects: LCSH: Bounty hunters--Fiction. | Transgender
    people--Fiction. | Abused children--Fiction. | Human
    trafficking--Fiction. | Women--Fiction. | Arizona--Fic-
    tion. | BISAC: FICTION / Crime. | FICTION / LGBT /
    Transgender. | GSAFD: Suspense fiction.
Classification: LCC PS3611.E386 C53 2018 (print) | LCC
    PS3611.E386 (ebook) | DDC 813/.6--dc23.

For my wife, Eileen

And for all of my transgender,
genderqueer, and non-binary siblings.

I see you.
I'm with you.
I love you.
You got this.

1

A blond woman opened the door, her swollen left eye shining with the rich color and texture of an overripe eggplant. Dried blood trailed from her twisted nose, over her split lip, and onto her faded Disney Cinderella T-shirt. Purple, green, and yellow bruises on her arms and legs documented a history of abuse.

"Jesus Christ! That looks like it hurts." I stood on her doorstep in Phoenix's Sunnyslope neighborhood, sweat beading on my skin in the late-afternoon heat. "Freddie do that to you?"

"What do you want?" Her fat lip and broken nose made it sound more like "Wuh you wuhn?" She glared at me from her open doorway, resting a hand on her hip.

"You're Vanessa Nealey, right?"

"Who wants to know?"

"Gee, I figured the words Bail Enforcement Agent printed in big yellow letters on my Kevlar vest would've given it away." I handed her my business card with a sardonic grin. "Jinx Ballou, friendly neighborhood bounty hunter. Your boyfriend, Freddie Colton, missed his court date. Big Bobby Mills at Liberty Bail Bonds hired me to pick him up. Is he here?"

Vanessa crumpled the business card and tossed it at my feet. "Go to hell, lady." She started to shut the door, but I caught it with the toe of my boot.

"Listen up, princess! You put your home up as collateral.

If Prince Charming doesn't come along with me, your bond is forfeit. Know what that means? It means no happily ever after. Liberty Bail Bonds will take your house, and you'll be on the street. Is Freddie really worth all that?"

She held my gaze for several seconds before her expression softened. "He ain't here."

"You sure about that?"

Vanessa stepped aside. "You wanna look around? Be my guest."

I was tempted to take her up on her offer, just in case she was bluffing. Technically, I didn't need her permission or even a warrant. By law, people on bail were still considered to be in custody, which was one of several reasons I quit the Phoenix PD years ago to be a bounty hunter. Too many regs. Too much paperwork.

My gut told me Vanessa was telling the truth. Freddie's Trans Am wasn't in the carport, and I didn't get the impression she was ready to lose her home just yet. "Where is he?"

"Out drinking, prob'ly."

I rolled my eyes. Sometimes my job was like pulling teeth. "Out drinking where?"

"Don't know. Don't care. We done here?"

I considered pressing her, but the sun was turning the back of my neck into bacon. I retrieved my crumpled business card and planted it in her hand. "Might want to hold onto this. If Freddie shows up, you'll want to call me. Unless you'd prefer living on the street when it's a hundred and ten out."

I turned to go, then pivoted to face her again. "Tell me something. Why do you put up with his bullshit? How many times has he been arrested for beating you up? Six, seven times at least, according to his sheet. And yet you keep posting his bail, dropping the charges, and letting him back in to do it all over again. I don't get it."

"Freddie loves me." She raised her chin with royal indignation.

"Geez, you really believe that, don't you?"

"We done here?"

"Do yourself a favor, Vanessa. Toss his crap onto the sidewalk, change the locks, and don't bail him out again. He isn't worth it."

"Mind your own damn business, lady." She shoved me away and slammed the door.

I wiped the sweat from my face and pulled my walkie-talkie from my tactical belt. "Okay, guys! Let's pack it up. Girlfriend says he ain't here."

"Bullshit!" came a gravelly reply from my associate, Fiddler. "When've you ever taken the word of a skip's girlfriend, Jinx?"

"Not usually, but this time I think she's telling the truth. Car's gone. Looks like he beat the ever-lovin' shit out of her—again—and went out drinking."

Fiddler, whose real name was Robert Dixon, was a bounty hunter from way back and was considered a legend in the business. Medical issues had forced him to give up leading his own team. But he could still guard a back door, and his prowess as a fugitive hunter was an invaluable resource. At least when I listened to him.

"I bet money he's in there hiding like the little pissant he is." Fiddler shuffled around from the backyard, his beer gut bouncing with each stride. Gray hair hung like ragged curtains from his jawline and down the back of his denim shirt.

Nathaniel "Rodeo" Kwan, an army veteran I'd been training for the past few months, approached from the east side of the house. He was a slim guy, a few years younger than me, sporting a straw Stetson on his head and a shotgun loaded with beanbag rounds slung over his shoulder. "If he ain't in there, where's he at?"

"Not sure." I led them back to my seven-year-old silver Nissan Pathfinder. Nicknamed the Gray Ghost, it featured an extensive collection of dents, scrapes, missing trim, and peeling paint that rendered it invisible when I was looking for defendants on bail who'd missed their court dates.

I hopped into the front seat and started the engine. The blast of hot air from the vents made me wince. Rodeo claimed the seat next to me. Fiddler slid into the back.

Flipping through Freddie's paperwork didn't yield any clues about his usual hangouts. I pulled out my phone and checked his social media accounts.

"Ha! You can run, but you're too stupid to hide." I held out the phone to Rodeo, showing a status update posted twenty minutes earlier. "He's at some place called One-Eyed Jack's. Dunlap and Nineteenth. I love dumb criminals, don't you?"

"One-Eyed Jack's?" Fiddler harrumphed. "Jesus! That place is a bucket of blood."

"It's that bad, huh?" I asked.

"Bad?" Fiddler laughed darkly. "Used to be called Jack's Saloon till the owner lost an eye in a bar fight. Friend of mine took a knife in the belly there for ogling some dude's girl."

"Friend of yours, huh?" I shook my head as I navigated out of the neighborhood and turned north on Seventh Avenue toward Dunlap. "You hang out with some choice people, Fiddler."

"All turned out for the best, though," he continued. "After my friend got outta the hospital, he never cheated on his old lady again."

Rough bars didn't scare me. Okay, maybe they did a little. But after my high school boyfriend's father beat me half to death on our graduation night, I'd made it my mission to learn how to handle myself. I'd trained for years in krav maga and aikido. I also practiced parkour to help me escape situations that got out of control.

In my eight years as a bounty hunter, I'd been in countless fights, often with guys much bigger than I am. I'd been stabbed a few times. Caught bird shot in the shoulder once. A moon-shaped scar on my lower back marked where a .44 Magnum slug had clipped the edge of my Kevlar vest. Typical hazards of the trade.

Nevertheless, I was the team leader. It was on me to determine how to take Freddie the abusive asshole into custody, ideally without starting a brawl with a bar full of his drinking buddies.

A plan formed as I waited for the light on Dunlap and Fifteenth Avenue to turn green. I'd tried it a few times before with mixed success, but it beat any alternatives I could come up with. "Okay, kiddos, we're going with a honey trap," I announced.

"Aw, shit!" Rodeo and Fiddler said in unison.

2

"You lost your damn mind, girl?" Fiddler growled. "Those animals'll eat you alive and ask for seconds. Besides, Conor would have my ass if I let you go into that bar alone."

Conor Doyle was my boyfriend and a fellow bounty hunter who had worked with Fiddler back in the day. Until we started dating a year ago, Conor was also my boss.

When our relationship caused friction among the other team members, I started my own fugitive apprehension crew with Conor's help.

"In case you hadn't noticed, Fiddler, this is *my* crew, not Conor's." I balked. "*I* sign your paychecks. I call the shots."

"With all due respect, Jinx," Rodeo said, "a honey pot doesn't sound like a smart strategy for this situation. Too many ways it can go sideways. I'd hate to see you get hurt."

I wiped the sweat from my face. "I'm open to suggestions."

"I say we go in with guns drawn and drag his sorry ass out of that shit hole they call a bar." Fiddler chucked Rodeo on the shoulder. "Give 'em a little shock and awe, right, soldier boy?"

"Yeah, right," I scoffed. "One of us might even get out alive to collect the bounty."

"GPS says One-Eyed Jack's is over there." Rodeo pointed at a shopping center to our left, and I slipped into the turn lane. "A more prudent approach would be to wait and grab him as he's leaving. Maybe he'll be too soused to put up much resistance by then."

I shook my head. "That could take hours. Phoenix Comicon starts tomorrow. I'm not cosplaying as Wonder Woman with bags under my eyes. Nobody wants to see that."

I turned into the shopping center lot and parked on the other side of Colton's Trans Am, out of sight of the bar's front door. The AC was only now blowing cold. I leaned in and savored the cool air on my face.

"We're going with the honey trap. So you got a choice. Either be my backup and get paid, or you can catch an Uber home and I'll keep the whole bounty for myself."

"I got your six, Jinx," Rodeo said after a tense moment of silence. "Honey trap it is."

Fiddler's phone rang. He answered it in hushed, angry tones. I couldn't make out the words but figured it was one of his ex-wives calling to bitch about something.

When he hung up, I asked, "Which one of the former Mrs. Fiddlers was that? Molly, Daisy, or Daphne?"

"Huh? Oh, uh, Daisy."

"Child support again?" Rodeo asked with a smirk.

"Something like that."

"So you in or out, Fiddler?" I turned in my seat to look at him directly. I'd been getting tired of his nonsense lately. Half the time he didn't answer his phone when I called. And when he did show up, he smelled like the crowd at a Phish concert.

"Aw, what the hell! I'm in," he grumbled. "But don't say I didn't warn ya."

"Duly noted." I pulled off my ballistic vest and handed it to Rodeo.

"I got a bad feeling about this, Jinx," Rodeo said.

"Zip it, Han Solo. We each do our jobs, no one gets hurt." I handed him my Ruger .40 caliber, my Taser, and my tactical belt. "Toss me my purse."

He pulled my black cloth purse from the glove box and

offered it to me. "But if what Fiddler says about this place is true—"

"Relax, I still have the .357 revolver in my ankle holster if things go sideways. Hand me the cuffs from my tactical belt." He did, and I slipped them into my back pocket.

"Now for a little macho-man kryptonite." With the makeup kit from my purse, I added some smoky eye shadow and thickened my lashes and eyeliner to make my eyes pop. I finished off the look with some slutty red lipstick. Normally, I was more sporty gal than girly girl, keeping the makeup to a minimum. But I could still crank up the femme when the job called for it. "How do I look?" I asked.

Rodeo studied my outfit and makeup, turning my face one way then another. He removed the band from my ponytail and let my black hair fall loose on my shoulders.

"Makeup's good—hot but not too over-the-top trailer trash. The oversized Diamondbacks jersey is okay, barely. But the dad jeans and biker boots don't exactly scream 'sexy,' especially for pulling a honey trap. A lacy blouse, Daisy Dukes, and strappy sandals would be better."

"Yeah, well, I don't have any of those with me, do I, Mr. Project Runway?"

He tilted his head, squinted, then tied a knot in the bottom of my jersey, exposing my midriff. "Gonna have to show some skin, girl." He flicked open a jackknife and pointed it at my chest.

My eyes widened. "What the hell?"

"Chill, girl." He pulled at the front of my collar with his free hand, cut a six-inch vertical slit in the top of the jersey, then folded under the newly made corners. "Just exposing a little cleavage. If you're gonna go fishing, you gotta use the right bait."

"Dude, I borrowed this jersey from my brother. Cost him a hundred bucks. He's going to kill me."

"Yeah, but now you look less like a construction worker." He popped his Stetson onto my head. "And more like a hot piece of ass."

I smirked, unsure how to take his comment. "Thanks, I guess."

"Enough with the fashion show," Fiddler grumbled. "We gonna do this or not? I got shit to do."

"Fine. I'll go in and draw Freddie out. Rodeo, I want you in front to help me muscle him into the Gray Ghost. Fiddler, guard the rear door in case Freddie makes me and bolts out the back."

I turned off the ignition, and we climbed out. The heat hit me like a blast from a hot oven. I hoped my face didn't melt before I got inside.

"All right, everybody in position. Let's take this guy down and call it a day."

Fiddler moseyed past the Subway shop at the end of the strip mall on his way around to the back of the bar. Rodeo took a position near a support column, shotgun at his side, where he watched me hustle toward the entrance.

A mountain of a bouncer sat on a stool beside the door, staring at his cellphone. As I approached, he stood and looked up. "ID?"

I handed him my driver's license. The bouncer glanced at it then looked me up and down.

A tremor of nervousness rippled through me, accompanied by a memory of me with my best friend, Becca Alvarez, on our way to see the movie *Anywhere but Here* at the dollar theater. I was eleven and still new to going out dressed as a girl. Despite Becca's reassurances that I looked very feminine, I was terrified someone would figure out I was transgender.

I had handed our tickets to the woman in the theater lobby. She looked down at me and stopped in the middle of tearing the tickets, no doubt deciding whether I was a boy or a girl.

I stood there feeling like a deer in the headlights until Becca nudged me and whispered, "Smile.."

I did. The ticket taker reciprocated. "Enjoy the movie, girls."

I brought my mind back to the present and forced a smile. The bouncer handed me my driver's license without a word and returned to his phone.

I breathed a sigh of relief and opened the heavy front door. As my eyes adjusted to the dim interior, I realized Fiddler wasn't kidding about the clientele.

A dozen or so men looking like escapees from a supermax prison sat at mismatched tables, their eyes following me to the bar. Some chatted up young women with a definite pay-for-play vibe. A couple of bikers in leather vests and bandannas crowded around a pool table along the far wall. The place reeked of stale beer and dollar store perfume, with a metallic undertone I suspected was blood.

On a flat screen mounted above the bar, the Arizona Diamondbacks were losing to the Phillies, while Keith Urban belted out a tune on the sound system.

It wasn't the first time I'd been in a place like this. Certainly not the last considering my line of work. I should've been terrified. Not the kind of joint a trans woman should linger in if she valued her life. But I was on the job, and my pulse raced with the thrill of the hunt.

3

My quarry, Freddie Colton, sat at the bar, nibbling pretzels and nursing a bottle of Bud Light. He looked to be in his midthirties, tall with muscular arms and wearing a royal-blue work shirt with his name stitched above the left pocket. His mug shot didn't do him justice. Few did, I supposed. But he was definitely easy on the eyes in a rugged, Brad-Pitt-gone-bad sort of way. A girl could get herself in trouble if she didn't know better.

His eyes were glued to the ball game on the flat screen. I hopped onto the barstool between Freddie and the TV and flashed him a polite smile before waving down the bartender.

The bartender had the face of a horse, a patch over one eye, and the scowl of a drill instructor. His cutoff denim shirt revealed a tattoo of a buxom woman waving a Confederate flag. I asked him for a Michelob.

Freddie angled his body toward me. "Jack, her drink's on me," he said in a baritone as smooth as silk. He met my gaze after a longing glance at my chest. "Don't think we've met. The name's Freddie. What's yours, sweet cheeks?"

"Hi, I'm Melody!" I cranked the pitch of my voice and my Southern accent up to bubbly bimbo levels.

"Melody? What a sexy name for a sexy babe. Damn glad to meet ya."

"Yo, honey!" a young guy shouted from one of the tables,

patting his own lap. His tongue flicked across his upper lip. "Don't waste your time with Freddie. He's old. Come party with me. I'll show you a real good time."

"Quit trying to cut in on my action, Mancini!" Freddie's face colored with indignation. "Don't mind him, Melody. He's a dumb ass."

His action, I thought. *Keep dreaming, buddy.*

"How come I ain't never seen you here before, girl?" He shifted closer to me and slipped a hand onto my thigh.

My internal warning system went off with a surge of adrenaline. I resisted the urge to twist his wrist in a pinch hold and drive the heel of my palm into his nose. Instead, I plastered a coy smile on my face. "Just moved to town."

He leaned in, inches from my face. "Oh yeah? Where from?"

"A little place in Texas no one ever heard of." His cologne smelled like an earthy blend of fine leather, moss, and musk, causing my body to respond in ways it shouldn't with a guy like him.

"What brings you to Phoenix this time o' year?"

"I'm a nurse. I start work at John C. Lincoln on Monday." It was a story I'd used before. My mother was an RN, so I knew enough medical lingo to bluff my way with a guy like Freddie.

"Is that so? Well, welcome to Valley of the Sun, Nurse Melody." His hand slipped farther up my thigh, causing the grip on my beer bottle to tighten. "You're just in time for summer."

"Yeah, can't believe it's hit a hundred and ten already and it's only June."

"I think things are 'bout to get a whole lot hotter." He squeezed my thigh, sending an unexpected wave of heat into my pelvis.

"Hotter. Yeah, uh, sure is." It came out breathier than I intended. *What the hell's wrong with you, girl? Keep your mind on the job.*

"Wanna continue this conversation in private?"

"Um, definitely."

"I'd invite you to my house, but my roommate … Not a lot of privacy, you understand."

You are such a liar, Freddie Colton. "I have a motel room just off I-17. Will that do?"

His gaze narrowed. "You ain't hustling me, are you? Cause I ain't the kind of man to have to pay for it."

"What? You think I'm a hooker? As if. I'm a medical professional." I turned to leave.

He grabbed my arm with a grip strong enough to leave a bruise then released it. "Shit, I'm sorry. Don't know what I was thinking. Forget I said it."

I gave him a side-eye and a reluctant, forgiving smile to replant the hook firmly into my prey. "Well, okay."

"That mean your offer still stands, Nurse Melody? I'd love to see your bedside manner." He set some bills on the bar to pay for our drinks.

"Sure, why not."

He held the door for me as we stepped outside into the glaring sunlight.

"My Trans Am's over here." Freddie pointed across the parking lot.

I let him take the lead as I reached for the handcuffs in my pocket. Rodeo stepped into our path, shotgun raised. "Freddie Colton, you're under arrest."

"Aw, hell no!" Freddie nearly knocked me over as he pivoted and raced back into the bar, overturning tables and chairs in his wake.

With Rodeo on my heels, I chased after Freddie, using my parkour skills to maneuver past obstacles and dodge pissed-off patrons.

I followed him down a narrow hallway, past the restrooms. He was thirty feet ahead of me when he blasted out the back door. I hoped Fiddler was ready to grab him on the other side.

When I rushed out the exit, Freddie was hightailing it down the alley with Fiddler nowhere in sight. I took off after Freddie, cursing Fiddler under my breath.

I quickly gained on him, but bringing him down wasn't going to be easy. He was a big guy, and his rap sheet told me he was a scrapper. I scrambled up a stack of wooden pallets onto a dumpster and vaulted into the air. I landed on his back like a cougar taking down an elk. He fell face-first onto the pavement and struggled to throw me off. I slapped the cuffs on him.

"Jesus Christ! What the fuck, Melody?" He tried to get up, and I put a knee in his back.

"Bail enforcement, asshole! You missed your court date. You're going back to jail."

"Like hell I am." Freddie tried to buck me off. "I'm gonna beat you bloody."

I drew my revolver and pressed it against his cheek. "Settle down, Freddie. I'd hate to have to shoot you."

"Can't collect your bounty if you kill me, bitch."

"Who said anything about killing you?" I flipped him over to face me. "I could put a .357 slug in your elbow or in your knee. Won't kill you, but it'll hurt like hell for a very long time." I pressed the nose of the revolver against his crotch. "Or maybe here. After all the times you beat up Vanessa, it's the least you deserve."

"You cunts are all alike. It's a goddamn conspiracy."

"Conspiracy! You're so full of shit." A laugh escaped my throat. "What'll it be, Freddie? You going to come along peacefully, or do I blast your junk into steak tartare?"

His eyes blazed at me until I pressed the gun harder into his crotch. "Five seconds. Four. Three. Two."

"All right, all right! I'll come along peaceful. Just don't shoot."

"Good dog." I patted him on the head and pulled him to his feet, keeping a firm grip on his arm. "I knew you'd see reason."

The pounding of boots on pavement approached from behind. I pivoted and raised the revolver only to see Rodeo rushing toward us, shotgun in hand.

"Ya got him?" he asked.

"I got him. What took you so long?"

"Got kinda crazy in there. Where the hell's Fiddler?"

Before I could answer, a mob burst out the bar's back door and headed in our direction. Jack the bartender marched in the lead with a sawed-off twelve-gauge leveled at us. Freddie's buddy, Mancini, swung a baseball bat menacingly. Others brandished an assortment of knives, broken bottles, and pool cues.

Rodeo and I pointed our weapons at the approaching throng. I held Colton by the back of his collar, using his body as a shield.

"Stop right there! Bail enforcement!" I shouted in my most commanding voice. "Drop your weapons and go back inside."

They stopped but didn't drop their weapons.

"Let him go, sweetheart," Jack said, "and we may just let you live."

"Yeah, after we fuck y'all up good," Mancini added.

"The lady told you to put down your weapons," Rodeo said. "I suggest you do it."

"Fuck you!" Mancini replied, whacking his bat on the ground.

"Which one of you wants to die first?" I aimed the .357 at Mancini. "How about you, Babe Ruth? Wanna try my fastball?"

Mancini glared at me for a few seconds, then dropped the bat with a hollow clunk that echoed in the alley. He held up his hands in surrender.

"Didn't think so. How about you, Jackie Boy? Wanna take one for the team? Show 'em what a tough guy you are?"

Jack tossed his shotgun on the ground. The other men dropped their weapons and held up their hands.

I smiled. "Good boys. Now go back inside."

With a lot of cursing, grumbling, and single-finger salutes, they complied.

Once the back door had shut, I breathed a sigh of relief and turned to Rodeo. "Well, that was exciting."

"Ya think?" He smirked, reclaimed his Stetson, and gathered up Jack's sawed-off and Mancini's bat. "Where's Fiddler?"

"Son of a bitch was gone when I got out here." I kicked a

discarded whiskey bottle, sending it smashing into the back wall of the building. "I'm going to wring his fat neck next time I see him. So sick of his bullshit."

"The other day, he told me he was working the Holly Schwartz job. Maybe that call he got was a tip. Not that it justifies him going AWOL."

The Schwartz case had been a recent news sensation. Holly Schwartz was a seventeen-year-old with a rare neuromuscular condition that left her wheelchair-bound and mentally impaired. She and her mother, Bonnie, were darlings of the charity fundraising scene, appearing on countless telethons and national talk shows to entertain, inspire hope, and attract donations.

Six months ago, Bonnie was murdered. According to the news, a black man had broken in to abducted her. Her mother was stabbed and killed fending him off. Holly escaped somehow and called 911.

The situation went from tragic to bizarre when Phoenix police arrested Holly for her mother's murder. Fans of the mother-daughter duo protested, claiming police were further victimizing a traumatized orphaned girl.

The latest development was that Holly had vanished shortly before a competency hearing.

"Did Liberty post Schwartz's bond?" I asked.

"No, some other agency did. Not sure who," Rodeo said as we perp-walked Freddie around the back of the building.

"But Fiddler's working the job? On his own?"

"For the past few weeks." Rodeo shrugged. "He's been having money problems, Jinx. Combination of medical expenses and gambling debts."

"Why am I just now hearing about this?"

Freddie guffawed.

I smacked him on the back of the head. "Shut the hell up."

"Fiddler and I met for beers last Saturday," Rodeo explained. "He gets chatty after he's had a few. That's when he told me."

"Well, he can take his gambling problems and shove them up his ass. I'm done with him. I need people I can depend on."

We rounded the corner and approached the Gray Ghost. Rodeo opened the back hatch and tossed in the shotguns and the bat. "By the way, when's *Phoenix Living* publishing that article about you?"

Phoenix Living was an alternative weekly covering local culture, news, and politics. A month earlier, Thom Hensley, one of their reporters, had interviewed me for a cover story on female bounty hunters.

I grinned. "Comes out tomorrow. I gotta admit, I'm a little excited to see what Hensley wrote."

"Our very own celebrity." Rodeo patted me on the back. "Try not to get too big a head."

"Yeah, right. I'm just hoping some other bail bond agencies read it and send some jobs our way. Liberty's been a bit lean lately."

4

Shortly after sundown, we delivered Freddie Colton without
incident to the Madison Street Jail in downtown Phoenix.
The duty officer gave me a body receipt, which I would
turn over to Liberty Bail Bonds the next morning in exchange
for a six-thousand-dollar check. Not bad for a few days' work.

On the way home, I dropped Rodeo off to pick up his tur-
quoise Mazda Miata at the Hub, a coworking space a couple of
miles north of the jail, where I rented a desk.

"Dude, when are you going to buy a real car?" I teased when
I pulled into the lot next to his car.

"Are you kidding? My Miata gets me plenty o' action."

"Oh really? From where? The Lollipop Guild? That car's so
tiny it should have the Hot Wheels logo plastered on the side."

"Trust me, it ain't the size that matters. It's all in the ride."
Rodeo grinned like the Cheshire cat. "Speaking of which, wanna
go grab a drink somewhere? Stallions, maybe?"

Stallions was a country-style gay bar with a mostly male
clientele, though it wasn't unusual to see women there too. I'd
been several times to dance and drink. Even brought Conor
once or twice. Fun place with good music and nice people, but
I wasn't in the mood tonight.

"Thanks, but my skin feels like the salted rim of a margarita
glass. I just want to go home and take a shower." Especially
after Freddie had been pawing all over me. "Besides, Conor's

coming over later. Rain check?"

"Date night. Got it." Rodeo smiled knowingly. He stepped out of the truck and grabbed his shotgun from the back.

I rolled down the window. "I'll deliver the body receipt to Big Bobby first thing tomorrow. Should have a check for you no later than ten."

"Copy that. Have a good night, Jinx." He gave me a fist bump.

"You too."

He locked his shotgun in his trunk and got settled in the driver seat. As I waited for him to start his car before taking off, I checked my phone and noticed Conor had left me a voicemail an hour or so earlier. I played it.

"Sorry, love, but I won't make it tonight. I'm on a stakeout, looking for one of my skips. Could be an all-nighter. Cheeky bastard's been giving me the slip at every turn. I'll catch up with ya in the morning before ya go off with your geeky mates at Comicon. See ya!"

So much for date night, I thought grimly. Since Conor and I had started dating, we saw each other less than when I worked for him. Didn't seem right, but there wasn't much either of us could do about it.

With Conor a no-show, I opted for plan B, which involved devouring an entire pint of raspberry sorbet while binge-watching the latest season of *Orange is the New Black*. After a much-needed shower, of course. Yeah, this girl knows how to live.

I walked through the front door of my house on Cypress Street in Phoenix's quaint—and grossly overpriced—Willo District. My brother, Jake, who renovated and flipped houses for a living, got it for well below market value. It was in the Central Corridor, a stone's throw north of downtown, and was the closest thing to an LGBT-friendly neighborhood I'd found in Phoenix. Conor lived only a half mile away, so who was I to complain?

I shuffled through the living room and down a short hall-way to my bedroom. The artichoke-style ceiling light above my futon filled the room with a golden glow. I wriggled out of my clothes, stepped into the bathroom, and turned on the shower.

As the hot water washed off a day's worth of sweat—and the lingering memory of Freddie's hand on my thigh drained away—a loud noise elsewhere in the house caught my attention. A thunk followed by a man cursing. A chill ran through me. Conor was on his stakeout. No one else was expected. So who the hell was in my house?

I left the water running so as not to tip off my uninvited guest that I was on to him. I slipped out of the shower and pulled out a Glock I kept stashed under a stack of hand towels in a drawer by the sink. The pistol's slide sounded deafening as I chambered a round.

I froze and listened to get a fix on my intruder's location. A kitchen drawer banged open—the junk drawer, from the sound of it—then slammed shut. Then another drawer rattled open.

Go time! I charged down the short hallway and leveled the gun at a large man standing with his back to me in the dark kitchen. "Down on the ground, now! Hands behind your head!"

It wasn't until the man held up his hands in surrender that I noticed the coppery curls atop his head. In one hand was a bottle of wine. In the other, a corkscrew.

"Don't shoot me, mum," he said in a thick Irish brogue. "I'll go quietly." He turned to face me with a cheesy smile on his face.

I lowered the Glock, catching my breath as my heart thundered in my chest. "Jesus, Conor. What the hell? I thought you were on a stakeout."

"The bloke showed up. We grabbed him and took him to Glendale lockup." His grin deepened. "Shite! Look at ya! All naked and deadly."

I rolled my eyes, a little embarrassed, then marched back to the bathroom to put away the Glock and grab my robe.

Conor hugged me from behind, whispering, "Now that we're both excited, how about a ride, eh, love?" He kissed my ear. I could feel him getting hard against my hip.

"After you scared me half to death? Fat chance, buddy boy!" I said with a chuckle. I slipped out of his grip, pulled on my robe, and tied the sash in a loose bow.

He sat on the toilet, looking up at me. "Scared *you*? I was the one staring down the business end of a Glock. Almost shat myself."

"Serves you right for sneaking in." I sat in his lap. Damn, he smelled good. My body literally ached to feel him inside me.

"Can ya blame me, love? You're gonna be spending all weekend half naked with your geeky mates wantin' to cop a feel of Superwoman."

I playfully swatted him. "First off, it's Wonder Woman, not Superwoman. And second, I won't be half naked. Just showing a little cleavage. I can try on the costume for you if you don't believe me."

"That's all right. I saw it when you first made it. And it's brilliant. But right now, I'm in the mood for more than a little cleavage." His deft fingers untied the bow on my robe's sash.

We made our way to the bedroom and spent the next hour loosening all the knots that a day pursuing fugitives can put into a body. It always amazed me that a man as strong as Conor could be so gentle.

His fingers and lips played my body with the skill of a jazz musician, leaving me gasping with pleasure. When he slid into me, I grabbed his butt cheeks and pulled him in even deeper, rocking into a rhythm that sent my mind shooting into the stratosphere.

By the time we were done, I lay next to him, floating on the lingering buzz of two orgasms, my hand resting on the ginger curls of hair covering his belly.

"You hungry?" I asked, gazing absently at the scars on his chest caused years earlier by an IED explosion overseas.

He took a deep sigh. "What? Ya want to go again?"

"Not for me, silly. For food. I could make us some stir-fry or something."

He opened his eyes. "That sounds brilliant."

I threw on a worn gray tank top and matching yoga pants, made my way to the kitchen, and chopped up some vegetables and a chicken breast. As I fired up the gas stove and added some peanut oil to the wok, Conor wandered in wearing my robe.

"Don't you look cute." I tossed the chicken into the hot oil and stirred it as it sizzled. "Though the pink kinda clashes with your red hair."

"I suppose it does." He shrugged.

"You know that article comes out tomorrow. The one in *Phoenix Living* Thom Hensley interviewed me for. I'm excited to see what he wrote."

His smile faded ever so slightly. "Oh yeah? That's great, love."

"Something wrong?"

"Naw, nothing's wrong." Conor shrugged and snatched a piece of broccoli from the cutting board. "I'm glad you're excited."

Something in his voice told me he was hiding something. I set down the spatula and faced him, hands on my hips. "What aren't you telling me?"

"Nothing, love. Swear to Christ."

"Don't lie to me, mister. You're so full of shit your emerald eyes are turning brown. Now spill!"

"It's just … in the bail enforcement biz, it's a good idea to maintain a low profile, especially with the press. Those dodgy blokes'll do a number on ya, sure as shoot ya. You in particular don't need guys like Thom Hensley digging up your past."

"Good grief, you think I told him I was trans? Not a chance. All we talked about was how I got into bounty hunting and what it's like being a woman in a male-dominated business. Period."

He kissed me on the forehead. "It's just I've read this guy's work. He doesn't write fluff stories, Jinxie. He writes hit pieces. Exposés about bad cops, corrupt politicians, and evil corporations. He did that series on Sheriff Joe last year. Wrote one last month about a strip club owner who's running a human trafficking ring."

"This isn't a hit piece, Conor. Thom's a nice guy. You'll see." I tossed in the veggies and my secret combination of sauces, though I was starting to lose my appetite.

"Don't be cross, love. I'm just worried about ya is all."

"I'd rather you be excited for me."

He hugged me from behind and gently kissed my ear. "Then excited I am."

I dished up two plates and handed him one. "Let's eat."

"How'd your night go?" he asked between bites. "D'ya get your guy?"

"Rodeo and I did." I picked at my food. "Fiddler was on the back door. But when the shit went down, he was MIA. Rodeo thinks he's working that Holly Schwartz case."

"That bloody prick! Don't know what's gotten into him lately. Ya want I should kick his arse?"

"Naw, I got it handled."

"That's my girl!" He grabbed my hand and squeezed gently, making it impossible to stay mad at him.

"After I turn in the body receipt to Liberty in the morning, I'm grabbing a bunch of copies of *Phoenix Living*. Want me to get you one?"

Conor paused mid-chew, shrugged, and shook his head a little too vigorously. "Naw, I'll just read yours."

"You really think he's going to out me, don't you? Why would you think that? Is there something you're not telling me?"

"Just me being paranoid is all."

"Paranoid and overprotective."

"What can I say? Ya mean the world to me, love." A smile bloomed across his face, but it had no effect on me.

"Well, cut it out. It's getting on my nerves. I'm not a child. I'm a grown woman." I pushed my plate aside. Conor's paranoia and a day of chasing down fugitives in the heat were taking their toll on my body as well as my mood.

He winked at me. "On that we can definitely agree."

"I'm tired. I think I'll turn in early. You coming?"

"I'd love to, but there's some paperwork I have to finish up at my place. Deez and the boys'll be pissed if I don't have their checks ready for them in the morning." He walked over and kissed me. "Don't worry. I'm sure the article will be brilliant."

"Thanks." I hugged him. "I love you."

"Love ya too. Get some rest. I'll clean up the kitchen before I go."

5

There were so many things I loved about being a bounty hunter. I set my own hours, though sometimes that involved spending long nights sitting in a car, bored out of my skull and hoping I didn't have to pee. Also, I didn't have to wear a uniform or worry about warrants or writing up arrest reports. And there was nothing like the thrill of slapping the cuffs on a fugitive and bringing him in. The only thing better was getting paid to do it.

The next morning, I showed up at Liberty Bail Bonds on Jackson Street in downtown Phoenix. Big Bobby Mills, the owner, had run the agency there since Biblical times, or so he told people. The office always reminded me of a cross between a man cave and a barbershop, wrapped in wood paneling, circa 1975.

A half dozen wooden folding chairs formed a small lobby at the front of the office. Autographed photos of Big Bobby posing with various celebrities hung on one wall, his favorite showing him arm in arm with members of Lynyrd Skynyrd after he'd bailed them out for disorderly conduct and possession of a controlled substance.

Big Bobby's wife, Sara Jean, sat at an antique walnut desk separating the lobby from the rest of the office. She worked as the office manager, providing me with files for defendants who'd missed their court dates—and paychecks, after I'd delivered them back to jail.

Sara Jean was a sizable woman with a smile that could fill a room with warm fuzzies, and a Southern drawl as sweet as fresh-picked peaches. Whenever I stopped by, she'd fill me in on the latest about her grandkids, whose photos surrounded her workstation. As the only two women affiliated with the agency, we had formed a bond.

Above her desk hung a constellation of plaques and framed certificates recognizing the agency's contributions to local nonprofits including Valley Big Brothers Big Sisters, Phoenix Children's Hospital, and St. Mary's Food Bank.

When Sara Jean didn't smile at me as I walked in with Freddie Colton's body receipt, I knew something was bothering her.

"What's wrong?" I asked as I sat in the chair in front of her desk. "One of your grandkids sick again?"

"No." She kept her eyes on her computer monitor, typing away.

I set the body receipt on the desk. She glanced at it and kept typing.

"You and Big Bobby have a fight?"

"No."

I started to worry. Had I said or done something wrong? Last time we spoke a few days earlier, she'd been telling me about having lost three pounds. I'd joked that soon she'd be beating off the boys with a stick. Maybe she'd thought I was mocking her.

"You upset with me about something?"

Her fingers froze above the computer keys. Her eyes locked with mine, and I saw a self-righteous anger that made me scooch my chair back a few inches. Without a word, she pulled the new issue of *Phoenix Living* out of a desk drawer and slapped it down. My goofy mug was on the cover, though to be honest, I thought the photo made me look better than I did in real life.

"Okay. Was there something in the article that bothered you?" Had I said something negative about Liberty Bail Bonds? I didn't think so.

Sara Jean looked away. "All this time I thought you were a girl."

I glanced at the cover again and felt as if I'd been punched in the gut. The teaser headline read "Tranny Bounty Hunter Cleans Up the Town." *Aw, shit!*

"Sara Jean, I *am* a girl." I stood up, arms spread wide. "I mean, look at me. Do I look like a boy? Do I sound like a boy?"

"No, but according to this ... " She pounded the magazine with her finger so hard, I thought she'd break one of her manicured nails. "You got one of them sex changes."

I sighed, even as my heart revved in my chest like a race car engine. "I've always been a girl, Sara Jean. It's just that through some crazy mix-up of biochemistry or genetics, I was born with a boy's body. It's hard to explain."

She fixed her gaze on me once again. "Ain't nothing to explain. Boys is boys, and girls is girls. God made you what you are. Ain't no changing it."

"I wish it were that simple, Sara Jean, but it's not. I'm—"

"Perverts like you's what's wrong with this world. Making it dangerous for God-fearing folks to use public restrooms."

"A pervert? Seriously, Sara Jean, is that what you think I am?" I rolled my eyes. "Wanna know what trans people do in public restrooms? We pee. We poop. And we wash our hands, which is more than I can say for *some* people."

Her hands disappeared under her desk. "Don't know what you're talking about."

"What we don't do, Miss Dirty Hands, is obsess about what's between someone else's legs because trans people are smart enough to know it's none of our goddamn business."

Her face colored with indignation. "Ha! That's what the fake liberal media wants people to think. Like y'all are just poor innocent victims. But I see y'all for what you are—wolves in sheep's clothing. Or women's clothing."

I pressed my palm against my forehead. I wasn't going to win this argument. As much as I liked Sara Jean, I'd known people like her my whole life—mindless drones who'd been fed a steady diet of hate-filled bullshit and self-righteous hypocrisy so long they refused to hear anything close to the truth.

"Fine. You want to think I'm some deviant out to destroy Western civilization, so be it. I just want to get paid, okay? Can we at least keep this professional?" I slid the body receipt closer to her.

She glanced at the paper, then at me, her mouth a thin line of bitterness. She snorted, pulled out the company checkbook, and wrote out a check with such ferocious pen strokes I thought she'd set the paper on fire. With a snap, she ripped the check loose and handed it to me. "Here's your check, *sir*. Don't come back."

My jaw tensed. If there was one thing that pissed me off, it was being intentionally misgendered, especially by friends. Or former friends. "I'd like to talk to Big Bobby."

"Bobby don't wanna talk to you. He gave me explicit instructions. He ain't hiring you no more. We are good Christians and don't take kindly to deceivers and perverts coming in here acting all unnatural. All these years I trusted you. I shared things with you. Intimate things with you, you … you thing."

Okay, that did it. Gloves were off.

I stood up and glared at her. "Look here, you ignorant transphobic bitch! Maybe if you pulled your holier-than-thou head out of your ass once in a while, you'd see not everyone is as privileged as you, that the rest of us are just doing our best to survive."

My rant was apparently loud enough to draw Big Bobby charging out of his office like a bull. He pointed a thick finger at me. "Get outta my office, you degenerate! Don't you never come back."

"I'm still working some of your cases, Bobby. So I will be—"

"We can handle them without you. Don't you worry your pretty, little, uh …"

I smirked. "Aw, Big Bobby. You called me pretty. Are you sweet on me?"

His face resembled a blood blister about to pop. "Get out!"

I'd said my piece, and I'd been paid. "Fine." I kicked open the door, stormed out into the heat, and sat in the Gray Ghost, wrestling with a combination of anger, humiliation, and hurt.

I had dirt on both of them. Maybe it would get me my job back, maybe it wouldn't. But even if it did, did I want to work with such bigoted assholes? I really didn't.

Bile rose in my throat as the salacious headline on the *Phoenix Living* cover flashed back into my mind. How had I not seen this coming? Was I not allowed to leave that part of my past behind? Would it haunt me for the rest of my life? I pounded the dash until the throbbing in my hand pulled me from that spiral of endless, unanswerable questions.

I took a deep breath. I focused on my mantra—WWWWD. What Would Wonder Woman Do? She'd let it go. She'd focus on the task at hand, which in my case meant finding a job. While I'd freelanced for several bail bond agencies over the years, the majority of my revenue had been coming from Liberty. With Big Bobby and Sara Jean giving me the heave-ho, I'd have to hustle up new business with my old contacts to make up the loss.

But first, I needed to get a copy of *Phoenix Living* and find out what in hell Thom Hensley had written about me.

6

I picked up a copy of *Phoenix Living* at a QT convenience store on McDowell. The clerk smiled, glanced at the cover, then back at me with a surprised look on his face. "Is that you?"

I nodded, impatient to read the article. "Yeah, it's me."

"So you're—"

"Really in a hurry. Thanks!" I hustled out the door for the sanctuary of the Gray Ghost.

I frantically flipped to the article. My heart thundered in my chest. My gaze danced erratically across the page. *Goddammit, girl, just chill out and focus.* I took a deep breath and started reading.

Most of what Thom Hensley had written came from our interviews. But then I came across the sentence: "Not only is Jinx Ballou among the few female bounty hunters in Arizona, she is also the only one openly transgender."

Openly transgender? What the hell? I pounded the dashboard so hard it sent a jolt of pain through my arm to my shoulder.

I'd met with Hensley three times, once at an upscale restaurant in Scottsdale, then twice more at his office for follow-up questions. He'd been charming and respectful, displaying a critical yet open mind and an attention to details.

"I find the idea of a female bounty hunter intriguing and encouraging," he told me over blue corn taquitos at our first meeting, setting a digital recorder between us. "We need more people like you breaking glass ceilings."

"Everybody's got to earn a paycheck somehow," I joked. "Besides, it's not like I'm the only woman in the business."

"You ever meet Domino Harvey?"

"No. She died a few years before I became a bounty hunter."

"What about that gal up in New Jersey? God, what's her name?"

"I know who you mean. Met her once when one of my fugitives fled to Trenton." I chuckled sardonically. "Not the most professional bounty hunter I've worked with, but she gets the job done … somehow."

"What inspired you to become a bounty hunter?"

My face warmed with embarrassment. "I was a nerdy kid reading comic books, dreaming of becoming a real-life Wonder Woman. When I realized at age six that wouldn't happen, I set my sights on becoming a homicide detective. I earned a bachelor's in criminology from Arizona State, then joined Phoenix PD."

"You were a cop?" He cocked an eyebrow. "Why'd you leave?"

"Funny thing about police departments. They don't let you go straight from the academy to being a plainclothes detective."

"You don't say," he replied with a chuckle.

"I knew this, obviously. But what I didn't realize was how miserable I'd be as a patrol officer. Me and uniforms? Not so much. Then there're all the rules and regs I had to follow. Wonder Woman never bothered with probable cause or arrest reports."

I stared blankly across the room, the memories replaying vividly in my mind. "The turning point came when my partner, Officer Luis Garza, and I responded to a violent confrontation between two rival gang members at Grumpy's Bar and Grill on the 300 block of West McDowell. By the time we arrived on scene, the suspects had been subdued by a couple of patrons— Conor Doyle and Robert 'Fiddler' Dixon.

"I took Conor's statement and learned he worked as a bounty hunter. I was intrigued. After two other uniforms transported the suspects to lockup, I questioned Conor further about his work. He explained he didn't have to wear a uniform, request warrants, or fill out arrest reports. I turned in my badge and joined his team a month later."

What I left out of my interviews with Hensley was that my aversion to uniforms and the regimental aspects of cop life stemmed from a near fatal semester at Phoenix Junior High Military Academy.

Before coming out as trans, I'd been acting out a lot. Drinking. Cigarettes. Weed. Anything to avoid dealing with my feelings of being a girl. When I got caught shoplifting a dress, my father, a psychologist, decided the discipline of a military academy would straighten me out and make a man out of me.

Instead, it sent me into a depression spiral that culminated in me breaking into the commandant's office, looking for a gun to kill myself with. All I found was a bottle of Vicodin. I washed down two dozen pills with a bottle of twelve-year-old scotch. Not that I really wanted to die. I just wanted to stop the soul-crushing pain I'd been struggling with my entire life.

I woke hours later in the infirmary, my throat sore from having my stomach pumped. My distraught father soon showed up, desperate to understand why I wanted to kill myself.

With my defenses down from the Vicodin and the humiliation of the failed suicide attempt, I shared my dark secret with him—that despite outward appearances, I'd always known I was a girl.

To my surprise, he didn't freak. Apparently, he'd suspected something was going on and had been doing research. After I was sent home, he rallied my mother and brother around me and got me started on androgen blockers. The next semester, I enrolled at Discovery Charter Middle School as a girl.

I stared at the newspaper, entertaining visions of exacting my revenge on Hensley—running him over with my truck, riddling his body with bullets Bonnie-and-Clyde style, pushing him off Camelback Mountain and enjoying the sickening splat as he hit the valley floor a thousand feet below.

How he'd discovered my transgender history was beyond me. Only a few people knew. One of them had spilled the beans, and I was determined to find out who.

When I finally calmed down, I drove north to *Phoenix Living*'s editorial offices in the Sun Glow Building on the corner of Third Street and Earll Drive. I pulled into the underground garage and locked my guns in the glove box, in case I was tempted to turn my murder fantasies into reality. Being fired was bad enough. Didn't need to get arrested for first-degree murder.

After a short ride on the elevator, I stormed into the offices with my copy of the paper rolled in my fist. "I need to speak to Thom Hensley," I said to the receptionist as calmly as I could manage.

Moments later, Thom came out wearing a pale-gray suit and a lime-green dress shirt.

"Hey! How's my favorite bounty hunter?" He extended his hand, looking extremely chipper. I wanted to put *him* through a chipper.

"What the fuck, Thom?" I shook the paper at him.

"Excuse me? Something wrong with the article?"

"What gave you the right to out me?"

"Ah." He frowned and gestured toward a hallway. "Let's talk in my office."

My face burned. I felt like screaming but accepted his invitation. He led me to a glass-enclosed office and drew the blinds. The office was small but smartly decorated. Journalism awards lined a walnut bookshelf along one wall. He settled behind his modern black desk and invited me to sit in one of the upholstered guest chairs. I remained standing.

"How dare you do this to me, you slimy little hack! Bad enough you out me, but you call me a tranny on the front page? You have any idea how offensive that word is?"

"I apologize for the use of that term. My copy editor writes the headlines, not me."

"I don't care if it was the pope. You had no right bringing up the subject in the first place."

He leaned forward, extending his hands in a conciliatory gesture. "Jinxie, sweetie, I did you and the transgender community a favor. Visibility is vital to greater acceptance. Look at Laverne Cox, Jamie Clayton, and Chaz Bono. They're not hiding who they are."

"Doesn't give you the right to out me. I got fired because of your story."

He pursed his lips in an apologetic pout. "Look, I'm sorry."

"Sorry doesn't help me. I want to know who told you."

"I'm afraid I can't reveal my sources. You understand."

I leaned over his desk, shaking the rolled-up paper at him as if he were a misbehaving puppy. "What I understand is that you're going to give me their name or you'll wish you had."

"Do I have to call security?" His hand hovered over a red button on his desk phone.

I gritted my teeth. A voice in the back of my head told me to chill. I sat in the chair. "Look, I just want to know who told. This is my life. Not some byline."

"Jinx, believe me when I say I never meant to hurt you or cost you your job. I know it's tough. But I have the utmost respect for your kind."

"My *kind*? What the hell do you know about my kind? Are you trans?"

"Well, no." He placed a hand on mine. "But look at the bigger picture. You're a trailblazer, paving the way for other transgender people to enter the profession. You should be proud."

I pulled my hand away while my grip on the paper tightened. "Don't try to charm me, Hensley. I want the person's name, and I want a public apology from you printed in next week's issue."

"Sorry. No can do."

"I'm going to sue your ass for defamation of character. You, your copy editor, the whole fucking newspaper."

"You can try, but you'd only win if what I wrote wasn't true.

Problem is, everything in that article is factual. And eventually, you'll realize I did you a favor."

"How 'bout I do the world a favor and jam this paper up your ass?"

His hand pressed the red button. "You should leave now."

I stood, my hands trembling, while my murder fantasies played on a loop in my head. "You're going to regret this, dipshit."

I stormed out of the office as two sides of beef dressed in black polo shirts appeared by the receptionist's desk. "Relax, boys. I'm leaving."

The security guards escorted me down the elevator and out to my truck, going so far as to watch me drive to the booth to pay for parking. In the ruckus, I hadn't gotten my parking ticket validated, so I had to pay ten bucks for the privilege of giving Hensley a piece of my mind. *Insult, meet injury.*

I hit the streets, unsure where I was going. *I should call Conor,* I thought. But I couldn't bring myself to do it. I kept hearing his voice in my head, warning me not to get too excited about the article.

Was this what Conor was hinting at last night? Did he tip off Hensley about my trans history? Surely Conor wouldn't betray me like that. But if not him, who?

The questions raced round and round my head like coked-up hamsters on an exercise wheel, until I decided to talk with the one person who could understand my predicament—my fairy drag mother, *Tía* Juana.

7

Juanita Valdez came up through the Phoenix drag scene in the 1970s and '80s, performing under the name Tía Juana. In the early '90s, she transitioned to living full-time as a woman. Eventually she became the owner of the Main Drag, one of the valley's biggest queer bars, where she also served as mistress of ceremonies a few nights a week.

I met Juanita when I joined the local transgender support group as a teenager. She took an immediate liking to me, declaring herself my fairy drag mother. She taught me how to walk and talk and blend in with the rest of the female population.

"You gotta work it, Miss Thang. Don't let them boys clock you as anything but total fish. Your survival depends on it," she'd warn me, usually after chastising me for not looking or acting femme enough.

Shortly after my reassignment surgery, she bestowed upon me my nickname, Jinx—a mash-up of my first and middle names, Jenna Christina.

Juanita lived in an elegant four-bedroom house off Seventh Street near North Mountain, where she offered housing to an ever-changing roster of trans people left homeless by their families.

I passed under an arch of climbing vines sheltering Juanita's front door from the morning sun. My watch read just past eleven, a decent hour for most respectable folks. Juanita, however, tended to sleep till the crack of noon due to the late hours she kept at the bar. I rang her doorbell, anyway.

Moments later, the door opened. Juanita stood tall and thin, combining the elegance of Lena Horne with the flamboyance and sultry voice of Tina Turner. Her brightly colored silk robe revealed long, dark legs, still shapely for someone in her midsixties.

She was not wearing makeup, a rarity for her and not a good sign. She could be moody before she'd had coffee and put on her face. Like, rabid-dog-psycho-killer moody. So I opted to tread lightly.

"Morning, *tía*. Did I wake you?"

"Please, *chica*, tell me that wasn't you leaning on my doorbell at this god-awful hour." She gazed at me, bleary eyed. "Haven't even put on my war paint yet."

"You look beautiful, anyway. Truly."

"Ain't you sweet. Full o' bullshit but sweet." She sighed and stepped out of the doorway. "Come on in, sweetie. Don't need you melting on my front stoop."

I followed her down a short hallway to a spacious, brightly lit kitchen that looked out onto a courtyard bursting with oleander, hibiscus, and Mexican bird of paradise. I took a seat at the breakfast bar while she filled two earthenware mugs with coffee. A copy of *Phoenix Living* lay facedown on the bar nearby.

"Cream or sugar, sugar?" she asked.

"A little cream, if you don't mind."

"You know I never do." She poured a smidge of half-and-half into the mug, then slid it over to me. "I always have mine black. This tired old queen needs all the kick she can get."

"Where are your housemates?"

"Rosalyn's at a job interview. Caden had a doctor's appointment. I think he's starting T soon." T was slang for testosterone injections.

"How's Ciara's new bookkeeping job working out?"

Juanita's mouth twisted into a cruel scar. "You didn't hear?"

"No."

"Some motherfucker beat her near to death last week in the parking lot where she worked."

"Shit. That was her?" My chest ached. "I can't believe it. How's she doing?"

"She came outta the coma after two days. Face is beat all to shit. Broken arm. Docs saying she may come home tomorrow."

"Damn. The police know who did it?"

"Cops don't know shit. No one saw nothing."

"You want me to ask around? Talk to some of my old contacts on the force?"

"Anything you can do would be appreciated, sweetie." Juanita settled onto a stool on the other side of the bar, cradling her coffee. "So what brings Miss Jinx Ballou to Casa Valdez this depressingly sunny morning?"

A dust devil of rage and humiliation twisted up through my mind. I flipped over the *Phoenix Living*. "I got outed."

"Oh my heavens!" she exclaimed in mock horror. "Someone call the queer police. There's been an outing! Should I administer mouth-to-mouth?"

"Gee, thanks. Just what I need is to be mocked." I slipped the issue closer to her. "Look at this shit. It's humiliating."

She tilted her head and met my gaze. "Humiliating? Why? Because now everyone knows the valley's badass female bounty hunter is a hot little tranny?"

"*Tía*, stop! You know I hate that word." Angry tears prickled behind my eyes. I was not going to cry in front of her, no matter how she pressed my buttons.

Her gentle hand touched my cheek. "My dear little princess warrior, I'm sorry, but there's nothing humiliating about people knowing you're transgender."

"It puts a target on my back. You were the one who pounded it into my head that my survival depended on people not knowing I was trans. Look what happened to Ciara."

"True, I did tell you that, but that was a long time ago.

Things have changed. Time for hiding in closets is over for seasoned warriors like you and me. We got to stand up and make a show of force. Let these motherfuckers know we're not going away." She tossed the copy of *Phoenix Living* across the breakfast bar. "Honestly, Jinx, I think you're just upset your little bubble of passing privilege got burst. A lot of us couldn't pass as cisgender if we tried."

"Maybe you're right, except the bail bond agent I work for fired me over the article."

"Well, fuck them! You'll find someone else to work for. You're good at what you do, right?"

I stared at my coffee. "Yeah, I suppose."

"And you're still dating that fine slab of Irish corned beefcake, are you not?"

I couldn't help but blush. "I am."

"You have a family that loves you and embraces you for who you are."

"Yeah."

"You have a roof over your head. Food to eat. A car to get you from point A to point B, yes?"

"Technically a truck, but yes."

"Then what the hell you bitchin' about, *chica*? You got a shitload more than most of us. I mean, damn, you transitioned before you hit puberty. Your folks paid for your surgery. You won the fucking lottery."

"I know, I know, but—"

"Look at me, Jinx. I'm sixty-four years old and can't get surgery because I'm HIV positive. Ciara, bless her tender heart, was nearly murdered. And you're whining about some crappy article and a narrow-minded bail bond agent? Bitch, please! Jinx Ballou, pity party for one!"

I felt sick and properly put in my place. I'd shown up here like a spoiled child with a broken toy when so many in the trans community faced homelessness, brutality, and worse on a daily basis. The room was silent for several minutes except for the chirping of a family of quail in the courtyard outside, the hen herding a half dozen bug-sized chicks to the shelter of the bushes.

Juanita broke the silence. "So why's *Phoenix Living* writing about you in the first place?"

I shrugged. "Thom Hensley called wanting to do a cover story about female bounty hunters. I said yes, figuring it'd boost business. But I never mentioned anything about being trans."

"Miss Thang, Hensley's an investigative reporter. He writes about corrupt politicians and Russian gangsters. You sat down with him and are surprised he dug up your little secret? *Chica,* please!"

"Okay, maybe I was a little naïve."

"A little?"

"Okay, a lot naïve. But still, I'd like to know who outed me to Hensley."

"Sure wasn't me. I never spoke to the man. Maybe that sweet boyfriend of yours."

I thought more about the night before, and my stomach soured. "He was acting squirrelly last night when I brought up the article."

"Then I suggest you ask him."

"I can't."

"Why the hell not? He's your boyfriend, ain't he?"

"I don't want him thinking I don't trust him."

"*Do* you trust him?"

"Yes. Maybe."

"Just ask the man. Don't play these mind games. Life's too short for that nonsense."

I finished my coffee. "You're right."

"Of course I'm right. *Tía* Juana is *always* right. Now"— Juanita gestured at my faded Pearl Jam concert T-shirt—"what is up with this outfit? Please tell me '90s grunge is not making a comeback. And where the hell is your war paint?"

"This is what bounty hunters wear. And it's too freakin' hot for makeup."

"Miss Thang, listen to your fairy drag mother and listen good. It is *never* too hot for makeup. A little waterproof eyeliner and some lipstick, at least." She tugged on my naked earlobes. "And did you learn nothing about accessorizing, or was I talking to myself all those years? I can loan you a pair of hoop earrings that would at least add some class to this sad little tomboy look you got going."

"Hoop earrings are too easy to get caught on something. Besides, I have some accessories in the Gray Ghost."

"Oh really? Such as?"

I smirked. "Black leather tactical belt from Bianchi with a molded plastic holster for my Ruger and two magazine pouches."

"Lord almighty, just kill me now."

"And I have bracelets."

She folded her arms and gave me a suspicious stare. "Really? Show me."

I pulled a pair of handcuffs from my back pocket. "See?"

"Out!" She pointed toward the front door. "I can stand this heresy no longer."

She was teasing, at least I thought she was. Sometimes it was hard to tell with her. But I needed to get going, anyway. I had to find a bail bond agency willing to hire me now that my big secret was out there.

At the door, I hugged her. "Thanks, *tía*. I can always count on you for a reality check."

"Darlin', my reality check bounced years ago." She cradled my face in her long, delicate fingers. "Go out there and get you a new client. Show those *pendejos* you won't be bullied."

"I will."

"And be safe out there in that crazy-ass world, you hear?"

"Always.

8

After Juanita's, I dropped by my house for a change of clothes. Since I was trying to drum up business, something a little dressier than my Pearl Jam shirt and jeans was called for. I was no fashionista, so my selection of business attire was limited. I debated between the federal agent style of a dark suit and blouse or something more casual like a polo shirt and jeans. I compromised with a white button-down shirt and khakis.

Juanita's comments inspired me to put on some makeup, but I kept it minimal. A little eyeliner. Mascara. Neutral lipstick. I was proud to be a woman, but I tended to follow my mother's philosophy of "less is more." As for my hair, I went with a simple ponytail. I was applying to be a bounty hunter, not a receptionist.

When I was satisfied with my look, I headed out into the blistering summer heat with a leather notebook filled with a thrown-together résumé and copies of body receipts I'd earned over the years.

One by one, I worked my way down a list of bail bond agencies I'd contracted with in the past, starting in downtown Phoenix, then heading east to Scottsdale, Gilbert, Tempe, and Mesa. When that yielded nothing, I doubled back and tried bail bond shops in Avondale, Goodyear, Glendale, Peoria, and Surprise.

None of my conversations were as confrontational as the

one I'd had with Sara Jean and Big Bobby, but the bail bond agents' averted eyes and clipped tones told me everything their words didn't—I'd been blackballed.

By midafternoon, I'd had enough. My voicemail showed three messages from Conor. I ignored them. I should have been slipping into my Wonder Woman outfit and celebrating sci-fi/fantasy culture with the costumed hordes at Phoenix Comicon. But even that held no appeal when I had no idea when I'd get my next paycheck.

While I calculated my next move, my phone rang. Caller ID showed it was my father.

"Hi, Dad, what's up?"

"Hey, cupcake. I'm calling to say how impressed your mom and I are with the article in *Phoenix Living*. When you told us you were interviewed, I didn't realize you talked about being transgender. Kudos to you for being so bold."

"Yeah," I grumbled. "Wasn't exactly how I planned it."

"Why? What's wrong?"

"I never told that reporter I was trans. He dug it up some other way."

"How do you feel about that?" My father, ever the psychologist.

"Angry, hurt, maybe a little scared. The bail bond agency I worked for fired me when they found out. I've been banging on doors all day trying to find work."

"Maybe it's for the best."

"The best? How is this for the best? How'm I supposed to pay my bills if I can't find work?"

"Being in the closet is no way to live, always afraid someone's going to find out your deep, dark secret. Before you came out to us, you were so miserable. Living with a secret is like a cancer. It eats away at your self-esteem and peace of mind. You're a beautiful, smart woman who happens to be transgender. I want my daughter to be proud of who she is."

I sighed. "I am proud, Dad. It's just I work in a very macho, testosterone-driven business. Not everyone gets it, you know?"

"Maybe you could go back to being a cop."

"I don't want to be a cop. I like what I do."

"And that's important, I know." I heard him sigh. "Trust the process, sweetheart. One thing this transition taught you was that you can get through anything. It made you tough. Sometimes I wonder if it made you too tough."

"I'm okay, Dad. I'll figure this out."

"I know you will. Oh, by the way, your mother wanted me to tell you she's been shopping again for you."

"Dad, no! I told her to stop. She keeps buying me those god-awful polyester dresses that look like they're from the 1950s."

"She's trying to be supportive. Just humor her next time you see her."

"I'd hate to reinforce bad behavior. Isn't that what you always say?"

"You got me there, cupcake." He laughed. "I'll try to talk to her. You'll be by for Sunday brunch?"

"I will."

"See you then, sweetie. Love you."

"Love you, too, Dad."

When I hung up, I decided a little bang-bang therapy might improve my mood. I drove north to Glendale and spent two hours punching holes in paper targets at the Westgate Shooting Range. There was something deeply satisfying about the explosive power of firing off a few boxes of ammo. Especially when the figures on the targets looked a lot like Big Bobby Mills.

By the time I was done, my wrist was throbbing and my bank account was a hundred bucks leaner. But I no longer felt the need to go all Bruce Willis on anyone, so the world was that much safer for everybody.

I hopped into the Gray Ghost and sent texts to Becca and Conor, saying I'd had a crappy day and asking them to meet me at Grumpy's Bar and Grill. Both responded with confirmations they'd be there. Becca rapid-fire texted me, desperate to know what was wrong. I replied that I'd fill her in at Grumpy's.

With my dinner plans in place, I called Rodeo. He answered after a couple of rings.

"Jinx. Uh, hey."

"I got paid for the Colton job. You can pick up your check tomorrow at the Hub."

"Just mail it. You got my address."

I sighed. "You know, don't you?"

"Know what?"

"Don't be coy with me, Rodeo. You heard Big Bobby fired me."

"He called me down to the office and told me. I'm sorry, Jinx. But you had to know there'd be consequences for coming out so publicly as … well, you know."

"Come on, Rodeo. You're a big boy. You can say the word. I'm transgender. Big friggin' deal. Is this going to be a problem between us?"

"Of course not. Happy to have you as part of the LGBTQ family. Truth be told, I'm a little disappointed you told that reporter before you told me."

"I never told that reporter I was trans." My grip tightened on the phone. I took a deep breath, not wanting to go down that rabbit hole again. "Anyway, I've been beating the bushes all day to drum up some new business for us. Should have something lined up soon." I hoped.

He didn't respond right away. I wondered if the call had dropped. "Rodeo? You still there?"

"Actually, I'm still working for Liberty." His voice was pinched.

"You what? How?"

"Big Bobby hired Fiddler and me as full-time employees. He's bringing everything in-house. I'll get a regular salary, health insurance, paid time off, the works."

"But you work for me, Rodeo," I said between clenched teeth. "I've been training you for six months."

"And I'm grateful. It's just that…"

"What?"

"Big Bobby said if I continued to work for you, he'd blackball me as well. I'm sorry, I can't risk it."

"How can you, as a gay man, turn a blind eye to what he's doing to me? What happened to loyalty and community solidarity?" My eyes felt as if they were throbbing.

"First off, I'm not gay, Jinx. I'm bi."

My face warmed at my misguided assumption. "Sorry. My bad."

"Second, loyalty doesn't pay the bills. I need the money and the bennies. My daughter's got severe nut allergies. Have you seen the price of EpiPens lately? So unless you've got big-paying jobs already lined up—"

"I got some leads," I lied. "And I've still got a few smaller outstanding jobs from Liberty."

"Jinx, they've been reassigned to Fiddler. He's the one leading the Liberty in-house team."

"Fiddler's leading the team? After he left us in the lurch on the Colton job?"

"He had an emergency come up."

"Yeah, an emergency. He's been having a lot of those lately. Working on his crew is the worst idea in the history of shitty ideas. You're an idiot if you can't see that."

"You think insulting me will get me to change my mind?"

"Rodeo, you're gonna get yourself killed working with him. What'll your daughter do then?"

"I survived Afghanistan. I can handle Fiddler. And FYI, he wants you to mail him his check too."

"Fiddler can kiss my ass. I'm not paying him squat after he disappeared yesterday."

"He's not going to be happy, but I'll let him know."

"You do that, Mr. Benedict Arnold." I hung up. I hadn't eaten since breakfast and was feeling seriously hangry. I needed food and friendly company.

9

I threaded my way south through rush hour traffic to Grumpy's. The place was packed. I nabbed the last empty booth and ordered my usual—a Grumpy Burger all the way, Cajun fries, and a Four Peaks White Ale to wash it down.

Grumpy, a pudgy Vietnam Vet with silver mutton chop sideburns, had opened the bar and grill after being discharged from the army in 1973. The place had become a local landmark, having won *Phoenix Living*'s "Best of Phoenix" award in the Bar and Grill category more than twenty times.

As I waited for Becca and Conor, my mind drifted back to the article and my argument with Hensley. I tried to compile a list of people who might have outed me.

The thought that any of my close friends or family might have blabbed to Hensley about my trans past decimated my appetite.

I looked up and caught Grumpy looming over me as I nibbled unenthusiastically on a french fry.

"Something wrong with my cookin', kitten?" He chewed absently on an unlit cigar.

"Don't start with me, Grumpy. I've had a crap day."

"That so? Something 'bout that article in *Phoenix Living*, I reckon."

I buried my head in my hands. "Geez Louise, not you too."

"Ah, don't go fretting, girl. I don't care what you are or

what you been. Long as your money's green, you're all right in my book."

I sighed and offered him a weak smile. "Thanks, Grumpy. At least somebody doesn't think I'm trying to corrupt Western civilization. Big Bobby at Liberty Bail Bonds fired me over this. Can you believe it?"

Grumpy huffed. "World's full of assholes, kitten. Just gotta move on." He raised an eyebrow. "You can still pay for that dinner, right?"

"Yes!" I laughed sardonically. "I'm fired but not broke. Not yet, anyway."

"Good." He wandered toward the kitchen. "You're a smart girl. I'm shore you'll figure it out."

"Sorry I'm late." Becca slid into the other side of the booth. She fanned her flushed, sweaty face with a menu. "Traffic's a bitch, it's a hundred and eight outside, and my car's AC chooses today to crap out."

"Guess I'm not the only one having a lousy day."

"Yeah, you mentioned that in your text. What's going on? You and Conor having trouble?"

After she placed her order for a black-bean-and-corn salad, I filled her in on the day's events, including my suspicions about Conor.

"Oh, sweetie, I'm so sorry. You'd think *Phoenix Living* would know better than to out someone," she said between bites of salad. "And why would Liberty care about you being trans? It's ancient history."

"Beats me. And people wonder why I keep it private." I buried my head in my hands.

"You don't really think Conor told, do you?"

"I don't know. Someone did."

"It wasn't me. When that reporter guy called—"

"Wait!" My heart skipped a beat, and I looked up at her. "Hensley called you?"

"Yeah, said he was doing background research."

"How'd he get your number?"

"I figured you gave it to him."

"Geez, who is this guy? Anderson Cooper? What'd you tell him?"

"That we both work at the Hub, you doing your bounty hunter thing and me working as an IT security consultant. What else? I mentioned I sometimes do skip tracing for you. He asked how we met. I said we'd been best friends since junior high. But not a word about you being trans. I'd never betray your trust, I swear." She held up her hand as if taking an oath.

"I know you wouldn't. But someone did, and it's bugging the hell out of me. And the way Conor was acting last night …" Bile burned in my throat.

Conor slid into the booth next to me, which suddenly felt very cramped.

"Jesus, love, ya look wrecked."

He started to put his arm around me, but I pushed it away, unable to meet his gaze.

"What's going on, Jinxie? Is this about the bit in *Phoenix Living*?"

"So you read it?" It came out harsher than I intended. I locked eyes with him.

"I did. On balance, I thought it was a great story. Painted ya as the brilliant, badass bounty hunter you are."

"Yeah," I said sardonically. "Except for the part where Hensley outed me and called me a tranny."

"Aye, except for that." He grimaced and let his gaze slide away.

"Did you tell him?"

"Tell him what? That you're trans? Ya know I'd never."

"But you knew he'd out me, right? That's why you were acting so weird last night."

Conor sighed. "Hensley called and asked what it's like dating a trans girl. Don't know how he knew, but I told him it was none of his bloody business."

I punched him in the chest. "Why didn't you warn me?"

"I was hoping he wouldn't print it. Ya want me to have a go at him?"

"No, I already did. Tried to get him to tell who outed me, but he refused and had security escort me out of the building."

"I could try to hack into his computer remotely," Becca suggested with a devilish grin. "Maybe I can find out some answers for you."

I shook my head. "Don't bother. At this point, it doesn't really matter. It's out there. I just need to focus on getting some new clients now that Liberty fired me."

"They didn't!" Conor gasped. "Bloody bastards."

"Not only that, they hired my team out from under me. Rodeo and Fiddler are now Liberty Bail Bonds employees."

"I'm so sorry, love." He put his arms around me, and I let him this time. It felt good. "Ya still going to Comicon?"

I shrugged. "Maybe. Tomorrow's priority is to find someone willing to hire me, then assemble a new team. Right now the prospects aren't looking promising. Everyone I talked to today gave me the cold shoulder."

Conor kissed my ear. Becca clasped my hand. If nothing else, it was always good to know who had my back.

"Ya try Bennett Bail Bonds in Mesa?" Conor asked.

"Yes."

"West Valley Bail Bonds by the sheriff's substation in Surprise?"

"Told me they didn't have anything for me, but they'd 'keep me in mind,'" I replied with air quotes.

Conor nodded knowingly. "How about Second Chance down on Washington by the ball park?"

I nodded. "Same results."

"Why don't you go back to working on Conor's team?" Becca suggested. "You're always complaining how y'all never see each other."

Conor grimaced but didn't say anything.

"Definitely not," I answered after an uncomfortable pause.

"Things got awkward after we started dating. Then when Deez got shot, everybody blamed me."

"Who's Deez again?" Becca asked.

"One of my guys." Conor shook his head. "And it wasn't your fault, Jinx."

"And yet suddenly I was Yoko Ono."

"Why? What happened?"

"We were making entry into a fugitive's house. He was a meth cook." Flashes of that day assaulted my mind. The reek of acetone and ammonia from a meth lab set up in a shed in the backyard. An explosion of glass as we made entry through an Arcadia door. A frightened child in the clutter-filled living room. Our team shouting commands to get on the ground, followed by people screaming.

"A guy in an upstairs bedroom got the jump on me and threw me to the ground. I should have been able to handle the situation, but I ... I'd spent the night before at Conor's and was ... I hadn't gotten enough sleep." I could hear my voice shake. My face felt hot. "Deez tried to pull the guy off me and got a bullet in the neck for his troubles. He spent two weeks in ICU."

"But he's right as rain now, love. All water under the bridge," Conor said. "Maybe Becca's right. Give it another go."

"I don't think so," I said with a weak smile. "Tommy Boy, Deez, and Byrd are all great guys. I just don't think it would work, especially now that I've been outed. Best I stick to running my own show."

"Well, shite." He doodled aimlessly with a french fry in the ketchup on his plate. "There's one place I don't think ya tried."

"Where?" I asked.

"Assurity Bail Bonds."

I scrunched my nose. "Didn't they go out of business a while ago?"

"The owner, Aaron Levinson, became ill a couple years ago and closed shop. After he died a few months back, his daughter, Sadie, opened a new office at the Arizona Center. Word on the street is she's got a defaulted bond worth a few hundred grand about to come due."

"Sweet." I grinned. "Best news I've heard all day."

"Just one thing." His mouth became a thin slit across his face. His gaze clouded with concern.

"What's that?"

He fidgeted in his seat. "Don't mention my name when ya talk to Sadie."

"Why not?"

"Just a misunderstanding from way back. Nothing important."

"Nothing important? Really?" I cocked my head. "So not important that I shouldn't even bring up your name? What kind of bullshit answer is that? Come on, dude, spill!"

"I can't, love. Honestly. Just trust me. She's a good person to work for. I doubt she'll care if you're trans. But keep my name out of it. It's all I'm asking."

"D'you sleep with her, big guy?" Becca asked, pointing her fork at him.

His face colored. "I'm not saying anything. If ya don't want to work for her, don't. Just trying to be helpful is all."

"Fine, I'll pay her a visit tomorrow." I eyed him suspiciously, unsettled by his need for secrecy. I needed the work.

10

fter dinner, I hugged Becca goodbye and followed Conor
back to his place, just a half mile from my house.

Part of me needed some TLC after the lousy day I'd
had. But I also hoped to uncover this mysterious history between
him and Levinson. I didn't want to ask her for work only to get
blindsided later by some bullshit in their collective past. Better
to know what I was getting into beforehand.

The sun had dipped below the horizon as we pulled up to
Conor's house, leaving the neighborhood in the soft, hazy glow
of dusk. On the outside, his house looked like any other on the
block. Brick facade with sage-green trim and a line of manicured
shrubs, surrounded by a lawn of sun-scorched Bermuda grass.
A few mesquite trees dotted the yard.

Inside the house, the walls were bare. No photos or artwork.
No plants. Saltillo tile covered the floor throughout. His furniture
was sparse but functional, consisting of a bed and nightstand
in the bedroom, and two recliners and an entertainment center
in the living room. His office had a bare IKEA desk, a metal
folding chair, and a filing cabinet. The whole place was dull,
empty, and lifeless—not so much a bachelor pad as a bunker.

"Ya want a drink?" he asked coolly as we stood in his kitchen,
avoiding eye contact. It felt like our first date but more tense.
He pulled a bottle of Jameson's from a cabinet.

"What I want is for you to tell me what happened between

you and this Levinson woman. You have a bad breakup or something?"

His face colored. "I don't want to talk about it, Jinxie." He poured whiskey into a couple of glasses and offered me one.

I slammed my glass onto the counter hard enough to slosh whiskey onto the worn laminate surface. "You're always full of secrets, Conor, and I'm sick of it! You didn't tell me Hensley knew I was trans. I had to learn about it from Sara Jean Mills. And now this crap? Quit stalling and tell me. I'm your girlfriend, for Christ's sake."

"There are things I don't discuss. This is one of them." He drained his glass and poured another before taking it into the living room. He plopped down on a recliner and stared at the floor. I followed him.

"I get why you don't talk about growing up during the Troubles in Ireland or your experiences with Dark Horse Security in Iraq. But this? Give me a freakin' break, dude. Whatever happened between you and Levinson, I'm a big girl. I can take it."

"Leave it alone, Jinx! I'm not bloody telling ya!" He glared at me so hard it felt like a blow to my chest.

I took a step back. "Why you got to be so secretive?"

"We all got secrets, love. I kept yours all these years. I'm asking you to respect mine."

"Bullshit! I trusted you with my secret. But you won't trust me with yours."

"This ain't about trust, love," he growled. "What happened between Sadie and me's got nothing to do with you."

"If I'm going to be working with her and dating you, it sure as hell does. I need to know what I'm in the middle of because, sooner or later, it's going to come out. I'd rather find out now than get blindsided later."

"Then don't work with her."

"No one else will hire me!" My shouts echoed off the bare walls, followed by a silence broken only by the bass beat of my pulse in my ears.

"I don't know what to tell ya, love," he said, barely above a whisper. His expression softened as tears rimmed his eyes. "Just leave my bloody name out of it, if ya go see her. That's all I'm asking ya. Please, just let it go."

God damn him and his puppy dog eyes. My anger softened. I took his free hand in mine. "Fine, I'll let it go. For now."

I woke at three the next morning after dreaming I'd discovered who'd outed me to Hensley. Unfortunately, my betrayer's identity evaded my conscious mind. I lay there trying to pull it from the jumbled fragments of the dream, but whatever eureka moment I'd had was gone. Probably nonsense, anyway.

At three thirty, I climbed out of bed and fixed a pot of coffee. I felt untethered. My private medical history had been exposed for everyone to gawk at. My career was in free fall. And now my trust in Conor was crumbling. Juanita's reminder that some had it worse than me didn't make the raw ache in my soul any less.

By the second cup of coffee, I wasn't feeling any better. So I grabbed some shorts, a tank top, and spare running shoes I kept in Conor's closet and went for a parkour workout.

The Willo District where Conor and I lived offered mostly level ground with few obstacles to bounce off of. Not an ideal parkour playground. Residents weren't overly fond of traceurs, as we parkour practitioners called ourselves, vaulting over their cars or dashing through their backyards. Block walls, palm trees, and a neighborhood park had to suffice for practicing flips, climbs, and other maneuvers. Anything to get my heart pumping and my mind focused in the moment rather than on my troubles.

After an hour's workout, I returned to Conor's. By the time his alarm went off at six, I had showered, inhaled a liter of water, and scarfed down a bowl of cereal. I was sneaking out the front door when I heard, "Leaving without saying goodbye, love?"

He stood shirtless, leaning against a wall. Despite the old scars on his chest and legs, he looked sexy as hell. Part of me wanted to jump his bones. Another part wanted to strangle him until he confessed what had happened between him and Levinson.

"Morning, sweetie. Didn't want to wake you. Lots to do today."

"Gonna talk to Sadie about hiring ya?"

I sighed. "Right now, it's my best option. So, yeah." When he raised an eyebrow, I added, "And I won't mention you. Promise."

"That's my girl. Now c'mere and let me give ya a kiss for luck."

I stepped back inside and kissed him deeply, even as a laundry list of emotions twisted my insides.

When I pulled away a moment later, he asked, "Ya going to the convention afterwards?"

"Definitely, assuming Sadie hires me. I need to seriously geek out with the three C's—cosplay, comic books, and my favorite celebs."

"Well, you're *my* favorite celeb."

My face flushed. "I'm just a girl who likes to catch fugitives and play dress up." I gave him a final peck on the lips and promised to let him know how it went with Sadie.

11

I stopped by my place for a change of dressy-ish clothes and stashed my Wonder Woman costume in a duffel bag before heading downtown to Assurity Bail Bonds's office at Arizona Center. If my meeting with Sadie Levinson went well, I could walk the half block south to the Phoenix Convention Center and enjoy the rest of Comicon. Tracking down Assurity's wayward defendants could wait until Monday.

The parking garage was near capacity when I arrived, no doubt packed with vehicles belonging to convention attendees. I found a space on the top floor, left the duffel on the passenger seat, and grabbed my notebook.

Assurity Bail Bonds was tucked in a corner on Arizona Center's second floor. A string of bells tied above the door jingled as I entered. The office consisted of a twenty-by-thirty-foot room with a single desk, three chairs, a coffee station, and a few vertical filing cabinets. Framed prints of paintings by Monet, Picasso, and Gaugin decorated the glossy white walls.

A slender woman in her forties with a no-nonsense expression on her face sat behind the desk with a stack of files beside her computer. Short wedge haircut. Red metallic framed glasses. Tailored maroon jacket over a white button-down blouse. A model of the modern professional woman. I hated to admit she left me feeling a little intimidated.

"Sadie Levinson?" I asked.

She glanced up at me and put a hand to her chin. "Hmmm … too casual for an attorney. Too dressy to be posting someone's bail. Whatever you're selling, I'm not buying."

"Not selling anything, actually. I'm Jinx Ballou, bail enforcement agent. I understand you have a sizable bond that's defaulted."

She leaned back in her chair. "Who told you that?"

"Well, you know, people talk." I forced a laugh, trying to act casual as I sat in front of her desk.

"Indeed. Been talking quite a lot about you lately, Ms. Ballou." She pulled a copy of *Phoenix Living* out of the wastebasket by her desk. "Took me a moment, but I recognize you now."

Oh boy. Here we go again. "Look, Ms. Levinson, I'm a damn good bounty hunter with eight years' experience. I've tracked fugitives from one end of this country to the other. The fact that I transitioned nearly twenty years ago doesn't change that."

"You're right, it doesn't." She slid the newspaper to the corner of her desk. "Personally, I don't care what you are or what you have between your legs. I do care about not going out of business. Right now that's a real possibility if I have to pay this defaulted bond. The bounty hunter I originally hired for this case wasn't as reliable as I'd been led to believe."

"You're talking about Fiddler, right?"

"You know him?"

I scoffed. "Let's just say you're not alone in your assessment of him."

"I have a lot on the line with this bond. I need someone I can trust, someone who gets results."

"I get results." I pulled out copies of body receipts I'd accumulated over the years and set them in front of her. She looked them over. Our eyes locked, and I felt a connection as she pulled a file from the stack on her desk.

"Very well. I gather you're familiar with the Holly Schwartz case."

"The disabled teenager charged with stabbing her mother to death."

"That's her. She missed her competency hearing a month ago. I'm on the line for half a mill."

A half-million-dollar bond meant a bounty worth fifty grand. Cartoon dollar signs ka-chinged in my brain. "I'm listening."

"I need her back in custody no later than end of day Tuesday."

The dollar signs went thunk and vanished. "Tuesday? Are you freakin' kidding me? That's only five days from now, including today."

"I'm very aware of that fact."

Finding someone who'd been in the wind for a month was tough. Doing it in five days? The Catholic Church sainted people for lesser miracles. But considering my limited employment opportunities, I had little to lose and a whole lot to gain. "I'll take it."

She handed me the file. I scanned a copy of the arrest report, the bail application with Holly's photo, and printouts of emails from Fiddler updating Sadie on the case. Between his lack of punctuation, convoluted syntax, and rampant typos, much of what Fiddler wrote was incomprehensible. Honestly, didn't nobody learn this guy some English?

"What's your take on the aunt? What's her name?" I flipped back to the bail application. "Kimberly Morton."

"Until Bonnie Schwartz's death, Ms. Morton had very little contact with Holly, despite being Bonnie's sister. Even with all of the media appearances, Bonnie was very protective of her daughter, never letting her out of her sight for a minute."

"And yet Morton puts up her home as collateral for bail? That's awfully generous. You think she knows where Holly is?"

"Based on what Fiddler told me, Ms. Morton cares a lot for Holly and what she's been through, despite their estrangement. Would she risk losing her home to protect the girl? I don't know for sure, but I doubt it."

"You think Holly was kidnapped?"

"Morton never received a ransom request as far as I know. Still, Fiddler uncovered reports of two other young women in the Schwartzes' Maryvale neighborhood who've gone missing in the past year. According to the arrest report, Holly claimed a black man was trying to kidnap her when her mother was killed."

"Any idea who this mysterious black man might be?"

"Fiddler didn't turn up anything. The detective on the case believes Holly made up the story."

I flipped to the arrest report and found the name of the detective assigned to the case—Pierce Hardin. I stiffened. I did not want to talk to him if I could avoid it.

"All right, I'll try to bring Holly in by Tuesday."

"I don't need you to try." Sadie looked as if the weight of the world sat on her brow. "You need to bring her in by Tuesday, or we're both out of a job."

I stood and offered her my hand, which she shook. "Understood."

As I turned to leave, she said, "One more thing. I don't want Conor Doyle working on this."

I tried to look innocent. "Conor who?"

"Don't play coy with me, Ms. Ballou. I read the article." She held up the newspaper and waved it in the air. "I know Conor's your boyfriend."

"Okay, fine, he's my boyfriend. What the hell's the deal between you two, anyway? Y'all have a bad breakup? He boil your pet rabbit or something?"

Her face was a stone wall. "Suffice it to say, I don't trust him and neither should you. He's not who he says he is."

"What the hell's that supposed to mean?"

"I can't say any more. Just take my word for it."

"Now who's being coy? He's my boyfriend. If there's something I should know about Conor, I'd like to hear it."

She pulled off her glasses and pinched the bridge of her nose. "You want to date him, that's your choice. But I don't want him involved on this job. That's final."

"Look, lady, you want me to find Holly Schwartz—in five days, no less—I'm going to need help. Right now Conor's all I got."

Sadie held out her hand, reaching for the file. "Fine. I'll give the job to someone else. I'm not having Conor anywhere near my cases."

I grimaced. She was probably bluffing. She seemed as hard up as I was. Then again, I could really use the fifty grand, even if it was a long shot. "All right. I'll locate Holly without him."

"See that you do. I find out he's working with you on this, I'll pull it. You hear me?"

I held up a three-finger salute. "Scout's honor."

12

I climbed the stairs of the parking garage, feeling conflicted about my new situation. On the one hand, I was happy to be working again, and with a bail agent who didn't care that I was transgender. The fifty-grand bounty wasn't anything to sneeze at, either.

On the other hand, what Sadie said about Conor bothered me. More than bothered me. It pissed me the fuck off. What the hell was she talking about? I didn't want to believe her. But there were parts of Conor's past that he didn't talk about. Like growing up during the Troubles in Ireland and some of the shit he saw in Afghanistan and Iraq. But what the hell did that have to do with who he was now?

When I reached the Gray Ghost, I flung the duffel bag with my Wonder Woman costume into the back so hard it bounced off the back window. No time to play superhero for the geeky masses. Comicon was on hold until I could track down a poor, orphaned, disabled girl and throw her back in jail. Sometimes this job fucking sucked.

Sitting in the driver's seat, I cranked the AC and opened Holly's file. Until the murder, she'd been living with her mom in a small house in the Maryvale neighborhood in west Phoenix. But after getting bailed out of jail, she'd been staying with her aunt, Kimberly Morton. That put Morton at the top of my list of people to talk to.

I'd check out Holly's old house in Maryvale later, though it was unlikely she was there.

I dropped by my house to change into a Gin Wigmore T-shirt and some cargo pants, then punched Morton's address into my GPS. She lived in a fancy-schmancy neighborhood off Tatum Boulevard in Paradise Valley, just east of Phoenix. I put my phone on speaker and called Conor.

"Good news! I got the job," I said when he answered.

"That's brilliant, love. Ya want to meet for lunch to celebrate, or are ya headed to Comicon?"

"Neither, unfortunately. I'm working the Holly Schwartz case. Only got five days to track her down."

"Shite! Five days. So, what's the bounty on her?"

"Fifty grand."

"Oy! That's a pretty penny. All to find some girl in a wheelchair?"

"You want in on it?"

So what if I swore on my scout's honor not to bring in Conor. The truth was, I never was one of those cookie-peddling Girl Scouts, anyway. Sure as hell was never a Boy Scout. Besides, something about this case didn't feel right.

If she was hiding out at Auntie Kimberly's house, Fiddler would have dragged her ass back to jail a long time ago. So either Kim Morton had connections with people who knew how to hide someone, or something seriously fucked up was going on. Going it alone could get dangerous either way.

"Ya didn't mention my name, did ya, love?"

"Not technically," I hedged.

"Jinxie, ya promised me ya wouldn't."

"Don't get your boxers in a bunch, dude. *She* brought up your name, not me. She knew we were dating from the *Phoenix Living* article. Maybe you shouldn't have gotten all blabby with Hensley, huh?"

I heard him sigh. "So she's cool with me being on the job?"

"Not so much. In fact, she expressly forbade it." My fists

tightened on the steering wheel, and I cut off some guy in a shiny new Beemer to get around a slow-moving landscaping truck. "Point of fact, she said you weren't who you said you are. What's she talking about, Conor?"

"Bollocks!"

"That's all you have to say? Bollocks?"

"She's daft, Jinxie. You've known me for years. Do ya honestly think I'm not who I say I am?"

"I didn't until all this bullshit. What happened between you two? I want an answer."

"Perhaps I should stay out of it. Don't want to jeopardize your business with Sadie."

I sighed. This wasn't going where I wanted it to. "Forget Sadie, Conor. I need backup on this, all right?"

"What's wrong, Jinxie?" he asked with a forced chuckle. "Ya worried a little girl in a wheelchair can take ya?"

"Yeah, right. Not her I'm worried about. There's something seriously hinky about this case. A disabled girl vanishes days before a hearing on her mother's murder? And after a month of hunting, Fiddler still can't find her? I got a bad feeling about this one. So are you in or what?"

"I've always got your back, love. Especially when things get dodgy. What's the plan?"

I told him to meet me at the aunt's house in Paradise Valley and gave him the address.

"I'll be there. But don't blame me if Sadie goes batshite crazy when she finds out I'm helping you."

"I won't tell if you won't."

Paradise Valley was an upscale suburb wedged between Phoenix and Scottsdale. Kimberly Morton's neighborhood, at the base of Mummy Mountain, consisted of sprawling stucco-covered ranch houses in various shades of tan, topped with red Spanish tile roofs and surrounded by manicured desert landscaping.

Among the shiny Porsches, Teslas, and Bentleys, my

scruffy-looking SUV stuck out like a turd in a champagne fountain.

I parked on the street next to Morton's semicircular driveway and tried again to decipher Fiddler's email updates to Sadie while I waited for Conor. I didn't learn much. Much of what he wrote was incomprehensible word salad. There were mentions of the house where Holly and Bonnie lived and a black van but nothing that made any sense. He'd smelled like weed when we'd gone after Freddie Colton. Maybe he was stoned when he wrote the emails. Maybe that was why he hadn't found Holly.

Ten minutes later, Conor pulled up behind me in his restored '68 black Dodge Charger. I grabbed my paperwork and put on my body armor and tactical belt, with my Taser on the right and my Ruger on the left in a cross-draw holster. A pair of wraparound shades and fingerless black leather gloves completed the ensemble.

The moment I opened the truck's door, the morning heat slapped me in the face like a wave. "God help me when monsoon season gets here."

"Hey, love," Conor said as we met by his car. He wore a tan polo shirt with the logo of his company, Viper Fugitive Recovery, embroidered in the left corner. "Ya look like you're ready to storm the castle. Ya expecting trouble from the aunt?"

"Not taking any chances." I adjusted the Velcro straps on the side of my vest. "Besides, I want her to know we mean business."

"Fair enough. I think I'll chance it without a vest in this swanky neighborhood."

"Suit yourself."

"So how do ya want to handle it? Ya want me around back?"

I shook my head. "I doubt Holly's here. But even if she is, she's not likely to outrun us in a wheelchair. Let's stick together for now, see what Auntie Kim has to say."

"Works for me."

We followed a flagstone walk to the front porch. I jabbed

at the doorbell a couple of times, then banged on the security screen door. "Open up! Bail enforcement!"

Moments later, a woman resembling a slender, uptown version of Bonnie Schwartz appeared on the other side of the security door. She was dressed in a brightly colored flowing silk sundress. The fancy threads contrasted with the haunted expression in her eyes. Her skin was sallow, and she looked as if she hadn't slept or eaten in weeks.

"Can I help you?" Her voice was a hoarse, lifeless whisper.

"Kimberly Morton?"

"Yes." Her gaze switched from me to Conor and back again. "If this is about my niece, I told the last guy, she isn't here."

"Look, lady, enough of this bullshit. You posted her bond with Assurity Bail Bonds, and Holly missed her court date last month. If I don't return her to custody immediately, you're going to lose your pretty little mansion." I waved the paperwork authorizing me to arrest Holly and slapped it against the screen.

Morton blinked back tears. "If I knew where she was, I'd tell you. Someone took her. That's all I know. I called the police, but they won't help. No one cares."

If she was lying, she was damn good at it. I offered her a sympathetic smile as my nagging conscience got the best of me. "Fine. I'm sorry. Tell us what you know. Then maybe we can find her and return her safely to custody. All right?"

I could see the wheels turning in her head, trying to decide if she could trust us.

"We just wanna help you and your niece get things sorted out, mum," Conor said in his sexiest brogue. "She's already been through so much, don'cha think? Please let us help."

The woman's distraught demeanor softened. I was jealous of the way his accent mesmerized other women. Then again, I fell for him the same way, so who was I to complain? And if it got us in the door, all the better.

Morton sighed and opened the security door. "Come in."

13

She led us from the spacious entryway to a living room as big as my entire house. Unlike my place, all the furniture and decor was coordinated in a kaleidoscope of off-white, beige, tan, and taupe. Native American pottery and other artwork lined bookshelves. The only vibrant colors appeared in a collection of abstract paintings mounted on one wall—explosions of red, orange, and blue on canvas.

She led me to a tan Ultrasuede couch. "Can I offer the two of you something to drink?"

"Some water would be great." Anything to get the taste of the desert out of my mouth.

She strolled to a wet bar on the far end of the room and pulled two cobalt glass bottles from a mini fridge and offered one to each of us. The water was some fancy brand I'd never heard of. I unscrewed the cap and took a long pull. Didn't taste any better than Dasani, but it was cold and wet, and that was all I cared about.

"When was the last time you saw Holly?" I asked.

A cloud passed over her face. "Two days before her competency hearing was scheduled. Holly and I had an argument about our attorney's decision to have her declared not guilty by reason of mental defect. Holly hated that. Kept screaming how she wasn't crazy or stupid, and insisted she didn't kill her mother."

"But Holly is mentally disabled, right?" I watched her body language. So far, she seemed to be telling the truth.

"Last time I spoke with my sister, Bonnie—which was a few years ago—she said Holly had the mental capacity of a five-year-old. Holly was fourteen at the time. Personally, I think she's smarter than her mother gave her credit for."

"It's been three years since you've seen your sister?" Conor asked.

"As kids, we were thick as thieves, she being just a year older than me. But in junior high, she shut me out and started hanging with a rough crowd—skaters and junkies, mostly. She ran away at sixteen, and I didn't see her for several years.

"Then out of the blue, I got a call from her not long after my late husband passed. Bonnie was pregnant. I figured she'd have an abortion, but she believed the pregnancy was a sign from the universe to get her shit together. Despite my busy schedule as a Realtor, I tried to be there for her during the pregnancy best I could."

"That's very generous of you," I said. "So what happened? How did you two become estranged again?"

"When Holly was six months old, she got really sick. Bonnie said she spit everything up and was having horrible seizures. Medical tests didn't show anything specific, so her doctors dismissed Holly's symptoms. They treated my sister like she was imagining things."

"How horrible," Conor replied.

"Bonnie didn't give up. She spent every spare moment looking up rare medical conditions on the web and poring over medical journals. It got to the point where her own health was declining. I made the mistake of telling her she was becoming obsessed. She didn't take it well. From then on, my contact with Bonnie and Holly was sporadic at best."

"Who killed Bonnie?" Conor asked. His question surprised me. It wasn't our job to determine Holly's guilt or innocence.

We just had to bring her in and let the courts figure out the rest.

"I only know what Holly told me. Bonnie was in their backyard, feeding the neighborhood cats. Holly was coloring at the dining room table when a large black man broke into the house. She screamed when he tried to drag her away. Bonnie came running and ..." Tears streamed down her face. My throat grew tight as I watched the raw emotion tear away her composure.

"Bonnie grabbed a kitchen knife to stop him. But he took it from her. Stabbed her several times in the stomach. Holly managed to lock herself in the bathroom and call 911."

"Why'd the police arrest Holly?" I asked.

"The police interrogated her for hours, treating her like she was a hardened criminal instead of a mentally impaired teenager. When I got a call from her and learned what was going on, I phoned my friend Zach Swearingen to represent her. He normally handles corporate cases, but he's the only lawyer I know, and he did some pro bono criminal work when he was younger.

"Once he was there, I figured they'd let her go. Instead, they arrested her. She was the victim, and they had the nerve to arrest her. What's this world coming to?"

"What about the girl's da?" Conor asked. "Is he in the picture?"

"Her da?"

"Her father," I explained, giving Conor a look.

"Bonnie never told me his name. Just said he was some guy she used to sleep with in order to buy dope. Bonnie used to have a drug problem. I think that's what caused Holly's health problems. I never pressed her for the father's identity. Not my business, you understand."

Something about the story didn't sit right with me, but I couldn't put my finger on it. "You love your niece, I gather."

"Of course, she's a good kid. And she's family."

"You'd do anything for her. Pay for her lawyer. Post her bail."

"Naturally!" Morton started to come alive. "Someone needs to be there for her. Sure as hell hasn't been the police."

"Would you risk losing your house to keep her from going to trial?" I pressed.

Conor shot me a glare that said back off. I ignored it.

Morton's face flushed. "You think I'm hiding her? I told you, someone kidnapped her. I called the police, this Detective Hardin, but he hasn't done a damned thing. Won't even issue an AMBER Alert."

"Did he say why?" Conor asked.

"He refuses to believe she was taken against her will."

"No ransom demand, though?" I pressed.

"No." The fire in her eyes dwindled. "That's what scares me more than anything. If they don't want money, then why take her?"

Morton pulled a pill bottle out of her purse and swallowed a couple of capsules. "I keep hearing about these sex traffickers—these men who sell girls into slavery. It terrifies me to think what she must be going through."

"How'd the kidnappers get in?" Conor asked.

"They broke the back door window. Snatched her right out of her bed. Didn't even take her wheelchair, for God's sake. I was asleep in the next room, but somehow I didn't hear a thing."

Yeah, I wonder why, I thought, eyeing the pill bottle still in her hand.

Morton's gaze drifted out to the backyard, where sunlight danced off the water of their pool. "I'm honestly at my wit's end."

I glanced around the room, looking for a security system. "You have any surveillance cameras?"

"I do. But the system wasn't armed that night for some reason. I don't know if it crashed or maybe Holly accidentally turned it off." She wiped a tear from her eye. "I can't tell you how many times I've wished I'd checked it before I went to bed that night."

"Can we see the room where she was staying?" Conor gave her that smile of his.

The damned woman blushed and smiled as she wiped her cheek. "I suppose it couldn't hurt anything."

14

I followed Kimberly Morton down a hallway to a bedroom ablaze with sunlight filtered through ivory curtains. A painting of galloping horses hung on the wall above the queen-size sleigh bed. The floral comforter was pulled back, revealing pale-yellow sheets. A nearby bookshelf held a collection of DVDs, middle-grade chapter books, and animal-themed knickknacks.

"After her mother died, I did what I could to make this guest room feel like home. She loves animals, especially horses. We were talking about getting a puppy before she disappeared."

Along the opposite wall stood a wooden desk with a stack of coloring books and a cup full of colored pencils. I picked up a coloring book that featured forest animals on the cover and thumbed through it. The use of color and shading was impressive, not what I expected from a mentally impaired teenager. "Did Holly color these?"

"Yes. She's quite talented. Something that her diseases couldn't take away, thank goodness."

I flipped to a picture of a mother bear and a cub and paused. On top of the brown coloring of the fur, streaks of red cut across the cub's stomach and front legs. Holly had also drawn something the color of rotten avocado streaming out of the cub's mouth.

On the next page, a family of deer crept through the forest. Thick red slashes marked the body of one of the fawns, while green and black lines spewed from its mouth. Holly had added the same bizarre touches on the following page. "Geez! What's up with this?" I held the book up to show Morton. "Bleeding, puking animals?" *Maybe she* is *nuts,* I thought.

"Oh, that poor child." Kimberly took the book and placed a hand on one of the drawings. "Must be a response to the trauma she's experienced."

"Uh-huh." I explored the dresser next to the bed. The top drawer was empty. The bottom drawer contained only a couple of shirts, one pair of shorts, and three mismatched socks.

I glanced at Conor, who stood next to the open wall closet. A couple of dresses hung from the rack.

"These all the clothes she owns?" Conor asked. "Seems a bit empty, if ya ask me."

"What?" Kimberly looked in the closet, then in the dresser drawer I was holding open. "No, she has plenty of clothes. I don't understand where they could be."

"You didn't notice her clothes were gone until just now? Seriously?"

"I ... I never thought to look in her closet. I just assumed they'd be here."

I shook my head. "Anything else missing that should be here?"

"No, not that I see." Kimberly's lower lip trembled as she looked around the room. *Is she for real, or is this all an act to throw us off the scent? How could she not have noticed this before?*

I stepped into the bathroom. Prescription pill bottles were lined up on the counter like a squad of orange plastic soldiers next to a weekly pill organizer. I looked at the labels but had no idea what they were for. "She take all these meds?"

Morton nodded. "That's what worries me most. She needs these. Without them she could ... assuming ... assuming she's still ... oh God!" Emotion choked off the rest of her sentence. She covered her face with her hand and slumped onto the toilet seat. "She has so many health problems. She can't survive without her meds."

I faced her and put my arms on her shoulders. "Can you think of anyone who would have taken her?"

"No! Of course not!"

I tried to think of more questions but couldn't come up with anything. I looked at Conor, and he shrugged.

"I don't know where Holly is, Ms. Morton. Maybe you're hiding her."

"I'm not!"

"Maybe she was kidnapped like you say. Either way, I intend to find her." I placed my business card in her hand. She looked up, and I locked eyes with her. "Call me if you think of anything that might help."

"I just want her home safe," she said, staring blankly at the shower curtain.

"You know when I find her, I'm taking her to jail, right? What happens after that is out of my hands."

Morton nodded. "I know."

"Come on." I led Conor out of the bathroom and into the living room. "She knows more than she's saying. How could she not have noticed Holly's clothes were missing?"

"Aye. And why'd they take the girl's clothes but leave her meds and wheelchair behind? Seems a bit dodgy. How about we talk to the neighbors? You go west, I'll go east?"

I mulled it over. "Yeah, all right. Meet you back at the cars in ten."

"And Kimberly?"

I glanced back down the hallway. "What about her?"

"I hate to leave her like this."

"She's a grown woman. I'm sure she can take care of herself. We got a fugitive to find and a bounty to collect. Come on. Let's canvass the neighbors."

"Whatever ya say, boss lady," he said with a grin.

I nudged him. "Don't you forget it."

When I stepped outside, my eyeballs felt as if they were boiling in my skull. Sweat trickled down my face as I hiked along the street for what felt like a mile but was probably closer to a couple of hundred feet. I pulled off my ballistic vest. My shirt looked as if I were competing in a wet T-shirt contest.

By the time I reached the neighbor's porch, my arms were bright red. I pressed the doorbell, and a moment later, a man in a green-striped shirt and chinos answered the door.

"If you're looking for landscaping work, I've already got somebody. Sorry."

"Seriously, dude? You think I'm here to trim your palm trees?" I held up my vest and pointed at the words Bail Enforcement Agent. "I'm a bounty hunter looking for your neighbor's niece. Her name's Holly Schwartz. Have you seen her?" I handed him Holly's photo.

He squinted at the picture and shook his head. "Nope. Doesn't look familiar."

"Really? She's been living next door for the past six months. Take another look."

He studied the photo for a minute. "Wait, I have seen her."

I felt a rush of hope. A break at last. "Really? Where?"

"On TV. 'Bout a year ago. One of them telethons, I think it was. That girl was on it, sitting in a wheelchair, singing 'God Bless America.' Skinny little thing."

I sighed. "Have you seen her recently? Say, in the past week or so?"

"Can't say as I have. Sorry." He handed me back the photo and shut the door before I could ask anything else.

I continued on to the next two houses, then doubled back to the neighbors on the other side of the street with similar results. Finally, I trudged back to our vehicles. My feet were so hot from the sidewalk, I thought my boots would melt. Conor was already waiting in his car, eating a bag of Flamin' Hot Cheetos.

I slipped into the passenger side and stuck my face in front of the vents blowing cool air. "Oh, thank goodness!"

"Any luck with the neighbors, love?"

"Asshole next door thought I was there to trim the bushes.

Can you believe that shit?" I lifted the bottom of my shirt and shook it, trying to send some of the cool air across my chest. "I swear one of these days I'm moving to someplace cool, like Seattle or Portland. Maybe Canada."

"Anyone seen Holly?"

"Not in the past few weeks."

"Shite! No luck on my end either." I could hear the bag rustle in his hand. "Care for a Cheeto? I find it helps me think."

"No, thanks. Just want to cool off."

"Maybe we should talk to Detective Hardin," he said. "Find out why he arrested her."

The memory of Hardin's gruff voice chewing me out for doing something stupid on a domestic disturbance call rattled in my brain. "I'll pass, thanks."

"Why?"

"What's it matter to us why he arrested her? Our job isn't to find out whodunit. I just want to track her down and bring her in. End of story."

"Ya know him, don't you?"

"What? No!" I sighed. "Okay, yeah, I know him. He was my training officer when I joined Phoenix PD."

"Why don't ya want to talk to him?"

"Doesn't matter. Maybe Holly's lawyer knows where she is. This Swearingen guy."

"A lawyer ain't gonna tell ya shite about his client's whereabouts, Jinxie. Let's talk to Hardin. If we can persuade him to let us look at witness statements, it might give us a lead."

I turned away from the air vent to glare at him. "Who's running this case? Me or you?"

He gave me a pacifying look, as if I were a rabid bulldog. "You are, love."

"Damn straight!"

I was being a bitch, but I was hot and frustrated about not being at Comicon. Not to mention being pissed at being outed. Poor Conor was in my line of fire.

"Holly's lawyer is bound by privilege. I doubt you'll get anything useful outta him."

"Then I'll just have to be very persuasive."

"Persuasive? What are ya gonna do? Threaten him? Charm it out of him?"

"I can be charming." I sneered at him. "When I want to be."

"Aye! Charming like a snake. And just as deadly."

"Hey, I charmed you, didn't I?"

"Aye, that ya did, love." He chuckled. "Care to place a wager?"

"I'll bet you fifty bucks I can get Swearingen to tell me where Holly is. Assuming he actually knows."

"I'll take that bloody bet."

15

Zach Swearingen's office was located in the Corporate Century Office Park on Shea Boulevard, just east of Scottsdale Road.

Conor was right. It was a long shot. Lawyers weren't chatty about their clients except in the courtroom. But I had a few ideas of how to loosen this one's lips.

First, I had to get past his secretary. After canvassing Morton's neighbors, I looked like a wreck and smelled even worse. It was time to get creative. I parked the Gray Ghost in the office park parking lot, grabbed my purse from the glove box, and got to work.

Moments later, Conor knocked on my window. "Oy! Jinxie! We goin' in or what?"

I rolled down the tinted window, and he gasped.

"Jesus bloody Christ! What happened? Ya look like you've been battered."

I smiled. "That's the idea." I'd used a combination of purple eye shadow and smudged eyeliner to give the illusion of bruises. "You still got that bag of hot Cheetos?"

"Sorry, love, I ate them all."

"But you still have the bag, right?"

"Aye. How come?"

"I need it."

He went to his Charger and returned a moment later with the empty bag. I stuck my hand into it, coated my fingers with the spicy red powder, and rubbed my left eye with it. "Holy fuck, that hurts!" I gasped.

"Bloody hell, Jinxie!"

I clenched my fist and gritted my teeth as I waited for the fiery pain in my eye to subside. It didn't. At least not right away. I tried to distract myself by thinking of the things I could do with my half of the bounty. Didn't help. "Ugh, that really hurts."

I peeked at my reflection in the rearview mirror, at least with my right eye. My left eye was red, puffy, and tearing uncontrollably. I really did look as if I'd been punched.

"Have you gone completely mad? What'd ya do that for?"

"You'll see." I grabbed my purse, leaving all my bounty hunter gear on the passenger seat, then locked up the Gray Ghost. "Just follow my lead."

Conor and I joined a petite elderly woman in the elevator, and I punched the button for the fourth floor.

The woman glanced at me then gave Conor the evil eye. As the door opened onto the third floor, the woman wagged her finger at him. "You should learn to keep your damned hands to yourself." She marched out of the car, and the doors closed behind her.

I chuckled.

"Please tell me I'm not the villain in this daft scheme of yours."

"Of course not," I said. "Story is that you're my new lover, protecting me from my abusive, hopefully soon-to-be-ex husband."

"Bloody hell."

On the fourth floor, I led Conor through the glass doors of Miller, Crouch, and Swearingen.

A sharply dressed man with a soul patch, wire-framed glasses, and a single diamond stud earring sat behind the receptionist desk. As soon as he saw me, a worried expression crossed his face. "Uh, can I help you?"

I drew on emotions from the darkest moments of my

childhood. My jaw tensed. My throat tightened, and I blinked back tears.

"I ... I do hope so," I said as I grasped Conor's hand. "I recently separated from my abusive husband. But he keeps coming after me and my new boyfriend."

"I'm so sorry." The receptionist offered me a box of tissues from his desk. I took one.

"Thanks. Unfortunately, the police won't do anything. I tried to get a restraining order, but it was quashed. My friend Kim Morton suggested I hire Mr. Swearingen to get it reinstated."

"I see. Well, do you have an appointment?"

"No, I ... I'm just so afraid. He ... he's threatened to kill me. Please, I must see Mr. Swearingen now."

"Of course." He picked up his phone and dialed an extension. "Mr. Swearingen, we have a woman in an emergency situation here. Says she was referred to you by Ms. Morton. Yes, certainly." He hung up. "You're in luck. One of Mr. Swearingen's court appearances got postponed. Go down the hall. Third door on your left." He pointed.

"Oh, bless you." I put my hand on his and gave him a teary smile.

As we walked toward Swearingen's office, Conor said, "Damn, love. That was Oscar-worthy. And more than a bit scary. Made me want to batter the imaginary wanker that done this to ya."

"Two years in the Aristotle Collegiate High Drama Club. You should have seen me as Rose in *Meet Me in St. Louis*." I used the tissue Chris had given me to wipe as much of the fake bruise makeup off my face as I could.

Zach Swearingen stood when we walked into his office. He wore a pin-striped black suit with a Rotary pin on his lapel. "Can I help you?"

I tossed the tissue in the trash can next to his mahogany desk. "Yes, we need help tracking down one of your clients."

"What? I thought you were a domestic violence victim."

"Sorry, didn't think your office manager would let us in if we told him we were bail enforcement agents."

"Bail enforcement agents? Get out of here before I call security."

"Why is everyone calling security on me these days? It's really rude."

"Maybe you should take a hint."

"Your client, Holly Schwartz, missed her court date last month," I said. "Assurity Bail Bonds hired us to bring her in. If we don't return her to custody by Tuesday, your friend Kim Morton loses her house."

"I have no idea where Holly Schwartz is. Most likely kidnapped by the man who murdered her mother. Maybe if the damned cops put out an AMBER Alert, we could find her."

Something about his gaze told me he was holding something back, but I had no idea what. Or maybe he was just a shifty-eyed lawyer. Or both.

"Mr. Swearingen," Conor said, "could ya tell us what ya know about her mother's attacker?"

He fiddled with a gold Cross pen on his desk. "According to Holly, he was about six-eight, medium-dark skin, wearing an orange shirt. Had a black wing tattoo on his right arm and a gold hoop earring in one ear."

"Anything else?" I asked.

"That's all she gave me."

"If ya think she's innocent, why are ya pleading that she's daft?"

Swearingen's face flushed. "Look, buddy, are you a lawyer?"

"Can't say as I am, no."

"Then don't tell me how to plead my case. You two clowns have wasted enough of my time." He stood and pointed toward his office door. "I want you gone."

"Fine," I said. "But if Kim Morton loses her house because of you—"

"Get out! And if you harm one hair on Holly Schwartz's head, I'll bring criminal charges against you both. You hear me?"

On the ride down the elevator, Conor held out his hand. "Pay up."

I rolled my eyes. "Yeah, right. He didn't know. That was a condition of the bet, remember?"

Conor harrumphed. "He knows where she is. I could see it in his eyes."

"There was certainly something he wasn't saying."

"So pay up. Fifty bucks."

"Good lord! I don't have it on me."

"Figures."

My eye was still irritated, and my head was starting to pound. "I'm calling Becca. See if she can do some skip tracing." I pulled out my phone and dialed her number.

"Not a bad idea," Conor said as we exited the elevator.

"This is Becca." She sounded glum.

"Yo, Becks, it's Jinx. I need you to do some skip tracing."

"Jinx." She groaned. "Today's not the best day. Can it wait?"

"Normally, I'd say yes, but I'm on a tight deadline. Got to catch my fugitive by Tuesday night. Chronic fatigue acting up?"

"Yeah. Not a good day. I'm all out of spoons."

She was telling me that her chronic fatigue syndrome was flaring up again and that her energy level was critically low. I felt bad about pushing her, but if I didn't locate Holly by the deadline, my career as a bounty hunter was over.

"I keep telling you, switch to knives. It's much more fun," I said, trying to cheer her up.

"Funny." She sighed. "I know I'll pay for it tomorrow, but for you, I'll risk it."

Years earlier, when she was first diagnosed with chronic fatigue—or myalgic encephalomyelitis, as it was formally known—I was one of the few people who didn't think she was just being lazy. I also tried to be there for her whenever she had a flare-up to make sure she had food and other essentials that she didn't have the energy to get for herself. Just part of our pact as besties.

"You're a goddess."

"Yeah, Hypnos, Greek goddess of sleep. Who am I looking for?"

"Holly Schwartz."

"The girl in the wheelchair whose mother was killed?"

"That's her. I need whatever you can find on her, her mother, and her aunt, Kimberly Morton. Pull phone records. Bank records. Anything that shows some recent activity." I gave her the relevant information from the bail application.

"Okay, I'll let you know what I find out."

"Thanks, Becca. You need anything? Groceries? Fast food? Porno?"

She chuckled. "Naw, I'm set, but thanks for asking. I'll be in touch."

I hung up. "Okay, she's on it."

"Brilliant. Let's go to the Phoenix police and talk to Detective Hardin."

"Ugh," I groaned. "I'd rather eat glass."

"What's the deal between you two?"

I cocked my head. "Asks the man who doesn't want to spill about his torrid affair with Sadie Levinson."

"We never had an affair. I worked for her father. Things got complicated is all."

"Complicated? The more you dance around this, the more I want to know. You realize that, right?"

"Fine." He strolled out of the lobby into the parking lot. The hot air made my eye burn more. "Don't tell me about you and Hardin. I'll just go back to working with my own team."

"Wait! Wait."

He stopped and turned. "Yes?"

I stared at the pavement, kicking at loose bits of asphalt. "He was my training officer, okay? That's how I knew him."

"And what? He was a bad cop?"

"Just the opposite. He's top-notch. Very by the book. Thing was, he was always on my case, criticizing every little thing I did wrong. Some of the other officers called him Officer Hard Ass. Now I guess he's Detective Hard Ass."

"Really that bad, eh?"

I looked up at Conor. "When I quit the force, he chewed me out. Called me a disappointment and said I was throwing away a promising career. He raked me over the coals for turning my back on the opportunity to be the department's first transgender officer. We parted with a lot of bitter feelings between us."

"So he knew you were trans?"

"Not a lot of secrets that side of the blue line."

"Was that why he was such a tosser to ya?"

"No, he was a bastard to everybody. Good cop. Really knew how to control a bad situation. But he didn't put up with a lot of bullshit. Turned being rude and sarcastic into an art form."

"Ah, so that's where ya get it from!"

"Funny. Not."

"I think ya should face your fears and talk to the man about Holly Schwartz. Maybe something in the case file can point us in the right direction."

"Fine. Let's do this."

He glanced at his watch. "Actually, I've got something else I gotta take care of, love."

I raised an eyebrow. "What? You just talked me into seeing Hardin. Now you're bailing on me?"

He shook his head dismissively. "Just a minor errand. Shouldn't be long."

"Whatever. I don't want to know." I hopped into the Gray Ghost and started it up, letting the AC blow out all the hot air before closing the door.

Conor knocked on my window. I rolled it down. "Yes?"

"Where ya going after you talk to Hardin?"

"The Schwartzes' house in Maryvale."

"I've got the address. I'll try to meet ya there."

"Whatever." I rolled up the window before he could respond, and drove off.

16

walked into the Phoenix Police Department building on Washington Street and found my buddy, Ortega, manning the front desk.

He glanced at me, and a smile opened up on his face. "How's it going, Ballou?"

I fist-bumped him. "Going well. I see you earned some stripes."

"Yeah," he said, patting the sergeant patches on his arm. "Passed the exam a few months ago. You looking good, mama."

"Shut the hell up, Ortega. God!" I blushed like a damned schoolgirl.

"You still chasing fugitives?"

"Matter of fact, that's why I'm here. I need to talk to Hardin about one of his cases. He in?"

"Should be at his desk." He handed me a visitor's badge. "Homicide unit. Third floor."

"Thanks." I attached the badge to my belt. "Good to see you, man."

My pulse quickened as I rode up the elevator and strolled through the homicide unit's maze of cubicles. Detective Pierce Hardin looked as though he was not having the best of days, and that was saying something. His skin was ashen. His clothes looked slept in. And there was a bottle of Maalox on his desk.

"Rough day, dear?" I asked nervously, resting an arm on the cubicle partition.

He turned a weary eye to me. "Ballou. And here I thought we got rid of you years ago."

"I'm back."

"Like a bad case of herpes. What the hell you want? I'm busy."

"Need some information on the Holly Schwartz case."

"Why you want that?"

"She jumped bail, and I've been hired to apprehend her."

He rolled his eyes. "I've been up all night working a triple homicide, and you want me to help you do your job? Ha!"

"Hey, when the people you lock up don't show up for court, somebody's gotta track them down. We all have a job to do so that justice is served."

"Justice, huh?" He rubbed his face, leaned back in his chair, and folded his arms. "What information you looking for exactly?"

"For starters, why'd you charge her?" Since I was here, I figured it couldn't hurt to ask. I grabbed a swivel chair from a nearby desk. "She's a mentally disabled girl in a wheelchair, for God's sake."

He pulled out the murder book, a three-ring binder filled with reports, photos, and notes on the case, and flipped through it. "Several reasons. The ME report shows the stab wounds coming from someone who was short or in a seated position, like a wheelchair. If the mother'd been stabbed by a large man standing, the angle of the wounds would have been completely different."

"So you don't believe her story about a black man in an orange shirt? A black wing tattoo on his arm sounds like a rather detailed description, if you ask me."

"No evidence of forced entry. Also, when we found the girl, she was covered in blood."

"So? Holly could have tried to stop her mother's bleeding," I suggested.

"So she claimed. But the blood on her shirt and pants wasn't just from transfer. It showed directional spray, consistent with castoff from a knife."

"Why would she kill her own mother? Her aunt says the two were thick as thieves."

"From my interview with Holly, I learned her doctor was scheduled to put a feeding tube in her. Holly didn't want one despite suffering from malnourishment. Claimed she didn't need it, that her mother was poisoning her to make her too sick to keep food down. Thus, motive."

"That's one thing I don't get. You grilled a mentally disabled teenager for sixteen hours?"

"First of all, don't lecture me on procedure, Ballou. I can shit regulations better than you can recite them. Secondly, we had a child advocate present. And third, she's not as disabled as people think."

"Are you serious?"

"Don't get me wrong, she plays the part very well. But trust me, there's a sharp, wicked little mind in that head of hers. I am not letting her get away with murder."

I sat there stunned. I wouldn't have believed it from anyone but Hardin. "So she killed her mother because her mother was making her sick?"

"That's my theory. And the evidence backs me up."

"And there's no connection to these two other women who were abducted from Maryvale earlier this year?"

"Feds believe those cases are part of a human trafficking ring they're investigating. There's no connection with the Schwartz case other than location." He took a slurp of coffee and made a disgusted face. "Anything else? I have murders to solve."

"Where would Holly hide to avoid jail time?"

"Try the aunt. The one who hired the attorney."

"I did. Didn't get the impression she's hiding her. What about the Schwartzes' friends or neighbors? I assume you canvassed the neighborhood after the murder."

"We did. Everyone loved her. But would they risk jail time

to hide her? I doubt it."

"Can I get a copy of the witness statements?"

"Hey, Hardin! The lieutenant wants to see you," a female detective called from across the room.

Hardin grumbled. "Wait here. And don't touch anything." He strolled into the lieutenant's glass-enclosed office and shut the door.

I figured he'd be in there a while. I grabbed the murder book and hustled to the photocopier in the corner of the bull pen. With a clack, I opened the binder and made copies of call logs from the victim's phone, fingerprint analysis, the medical examiner's report, and transcripts from interviews.

I heard the lieutenant's door open a crack.

"Shit." I stuffed the copies in my waistband under my shirt, put the originals back in the murder book, and hightailed it to Hardin's desk before he walked out of the office.

"Anything else you need to know?" Hardin asked when he returned. "I've got work to do."

"Yeah, how come you didn't issue an AMBER Alert?"

"Two reasons. One, she turns eighteen in a couple months. And two, I've seen no credible evidence that she'd been abducted. Either her aunt or someone else is hiding her. I did issue a BOLO, however. Notified the sheriff's department, state patrol, and border patrol. Anything else?"

"No, I'm good. Thanks for your help." I got up. "Good luck with the triple murder."

"Thanks. Nice article in *Phoenix Living*, by the way."

I rolled my eyes. "Don't remind me."

"What? I thought it was good. Nice to see people in your community getting decent representation. Especially in your line of work."

"Thanks, I guess." I started to walk away, then turned. "Hey, speaking of my community, you heard anything about the Ciara Vanderbilt case?"

He squinted. "Name's not familiar. Another one of your skips?"

"A friend of mine, actually. Trans woman beaten and left for dead in a corporate office parking lot."

"This is the homicide unit, Ballou. Unless she's actually dead, it's not my case."

"Oh well. Thought you might have heard something. Thanks, anyway."

"Good luck finding Holly Schwartz. You're gonna need it."

17

When I reached the Gray Ghost, Becca called. She sounded so fragile.

"Ran the phone logs for the Schwartzes. Bank records too."

"Great! Anything interesting?"

"Bonnie's calls were mostly to doctors," she said as she took an audible breath. "A few to a company called Compassionate Care." Another breath. "A handful to charities. Rare Disease Foundation. Campaign for Neuromuscular Research."

"No surprises there."

"Not many calls on Holly's phone. Most to her mother. A couple to a George Peavey. Not sure who he is yet." She paused for a moment and moaned quietly. "Final calls were night of the murder. One to Richard Delgado. Visiting nurse, I think. Last call was 911."

"What about the bank records?"

"Expenses were typical household—Walmart, Safeway, utilities. Deposits were mostly disability payments and checks from charity orgs."

"Can you email me that information?"

"Yeah."

"Thanks, Becks. I know you need to take care of yourself. I'm just under such a time crunch."

"I know."

"When you're feeling better, see what you can dig up on Richard Delgado and George Peavey."

"Gotcha. Bye." She hung up.

I hated pushing her like that, but I didn't know anyone else who could get me the answers I needed. Unfortunately, none of the info I had so far gave me a clue where Holly might be or whether she was hiding from the law or had been kidnapped. Time to visit the scene of the crime.

The Schwartzes' Maryvale residence was ten miles northwest of downtown Phoenix. The cars parked along their street consisted of junkers with crumpled quarter panels, missing bumpers, and cracked windshields. In this environment, the Gray Ghost was invisible.

The house was tan with brick-red trim. Candy bar wrappers and empty beer bottles littered the yard. Weeds grew four feet tall in places, while sunbaked earth showed in other spots.

I suited up with my body armor, tactical belt, and weapons. I doubted Holly was hiding in the old family domicile, but it was a possibility. Didn't want to be caught unawares.

From the driveway, I followed a paved walkway into a narrow courtyard, which shielded me from anyone who wasn't standing directly in front of the house. An aluminum ramp rose six inches to the front doorstep. Faded, tattered fragments of the Phoenix PD crime scene seal clung to the door, warning people not to enter without permission. But the techs had finished their work months ago. My only barrier now was the dead bolt.

I could have used the ram I kept in the back of the Gray Ghost but preferred to make a more low-key entrance, considering I was alone. I fished a couple of picking tools out of a leather pouch I kept in my cargo pants and set to work on the lock. The security pins made it trickier than the typical door lock, but soon the cylinder turned and the door opened.

Sunlight filtered through gauzy blinds in the room to my left. Tiny black flies buzzed around my face and ears. Despite the passage of time, the stench of death lingered in the air,

compounded by the suffocating heat from the lack of air con-
ditioning. I made a conscious effort to breathe through my
mouth. It didn't help much. It took all my willpower not to retch.

I flicked a light switch. No power. I pulled out an LED flashlight and swept the front room. A slate-blue couch stretched in
front of the double window to my left. I crossed the room to a
laminated wood bookshelf standing against the wall, filled with
stacks of board games and stuffed animals. Nothing indicated
where I would find Holly.

I stepped up to a dining area with a glass dinette table and
four brass-and-cloth chairs. On the table, three colored pencils
rested in the crack between pages of an open coloring book.
No eviscerated animals in this one. Just beautifully colored
abstract designs.

Next to the book lay a yellowing *Arizona Republic* newspaper featuring a photo of the Phoenix Suns' Cedric Wilson on
the front page. The article reported that the basketball star had
apparently undergone knee surgery following an ATV accident.

Something about Wilson's photo piqued my interest, but
I wasn't sure why. I was a fair-weather sports fan at best. I
scanned the article but didn't find anything relevant to my
case and tossed it aside.

I entered the kitchen, where the puke-green countertops
didn't help my growing sense of nausea. Neither did the dead
maggots in a graveyard of dried refried beans occupying a
saucepan atop the stove. *Why hasn't anyone cleaned up?* I
wondered. Maybe the property was still in probate.

I moved on to the family room on the other side of the
kitchen's breakfast bar. The smell of death was intense here. A
three-foot-wide brown-black stain on the floor marked where
Bonnie Schwartz had met her end. I stared at the bloody carpet,
playing out the multiple scenarios in my mind. Home invasion
or domestic disturbance? Either way, it was a tragedy.

A stack of mail lay on a water-stained coffee table. I sorted
through the envelopes and flyers, hoping for clues. Most of it

was junk mail promising amazing deals on hearing aids, solar panels, and dental services. A few medical bills were marked past due. One was an envelope from Compassionate Care, LLC.

There were also letters and cards hand addressed to Holly. I opened one. It was from a fan thanking her for the inspiration after she appeared on a telethon. The others offered similar thanks and well wishes. A few included cash and checks.

The last one I read was printed from a computer. It started innocently enough but soon got creepy and sexually explicit. It was unsigned. According to the postmark, this creep was local. My skin crawled. The stale air felt suffocating. I could feel the stench of decomp in my lungs.

I stuffed the stalker letter, the fan mail, and the bills into a pocket in my cargo pants. I'd go through them later to see if they pointed to anything. Maybe Becca could help.

A hallway led to Holly's room, where an adjustable bed took up much of the space. Inspirational posters hung on the walls. *Hang in there! Believe in yourself. Life is a miracle.* Whatever. I checked the brightly painted chest of drawers and then the closet. Both were empty.

I continued my search in the guest bathroom, a spare bedroom, and the master bedroom without finding anything of note.

In the master bath, I discovered a sliding panel in the wall, concealed behind a wicker vanity shelf. I kneeled down with my flashlight to get a closer look.

"Find anything interesting?" someone asked behind me.

My flashlight clattered to the floor, and I nearly jumped out of my skin. Bile rose in my throat as I snapped to my feet, ready to fight.

"Holy fuck, Conor! You scared the shit out of me. Again. I should put a bell on you."

"Nothing to be scared of, love. Just the man of your dreams." He wrapped his arms around me and leaned in to kiss me.

I pushed him away. "More like my nightmares, the way you keep sneaking up on me."

"What's wrong, Jinxie? Can't a guy get some love?" he joked.

"Jesus, Conor, a woman died here, and her daughter is missing. Have some respect." I sat down on my heels and slid back the concealed panel. With the beam of the flashlight, I discovered a small money-counting machine. I pulled it out to show Conor.

"Now why do ya suppose they have a counting machine hidden away in the loo?" Conor asked.

"Someone was apparently making enough green they needed help counting it."

"Ya probably right. Unfortunately, it doesn't tell us where our girl is."

"No, it doesn't." My pulse slowed as disappointment settled in. "God, I wish I was at Comicon right now instead of this sweltering house of death."

"Naw, ya don't. I heard on the news some bloke inside the convention center got nicked with four loaded pistols and a shotgun. Security's been ramped up a hundredfold. All props are now banned."

"Geez! What the hell's wrong with people?"

"It's a mad, mad world, love." He offered me a hand and pulled me to my feet. "Any luck finding your fugitive?"

"Bits and pieces of information but no workable leads." I led him back down the hall and out the front door. I felt light-headed. The oppressive heat and the god-awful stench were taking their toll. I managed one more glance around the front room and got the hell out of there.

It wasn't much cooler outside, but at least the air was fresh. Well, as fresh as the air in Phoenix ever was, what with the brown cloud of smog and all. As my eyes adjusted to the glaring daylight, I noticed a skinny white woman with blond dreads standing by the Gray Ghost and eyeing me suspiciously.

18

The woman wore a lacy halter top, Daisy Dukes, and flip-flops. A muddy kaleidoscope of ink ran down each pale arm. I guessed she was in her forties, but she could have been younger.

"What're y'all doing in Bonnie and Holly's place? Y'all cops?" she asked through a mouth of rotten teeth as we approached. Her voice was like gravel in a blender.

"Not exactly," I replied. "Holly's gone missing. Her aunt's worried, so we're trying to find her. Did you know Bonnie and Holly well?"

"Yeah, I knowed 'em."

I perked up. "Any idea where Holly might be?"

She crossed her arms. "What's it worth to you?"

About fifty grand, I thought. I pulled my wallet out of my pocket. I didn't generally carry my purse when I worked. It was unwieldy and just something to lose. All I had in the wallet was a ten and three ones. I handed her the ten. She looked at me as if I'd kicked her dog.

"A ten? That's all Holly's worth to you? Damn, I get more than that for a hand job."

"Good lord." I nudged Conor. "Hey, ya got any cash on you?"

"Ya mean aside from the fifty ya owe me from our bet earlier?"

"Come on, man, cough up some green so Trixie here can buy herself a new set of teeth."

"For your info, my name ain't Trixie. It's Shartroose." She spelled it for me. "You know, like the color?"

I didn't know exactly how the color chartreuse was spelled, but I was pretty sure that wasn't it.

Conor pulled out a wad of twenties. I snatched it from him and counted out three, then handed back the rest. She reached for the cash, but I held it away.

"First tell us what you know. Then we'll see what it's worth."

"What I know is I saw a black creeper van parked in front of their house that night. I seen the same van there several times before."

"You see who was in it? Or get a license plate?"

"No."

"That's it? You saw a black van?"

"Who you think I am? Jessica Fletcher or some shit? I told you what I know. Now gimme my money."

"That little tidbit isn't worth sixty dollars. Not even worth the ten."

"It's worth something."

"It's worth crap." I strutted around to the driver's side of the Gray Ghost, fanning myself with the cash. Conor stood to the side with a bemused look on his face.

"All right, fine," Shartroose said, following me into the street. "Driver had brown skin, long black hair."

"Any distinguishing features? What was he wearing?"

"I don't know. I was busy getting ready for a date, and it was dark besides. I think I seen him wearing an orange shirt one time before, though."

So far he sounded like the guy Holly described. "How old was he?"

"How'm I supposed to know?"

"Guess."

"I dunno. Twenties, thirties, maybe."

"What was he doing when you saw him?"

"I just saw him pull up and walk to the front door." Shartroose got quiet and mellow all of a sudden. "Makes me sad to think about it. Bonnie was real nice. Spent her life taking care of that poor girl. Then someone gone and kilt her."

"Have you seen Holly since then?"

"Not since that night. Heard she moved in with a relative in the East Valley."

I paused, hoping she'd offer something else. When she didn't say anything, I handed her a couple of the twenties. She looked at them as if they were trash.

"Forty lousy dollars? For all I told you?"

"Plus the ten I already gave you makes fifty. And trust me, that's being generous."

Conor grabbed the other twenty and handed it to her with his business card. "Thank ya, darlin', for all your help. Would ya give us a ring if ya see either Holly or the guy show up? We'll make it worth your trouble, I promise ya."

Shartroose's eyes got all sparkly as she nuzzled up to him. "Oooh, Mr. Lucky Charms, I like how you talk. I'll call even if I don't see them none. You and me can do a little partying."

I pulled her hand off Conor's thigh and shoved her away. "Thanks, but we got work to do." I turned to him. "Come on, Lucky Charms. Before I shoot you in your shillelagh."

"Bitch!" Shartroose shouted as she walked across the street.

Conor chuckled. "Not jealous are ya, love?"

I scoffed. "Of Shartroose and those nasty teeth of hers? Yeah, right. I'm sure you're just itching to kiss that mouth."

"Then why're ya getting your knickers in a twist?"

"Because it's four o'clock in the afternoon and I've spent the last hour in a house that smelled like hot death. If we don't come up with a lead soon, I'll miss out on fifty grand and any future jobs with Assurity Bail Bonds."

He put an arm around me, and I didn't resist. "Come on, Jinxie. I'll buy ya a beer at Grumpy's."

I was about to say yes when a man with long black braids and wearing a blue-plaid shirt came strolling down the sidewalk.

He spotted me and took off running the other way.

I raced south after him. Conor's Charger roared to life behind me, but I was focused on the man I was chasing.

With the weight and bulk of my gear, I had trouble keeping up with him. Shortly before the road took a sharp right turn, he cut between the houses and hopped a block wall. I drew on my parkour skills and vaulted it with half the effort he used and spotted him running across the backyard, a Chihuahua yapping at his heels.

When he flipped over the opposite wall, the Chihuahua turned its attention to me. I breezed past the dog as I heard a loud splash.

I cleared the wall and landed on a narrow strip of ground between the wall and a kidney-shaped pool. A tangle of green garden hose extended to the water's edge. My quarry splashed desperately in the pool, crying out for help.

I was tempted to let him drown, but if he knew where Holly was, I couldn't risk losing him. I extended a ten-foot leaf skimmer. He grabbed hold of it, and I pulled him to the edge of the pool.

"Jinx?" he sputtered as his braids floated in the water behind him. "Why you chasing me?"

"Why you running, Jessup?"

Before he could answer, a man came out of the house, pointing a double-barrel shotgun at the two of us. He was bald except for a wisp of white encircling his pale head. His plaid shorts were pulled up to his armpits. "What the hell you hooligans doing in my backyard?"

I raised my hands in surrender. "Hold your fire, mister. I'm a bail enforcement agent. Just fishing this guy out of your pool. Put down the gun, and we'll be on our way."

He looked from me to the man in the pool but didn't lower the shotgun. "Y'all get on outta here b'fore I exercise my Second Amendment rights."

I pulled Jessup out of the pool and led him out the front gate, dripping water along the front driveway to the street. "How's the water?" I asked, keeping a grip on his arm.

"I ain't done nothing, and you know it."

"Then how come you ran? If I didn't know better, I'd say you have a guilty conscience."

"It's a nice day. Thought I'd get some exercise."

"Running in a hundred degree weather, followed by a dip in a pool? You training for a triathlon?"

"It's a free country. Besides, you ain't got no warrant on me."

"Actually, I'm looking for a missing girl. Rumor is she was taken by a light-skinned black man with long hair and a tattoo on his arm." Though I had to admit, the ink on Jessup's arm wasn't a wing but more a Samoan tribal design.

"You talking 'bout Holly, ain't ya?"

"Yep."

"And you think I took her? Shit, Jinx. I sling a little dope now and then, but I ain't never took nobody. You know I ain't like that. 'Specially that poor child."

I had to admit, for all the times I'd gone after Jessup for jumping bail, it was always for nonviolent drug-related offenses. Still, junkies and dealers weren't above learning new tricks. "Where were you a month ago?"

"Month ago? Oh, I remember." A smile spread across his face. "Vegas, baby! Wanna see pics?"

"Show me."

He pulled his phone from his back pocket. "Shore hope it didn't get fried from me skinny-dipping." He tapped the screen a few times. "Hey, hey! Looka here!"

I took the phone and flipped through a series of photos of him posing with a couple of showgirls. The time stamp matched the date that Holly went missing. "You win anything?"

"I was up about two grand, then I lost it all and them some. House always wins, you know what I'm saying?"

"Any idea who might've taken Holly?"

He stared at the ground as he wrung the water out of his

Sean John plaid shirt. "Past few months, I heard word that someone's snatching girls off the street. Young ones, mostly. In a black van."

"I heard about the two. Feds are investigating it."

"Way I hear it, closer to ten I know about. Cops don't like to say. Don't wanna spook folks 'round here. But we know what's going down."

"You see that black van driving around? Or in front of Holly's house?"

"Possible. Not really sure." He looked up at me. "You gonna throw that girl in jail 'cause of her mama got kilt? Don't seem right."

I sighed. "Jessup, I got orders to pick her up. If she's in danger now, hopefully I can find her, return her to custody so her aunt can bail her back out. Maybe once they see she was kidnapped, they'll drop the charges."

"But you gotta do what you gotta do, huh?"

"'Fraid so, man."

He nodded. "I got your number from the last time. I hear anything, I call you, a'ight?"

"'Preciate, my friend."

He walked away and took off his shirt. The sunlight gleamed off his wet, dark skin.

I turned to stroll back toward the Schwartz house when he called out again. "Yo, Jinx! Just remembered something Holly say to me."

"What's that?"

"'Round Christmastime, we was all over at her mom's place. Holly say to me her daddy was gonna take her away to live in his mansion. Like he Daddy Warbucks or something."

"Her father? You sure?"

"What she said. 'Course she was a little loopy from the medication she was on. Maybe she made it up."

I stood there pondering. "She say his name or what he looked like?"

"Naw, nothing like that."

"Thanks. I'll catch ya later."

He flipped me a bird but was grinning while he did it. Then he passed between two houses into a vacant lot.

I met Conor driving his Charger coming from the other direction. "Ya lose him, love? I tried to intercept him with the car. Must've missed him."

"Wasn't our guy. Just Jessup."

"Shite! Get in. I'll drive ya back to the Ghost."

19

On the drive to Grumpy's, I called Detective Hardin again. Judging from his tone when he answered, his mood hadn't improved with the day. Then again, neither had mine.

"Hey, when you interviewed the Schwartzes' neighbors, d'you talk to a gal calling herself Shartroose?"

"The meth junkie? All I got from her was a lot of nonsense."

"She told me she saw a black van in front of the Schwartzes' house shortly before the murder. Driver matched Holly's description of the man who attacked her mother. African-American. Long hair. Orange shirt. Black creeper van. I think Holly's story may be legit." I chose not to mention the stalker letter or the money-counting machine. Reading other people's mail was a federal crime. And my breaking into the house when I had no reason to believe she was there was also frowned upon.

"You think suddenly after nineteen years I forgot how to do my job, Ballou? I got the ME telling me one thing. A junkie whore telling me something different. Who you think I'm gonna believe?"

"Just wondering if you overlooked something. How else is a girl in a wheelchair going to suddenly disappear? Maybe human traffickers. I hear there've been a lot more missing girls than you let on."

"Ballou, I'm exhausted and don't have time to listen to you play armchair quarterback. You wanna solve homicide cases?

Rejoin the force. Otherwise, do your speculating on your own time."

"This girl could be enduring God knows what."

"Goodbye, Ballou."

"Don't hang up on me, Hardin. Hello? Goddammit."

Grumpy's parking lot was already full by the time I got there. I parked the Gray Ghost on a nearby side street. Conor pulled in behind me. As we walked the half block to the restaurant, I filled Conor in on my conversations with Hardin and Jessup, as well as the creepy letter I found at Holly's house.

"I don't get it," I said as we walked across Grumpy's parking lot. "Hardin's absolutely convinced that this seventeen-year-old girl is guilty, even when most of the evidence points to someone else."

"Why da ya care what he thinks, love? We got to find the girl. Let the courts sort out her guilt or innocence."

"I know, but it pisses me off. I hate how people get railroaded when cops are too stubborn to look at evidence that contradicts their theory of the case." I pulled open the door. The air inside was cooler, but I still felt as if I were melting. Conor and I grabbed seats at the bar.

"Uh-oh! Here comes trouble!" Grumpy breezed past carrying a couple of plates of food, made less appetizing by that damned cigar dangling from his mouth.

"Don't start with me, Grumpy." I put my hair up into a ponytail to get it off my neck. "Could you crank up the AC, for Christ's sake?"

"I could, kitten, but then I'd have to double my prices. 'Lectricity ain't cheap." He handed the plates off to a server. "You want your usual?"

"Yeah, whatever."

He set down a couple of beers in front of Conor and me, then waltzed back into the kitchen. I pressed the bottle to my temple and gasped. The ice-cold glass against my sun-scorched skin was equally painful and orgasmic.

"Let's say ya find the girl," Conor said after a long pull on his beer. "Whatcha gonna do with your cut of the bounty?"

"Honestly, haven't thought much about it. You?"

"Pay off my second mortgage," he said. "I owe a lot on those renovations I did a while back."

"You're so damn practical. I think I'd like to buy a motorcycle."

"Ha! You'd look bloody deadly on a Harley."

"Fuck Harley. There's a shop north of the valley that sells custom motorcycles for women. I've seen the website. Amazing shit. And fast too."

"You'd look hot no matter what ya rode." He winked at me. "Now all we got to do is find where the little lass is hiding."

I pulled out the stalker letter I'd picked up at the Schwartzes'. "Look at this. He talks about adding her to his harem. Begs her to send him photos of her naked but warns her not to tell her mom. The girl's seventeen, for Christ's sake. Ugh!"

Conor took the letter and the envelope. His lips drew back in a snarl. "What a bloody gobshite! What kind of filth writes such a thing to a teenage girl?"

"I wonder if the author of this letter is the one who tried to grab Holly and killed her mother," I said.

"Could be. Maybe also connected to these kidnappings in Maryvale." He took a long pull on his beer. "But if it is the same bloke, why take the girl months later? From her aunt's house, no less?"

"To keep her from testifying? Who knows? But it's looking more and more like she was kidnapped. I have no idea where to look." I thought about it for a moment. "But I know someone who might."

I pulled out my phone. I still had Hensley's phone number from when we were arranging the interviews.

"Where would I find those sex traffickers you interviewed a while back?" I asked when he picked up the call.

"Who is this?"

"Jinx Ballou. Now answer the question," I growled.

"You trying to get me killed? Is that what this is?"

"No, I'm trying to save the life of a seventeen-year-old girl. Now where do I find these guys?"

"Like I told you before, I don't divulge my sources. Normally, it's for professional standards. But these human traffickers are sociopaths. They kill anyone considered a threat. They've murdered cops, judges, feds, you name it. I'm not putting my life at risk so you can collect a bounty."

"Hensley, either you can tell me, or I can find them myself, and when I do, I'll tell them you blabbed. Or you can tell me for real and I'll keep my mouth shut. I'm just trying to rescue someone they've taken."

"You're looking for Holly Schwartz, aren't you? I heard she missed a court hearing. You think she got kidnapped?"

"It's highly likely." The line was silent for a moment, except for his breathing. I liked that he was sweating over this.

"Okay, here's what I know. There's a guy named Volkov. Used to run strip clubs down in Tucson, then a few years ago, he expanded up here. But the strip clubs are a cover. He's been running a human trafficking empire for the better part of two decades. His family runs a major crime syndicate in Chechnya.

"He drove out all his competition in Arizona and several surrounding states. Most of the coyotes running girls from Central America and Mexico work for him. But they also grab local girls too. They send them to drop houses all over the western US, where they're forced into domestic work if they're lucky. Sex work if they're not."

"Where do I find this Volkov?"

"He's got an office in downtown Phoenix. But it's just the corporate office for his strip clubs. He keeps the girls in an old warehouse elsewhere."

"Where?"

"I don't know. They blindfolded me."

"You've been there? And you didn't do anything to save those women?"

"What was I going to do? I'm a reporter, not a cop. I was unarmed. They had automatic weapons."

"And you have no idea where he keeps these women? East Valley? West Valley?"

"West, I think. Past Goodyear, if I had to guess. Could be the other side of the White Tanks for all I know."

"You're really useless, Hensley."

"Look, if you promise not to mention my name, I can put you in touch with someone who knows more than I do."

"Well, fuck, why didn't you say so before?"

"If word got out that I shared this, it could ruin me."

"After the crap you've put me through, you think I'm worried? You are at the top of my shit list, buddy. And so is whoever ratted me out to you."

"For your information, no one ratted you out. I *figured* it out. You were enrolled at one school as a boy. Then months later you show up at a new middle school as a girl. It wasn't rocket science. As for my Volkov source, I'm not telling you his name if you're going to betray my trust."

"Fine, I won't tell. Just give me the name."

"He's a concierge at the Harrington Arms Hotel."

"Seriously? The Harrington Arms?" It was a hotel built in downtown Phoenix the year Arizona became a state. A century later, its posh amenities and five-star service still attracted elite guests from around the world. I'd never even been in the lobby, much less stayed in a room.

"What's this concierge's name?"

"Ricky."

"Ricky who?"

Conor perked up at the name. "Ricky the concierge? I know that little wanker."

"Never mind," I told Hensley. "So they really allow sex slaves at the Harrington Arms?"

"It's very hush-hush. But apparently some of their guests are willing to pay handsomely to have certain less-than-savory urges satisfied," Hensley explained. "Ricky contacts someone in Volkov's organization to take care of them. A defenseless celebrity like Holly Schwartz would fetch a high price."

"How come you never mentioned the Harrington in your newspaper?"

"Because Volkov made me promise not to, and I'm rather attached to my head. "

"So you're getting paid while women are being exploited. Congratulations, you're a douchebag."

"Hey, I've shared what I know with the FBI, okay?"

"Oh, you're a real humanitarian."

"How long has Holly been missing?" Hensley asked.

"About a month. Why?"

"He likes to move around the girls every few weeks or so. Chances of her still being in Phoenix are slim, I'm afraid."

"Let's hope for your sake she's still in town."

"What's that mean? If this gets back to me—"

"Quit your whining, Hensley, you little bitch. If I can't get my career back on track with this job, Volkov'll be the least of your worries." I hung up before he could protest further and turned to Conor. "So you know this Ricky fellow?"

"Aye, I've squeezed him for info a few times. Skinny little weasel with a pompadour. Like some little rockabilly wannabe. Not surprised he's mixed up with the likes of Volkov."

"His last name isn't Delgado by chance, is it? There was a Richard Delgado on one of the Schwartzes' call logs."

"Naw, his last name's Harris." He picked at the label on his beer. "So ya think Volkov has your girl, eh?"

"About the only lead I got at this point."

"Bloody hell."

"Why? What do you know?"

"Guy's a fuckin' psychopath. I've heard stories of what he does to girls who try to escape. Carves them up slowly like a Thanksgiving turkey while forcing the other girls to watch. 'Course, no one can prove it. Every once in a while, the feds raid his clubs, hoping someone'll talk. No one does."

I finished off my beer and slapped him on the back. "Well, that's why they pay us the big money. To go after psychos and bring our fugitives to justice."

"You're bloody serious?"

"As a fucking heart attack. I got everything riding on this case. No punk-ass Chechen gangster's getting in my way."

He finished his beer and pounded the bar. "All right then, love. Let's go talk to Ricky the dodgy concierge and get our girl."

20

We dropped off Conor's car at his place and drove to the Harrington Arms in the Gray Ghost. It was going on six o'clock, and most of the traffic was heading away from downtown. We rode the elevator from the underground garage up to the cavernous lobby.

My jaw dropped. I felt as if I'd walked into a cross between Buckingham Palace and a neo-Gothic cathedral. The place shimmered with gold. Towering columns rose forty feet from the marble floors to support the elaborate vaulted ceiling, lit with crystal chandeliers the size of my truck.

A grand staircase flowed from the second floor, spreading out at the bottom like a river delta. Twenty-foot-tall Art Deco paintings depicting the Phoenix of yesteryear hung from the walls above arched doorways. In the center of it all was a lounge area decorated with luxurious rugs and couches. People from all corners of the globe milled about, speaking languages I could only guess at.

"Jesus fucking Christ, is this Arizona or Renaissance Italy?" I whispered as I followed Conor, trying not to gawk like a tourist. "Where's the concierge?"

"Follow me."

To the left of the sprawling mahogany registration desk, a guy in his midtwenties stood behind a podium with a Mac laptop. He was dressed in a burgundy suit and wore his hair in the pompadour Conor had mentioned.

He looked up with a smug smile, which soured as soon as he saw Conor. "How may I—oh no. Not you."

"Jinxie," Conor said, "meet my buddy Ricky, the concierge. Ricky, old boy, this here's my gal, Jinxie."

"No offense, Ms. Jinxie, but I am here to serve our guests." He glared at Conor. "Not scruffy ruffians. Do I need to call security?"

Conor put his arm around the concierge's shoulder. "Ricky here helps the Harrington's guests access all sorts of hard-to-acquire items. Tickets to sold-out Suns games, guest passes to TPC, reservations for a chef's table at the hottest restaurants. You want it, this bloke'll get it for ya. For a price, of course."

Ricky signaled to a wall of muscle dressed in black standing on the other side of the registration desk. He ambled toward us, his thick arms ready at his side.

Conor continued, paying no attention to the approaching man in black. "Our boy here also helps his clients satisfy their dodgier appetites. Drugs. Dog fights. Prostitution. S&M. Every sort of kink ya can imagine."

"Uh, Conor ..." I pointed toward the security guard, who cracked his knuckles as he drew closer.

Conor beamed. "Ricky likes to indulge a bit too. I've got some lovely videos of him with the governor's granddaughter. What was her name, old boy?"

Ricky went rigid, his face coloring, his eyes locked on Conor. The concierge waved off the security guard, who returned to his post by the front desk. "What the hell you want?" he asked through gritted teeth.

"We're looking for a girl," I said.

"Hungry for a little threesome action, are we?"

"Not exactly." I held up a photo of Holly. "We're looking for this girl—Holly Schwartz."

Ricky cocked an eyebrow. "I know her. Why are you ... oh, wait a minute, she's been in the news lately. Something about her mother getting murdered. *Très* sad." He gave a mocking pouty face, making his bottom lip look very punchable. I resisted. Barely.

"She's also missing," I said. "Most likely kidnapped by a human smuggler named Volkov."

Ricky shrugged with a disinterested look. "I know nothing of such things."

Conor slammed the laptop shut, almost catching the concierge's fingers in it. "Cara! That's Governor Denton's granddaughter's name, isn't it? She's a cutie, though a bit young even for you, Ricky boy. And unless ya help us out, I'm sending our madame governor a video file of the two of you."

"For your information, it was consensual."

"Bullshite. The girl's fifteen, ya little wanker. You're what? Thirty?"

"Twenty-seven. Ish." Ricky's left eye twitched. "I really hate you."

"Coming from a gobshite like yourself, I'll take that as a compliment. Where's Volkov keep the girls?"

"If I tell you, Volkov'll kill me."

I flicked open a black-bladed knife and leaned into the little maggot, pressing the tip of the blade into the belly of his heavily starched shirt. "How long you think you'll live when I eviscerate you? Intestines dumping onto the floor, blood and fecal matter all over your pretty white shirt? My guess is ten minutes, maybe twenty. The whole time, you'll be screaming in agony, knowing no one can save you. Conor, you want to time him?"

"All right, all right! Jesus!" He cowered, his eyes tightly shut, trembling like an overbred Yorkie in a thunderstorm. "I-I'll tell you."

"You got five seconds, or I start cutting."

"Th-There's a warehouse. West of Buckeye. Not far from Arlington."

"Address!"

"It's ... it's in my laptop." He opened the Mac and brought up an address on Old US Highway 80.

Conor patted him on the back. "See? That wasn't so hard, was it, Ricky boy?"

"What about Holly Schwartz?" I pressed the tip of my knife harder. "Does he have her?"

Ricky winced. "The crippled girl?"

"Disabled," I corrected.

"There was a girl like that. Don't know if it was Holly." He swallowed hard. "But that was weeks ago. Volkov likes to move his girls around. Doesn't want 'em too comfortable."

"Let's hope for your sake he's still got her." I put away my knife and marched back toward the elevator.

"What's that supposed to mean?" Ricky cried. "Hey! Conor, what's she talking about?"

Conor caught up with me as I punched the down button between the two elevators. "Ya know, you're quite scary sometimes."

"People like him make me sick," I muttered, staring at the lit button. "I should have gutted him."

"If ya had, we couldn't go rescue Holly, now could we?" He put an arm on my shoulder. "By the way, if we're planning on stormin' the castle, we'll need some serious backup. Unfortunately, Deez and the boys are up in Salt Lake, chasing down a fugitive."

"Let me see what I can do." I pulled out my phone and hit a number on speed dial. On the third ring, I heard a familiar voice ask who was calling. "Rodeo, it's Jinx."

"Hey, Jinxie. How's it hanging? Oh, sorry. Was that inappropriate considering you're, uh, you know?"

"Oh good lord. Get over yourself." I sighed. "Listen, Conor and I need some support. You available?"

"I told you, Big Bobby won't allow me to work with you."

"Don't be such a pussy! Come on. We need you." The arrow on the antique floor indicator above the nearest elevator began dropping from fifteen. I doubted I'd get much signal once we stepped in the elevator. "We're hitting a Volkov warehouse to rescue Holly Schwartz."

"Wait, did you say Volkov? As in Milo Volkov?"

"You heard of him?"

"Only from reports of the mutilated bodies left in his wake. That's a whole lot of heat I don't need. I'll pass on this one."

"You chickening out, Rodeo?"

"Last time someone crossed Volkov, the guy's remains were scattered on top of Camelback Mountain."

"Volkov cremated him?"

"No, ran him through a wood chipper."

I cringed. But I was committed to saving this girl, especially since no one but her aunt seemed to give a shit. "Did I mention the bounty is fifty grand?"

"And how much of that can I spend when I'm dead? Not interested, Jinxie."

"Come on, Rodeo, think what this girl must be going through. What if it was your daughter?"

"But it's not. And I won't be much of a father if I've been ground into raw hamburger," he said firmly. "Good luck, Jinx. Try not to get yourself killed. I really like you." He hung up.

"Crap." I turned to Conor as the elevator door opened. "Rodeo's out."

"Smart man."

I gave him a sideways look while we rode down to our level in the parking garage. "You're not having second thoughts, are you?"

"Naw, but ya can't blame a bloke for not wanting to go up against a Chechen gangster."

"Suppose not. But I'm not giving up on this girl. I can't."

"I understand."

"Who else can we call?"

"Maybe it's better with just the two of us. Going in all guns blazing isn't the best strategy."

"So how we getting in?" The elevator door opened, and we stepped into the parking garage.

"I have an idea. You probably won't like it, though."

He explained his strategy. He was right. I didn't like it.

"That's your plan?" My voice echoed off the concrete walls and floor. "Are you fucking insane?"

"Ya got any better ideas, love?"

"Not at the moment, but I'm sure as hell not doing that." We climbed into the Gray Ghost. "Let's stop at your place, arm up, and see what we're up against."

21

The Gray Ghost's dashboard read eight o'clock when I pulled off the road a half mile from a fenced-in warehouse belonging to Eden Produce. Farmland stretched out in all directions, illuminated by silver moonlight. From the driver's seat, I stared at the front gate through a pair of binoculars.

The fifteen-foot chain-link fence was topped with razor wire. Inside the fence were parked two semis bearing the Eden Produce logo. It looked like one of dozens of produce warehouses in the area except for the armed guard manning the front gate.

"Guard at the gate's carrying an AK-47," I said. "No one along the fence as far as I can see." My phone rang. I checked the caller ID, saw it was my mom, and sent it to voicemail. I needed to focus on the task at hand.

Conor looked through his own binoculars. "Surveillance cameras along the fence and all visible points of entry into the warehouse."

"So I guess this is the place, huh?" I asked.

"Unless kale's gotten so pricey you need armed guards to keep out the crazed vegetarians, I'd say we're in the right spot."

"How many more inside, I wonder?"

"Crazed vegetarians?" he asked with a smirk.

"Armed guards, smart-ass."

"No way of knowing. Maybe this isn't such a good idea."

"I'm not giving up on this girl," I said.

"Darlin', it's not worth getting yourself killed. Not even for fifty grand."

"It's not about the money anymore. This kid's been either sick or abused her whole life, confined to a wheelchair. Her mother's been murdered. And now this? I don't care if I don't see a dime. I'm not abandoning her to a life as one of Volkov's sex slaves."

"And how ya propose we get past these blokes?"

"I guess we go with your plan," I said, although thinking about it made me nervous.

He shook his head. "I withdraw my suggested plan. Too risky."

"How else will we get in there?"

"It's not getting in I'm worried about. It's getting out."

"Since when have you backed down from a challenge?"

"This isn't a challenge, Jinxie. It's bloody suicide. I won't do it."

"Fine, I'll do this myself." I pulled off my ballistic vest and began mussing my hair. When I looked sufficiently feral, I hopped out of the truck and rubbed dirt on my face, clothes, and through my hair.

Conor sighed. "Jesus, Mary, and Joseph, woman. You can't do this by yourself. Won't work."

"Then work with me." I locked my gaze on him.

He walked up to me and cupped my face in his hand. "You're daft, ya know that? Completely mental."

"Aw, you say the nicest things." I forced a smile, even though my insides shook like Jell-O. I knew he was right. This whole thing was stupid. But I was sick of people telling me what I couldn't do, and pissed off at everyone turning a blind eye to the shit going on inside that warehouse.

"So your mind's made up, eh?"

"Damn straight."

"Then let's get on with this bloody nonsense." He lifted the back hatch of the Gray Ghost, pulled a Bushmaster M4A3

Carbine out of its case, and popped in a curved thirty-round magazine.

I tossed my tactical belt in the truck and stuffed the Ruger in the front of my waistband. My revolver was still in the ankle holster. I used my knife to cut a pair of zip tie cuffs in half, then slipped a cuff on each wrist. With the closed knife concealed in my right palm, I held my wrists together in front of me, giving the illusion I was restrained.

I looked up at Conor with my most defeated expression. Eyes lifeless. Shoulders slumped. "Convincing enough?"

He turned and cocked his head, studying me. "Hands should be behind your back."

I moved the Ruger to the small of my back and held my hands behind me, hoping the slower draw time on the Ruger wouldn't cost me my life. "Okay, how about now?"

I saw him shudder, though he tried to hide it. "I really don't like this."

"Why? You're the one with the assault rifle."

"Not me I'm worried about."

"I can take care of myself, big boy," I said. "Let's do this."

We climbed back into the Gray Ghost with Conor in the driver's seat.

22

onor pulled up to the gate. The guard shuffled over. "What the hell you want?"

"Caught this one trying to escape from one of the other drop houses," Conor said in his best American accent. "Boss man told me to bring her here."

"No one told me nothing."

Conor shrugged. "Don't believe me? Call Mr. Volkov, though I'm told he's wining and dining some bigwig Arab clients." He pronounced it "Ay-rab," and it was all I could do not to laugh. "I wouldn't disturb 'em if I was you."

"Please don't do this," I pleaded, playing the part. "Just let me go. I won't tell anyone."

"Shut the hell up!" Conor slammed me across the face hard enough to make me see stars. I tasted blood.

Conor's unexpected punch triggered long-forgotten memories. The trauma of getting pounded into a bloody pulp at my high school graduation party surfaced. Images flashed through my mind of a huge man driving his mallet-sized fists into my body, the antiseptic smell of a hospital, and the incessant beeping of a vitals monitor.

I'd been hit countless times in my work and always shook it off. *Why the hell is this any different?* I sobbed and hung my head in defeat. Part of the act, I told myself.

"Yeah, all right. I'll radio Perkins in the warehouse to have someone escort her inside." The guard reached for his radio.

"No can do, mate." Conor's American accent was slipping.

My gut twisted. *Don't blow it, dude,* I thought.

"I have orders to escort her all the way in personally," Conor said. "It's my arse if she gets away again."

The guard narrowed his gaze at Conor, then grunted his approval and waved us on. "Pull around back to the loading dock. Sanchez'll show you where to go."

"Thanks!" Conor drove through.

I took a deep breath, getting control of my emotions. One step closer to rescuing Holly.

"You okay, love?" There was concern in his voice. "Aw, shite! Your lip's bleeding."

"I'm all right." My grip tightened on the folded jackknife behind my back. "We're committed now. Just stick to the plan."

He drove around the warehouse to a large concrete loading dock with a staircase on the side. A dark-skinned man guarded the back door. Sanchez, no doubt.

Conor climbed out. Sanchez raised his rifle and pointed it at Conor.

"Whoa! The guy at the gate told me to bring this one around back. Clever girl snuck out of one of the other drop houses." Conor walked around and opened my door and roughly dragged me out of the truck. I kept my eyes on the ground.

"Yeah, okay. Bring her up," Sanchez replied.

Conor poked me in the back with his Bushmaster. "Move, cunt!"

I trudged up the stairs to where Sanchez was standing. He slung his rifle over his shoulder and cupped my chin, turning my face this way and that. "What happened to this *puta's* face?"

"Put up a bit of a fight when we caught her."

"You think you smart, *puta*?" Sanchez licked his lips. "Not so smart now, eh?" He grabbed my right breast and twisted hard enough to make me gasp. My grip on my knife tightened as I resisted the urge to fight back.

"Easy, mate." Conor pushed himself between us. "Let's not damage the merchandise any more than necessary."

"Fuck you, *maricón!*" Sanchez shoved Conor aside and grabbed my shirt collar. His breath smelled of spiced meat and tequila.

When he reached for my crotch, I flicked open my blade and lunged at Sanchez. He grabbed my arm, and we grappled until he kicked me away, sending me teetering off the edge of the platform and landing on my butt five feet below. I vaulted back onto the platform, knife still in hand.

Conor had Sanchez in a choke hold, but the guard broke free with an elbow to Conor's midsection. Sanchez picked up Conor's rifle and was about to shoot when I drove my knife into his carotid. Warm blood sprayed all over me, the wall, and the ground. He collapsed on the platform. A moment later he was still.

My heart raced as I looked around to see if anyone else had heard the scuffle. We appeared to be alone for the moment. Score one for the good guys.

Conor eyed me suspiciously. "You okay, love?"

"More than okay." I wiped my face on my shirt and caught myself grinning. "Okay, folks, let's see what's behind door number two."

I stashed my knife in my pocket and pulled out the Ruger. Conor opened the door, and I followed him in. The interior was dark and chilly, with rows and rows of twenty-foot-high shelving stocked with boxes of produce on pallets. Two forklifts sat idle in a corner.

"Where to now?" I asked.

Conor pointed his rifle down the aisle along the left wall. "Let's try that way."

With my finger on the trigger, I led the way past the stacks of produce. At the other end of the row stood a large caged area filled with people. I caught a whiff of body odor and urine.

"Who the hell are you?" A broad-shouldered man with his AK-47 raised appeared at the end of the row, between us and the cage.

I raised my Ruger, put two in his chest, and raced past him to where women and children of various ages huddled inside the chain-link cage. A girl about twelve years old looked up at me. Her eyes went wide. "Look out!"

I ducked as a burst of automatic gunfire shook the air. Bullets rattled the fence and ricocheted off the back wall. I turned and saw two other guards shooting at us. I pulled off three shots at one guard, hitting him in the neck and chest. I aimed at the other and was about to pull the trigger when his head whipped back in a cloud of gore as Conor brought him down with his Bushmaster.

The door to the cage was secured with a padlock. "Where are the keys?" I called to the girl who had warned me about the other guard.

"He has them!" She pointed at the guy Conor had shot. I heard shouting and the pounding of boots on concrete coming from all around us.

"Cover me!" I told Conor.

I stashed my Ruger in my waistband and searched the dead guard, shuddering as bursts of gunfire ripped through the air. My hands found a cluster of keys attached to his belt. I cut the belt with my knife and located the one that looked like a padlock key.

I popped the lock as a spray of bullets hit the fence around me. The people in the cage screamed, and we all dropped to the floor. I turned with my Ruger out and dropped another guard raising his weapon at me.

"FBI! Drop your weapons! Get on the ground!" One of the guards held up a badge.

"What the—" I wasn't sure whether to believe him or not.

"Drop your weapons, now! Get on the ground!" A female

voice came from behind me in the cage. I turned. A woman with dirty-blond hair and fierce eyes had a Glock trained on me.

"Fuck." I set my gun on the floor and lay down with my hands behind my head. Conor did the same.

"We're bail enforcement agents," I said. "Looking for a fugitive." I felt myself being cuffed.

"Took us months to infiltrate this organization, and you two screw up the op because some jailbird jumped bail?" the female agent asked.

I looked over and saw the other agent cuff Conor. This was so not how I pictured it would go down.

The lady fed pulled me to my feet and escorted me to the warehouse office. Once inside, she closed the office door and pushed me into a swivel chair. "Who are you?"

"Jinx Ballou. My partner's Conor Doyle. We're looking for Holly Schwartz. She was kidnapped by Volkov's organization. Who the hell are you?"

"Special Agent Deborah Velasco, FBI. You're looking at several felonies, Ms. Ballou. Murder, B&E, obstruction."

"Look, Agent Velasco, I'm sorry we wrecked your under-cover investigation. But we had reason to believe our fugitive was here. That gives us the right to enter. And you can't charge us with murder for defending ourselves."

Agent Velasco knitted her brow. "You're looking for the teenage girl charged with murdering her mother?"

"We have reason to believe she was kidnapped and was brought here."

"I hate to burst your bubble, but you were given bad intel. There was a disabled girl here a week ago, but it wasn't her. You just exposed a federal undercover investigation for nothing."

"Shit."

23

onor and I were transported, still handcuffed, to the FBI's Phoenix office, then put in separate interrogation rooms. Velasco and her partner, Special Agent Danny Gleason, repeatedly questioned me over our failed rescue attempt. When I realized my explanation was getting me nowhere, I invoked my right to counsel.

By that time, the bitter coffee and stale vending machine snacks had their intended effect. My back teeth were floating when my attorney, Kirsten Pasternak, stepped into the interrogation room. Yellow-framed glasses on a chain. Gray silk jacket over a white blouse. She stood a good three inches taller than Agent Gleason. I'd met her at the transgender support group and had found her an invaluable, if expensive, resource.

"I represent Ms. Ballou and Mr. Doyle," she told the agents. "I'd like a moment to confer with my client."

I gave her a rundown of the evening's events. Apparently she had already spoken to Conor and confirmed that our stories matched. She called the agents back into the room, and the three of them sparred while I concentrated on holding my bladder. Occasionally, I added a bit of information when Kirsten gave me the green light.

When Kirsten pressed the agents to either arrest me or release me, Velasco and Gleason agreed not to charge us for now. I made a beeline for the restroom to pee and clean the dried gore from my face and hands. My shirt and cargo pants were beyond repair.

It wasn't the first time I'd killed someone in my duties as a bounty hunter. Unfortunately, circumstances sometimes made lethal force necessary. I wouldn't lose any sleep over the deaths of a few punk-ass human smugglers.

When I trudged out of the restroom, Kirsten met me at the door.

"Am I free to go?" I asked.

"For now. Just don't leave town. There's still a chance they'll press charges."

"Great."

"So this Holly Schwartz you're chasing, she's the one that's been in the news, right? Charity poster girl allegedly turned killer?"

"That's her."

"Any idea who's representing her?"

"Some guy named Swearingen."

Kirsten barked a laugh. "Zach Swearingen? Last time that hack saw the inside of a courtroom, Bill Clinton was getting blow jobs in the Oval Office."

I shrugged. "Apparently he's a friend of Holly's aunt."

She handed me one of her business cards. "When you do find this girl, have her call me. Tell her I'll represent her pro bono."

"Pro bono? You don't represent *me* pro bono."

"You're a successful bounty hunter. She's a penniless orphan in a high-profile case. I could use the publicity."

I rolled my eyes but took her card. "Whatever. If she asks, I'll give her your card."

"Thanks." She patted me on the back. "Now try to stay out of trouble until we can get this matter resolved."

It was midnight by the time we got back to Conor's bunker. I headed straight for the shower to wash off the remaining blood, dirt, and the night's trauma. Only the blood and dirt came off.

I stood there letting the water wash over my body, trying

to make my mind go blank. But Conor's play-acting punch had unearthed a Pandora's box of memories I'd intentionally buried more than a decade earlier.

I'd been dating Peyton Dietz at the time. He was our high school's star basketball player and had been offered a scholarship to UNLV. I was looking forward to getting gender reassignment surgery after graduation before going on to study at ASU. When he asked me out, I felt like the luckiest girl in the world. Peyton knew about my gender transition and didn't care. He accepted me for the girl I was. Peyton's father, Barclay Dietz, was a different story.

Whether Peyton told him or Mr. Dietz found out some other way, I never heard. But a few hours into a graduation party at a mutual friend's house, Peyton got a call from his father, insisting the two of us meet him outside on the street. He made it sound urgent. Fearing it might be a family emergency, we rushed outside.

We found Mr. Dietz several houses down, standing beside his Jaguar with his arms crossed. Where Peyton was tall and lanky, Mr. Dietz was massive and muscular like a bull. Peyton said he'd been a middleweight boxing champion in his day.

Mr. Dietz ordered Peyton to wait in the passenger seat, saying he wanted a private word with me. Peyton protested, but Barclay Dietz wasn't one to put up with back talk. Peyton obeyed.

Mr. Dietz started with some innocuous questions. Was I having fun that evening? How was the food and the music? He even complimented my dress, an off-the shoulder peach number full of ruffles. Back when I wore ruffles.

Then his questioning turned darker. "What kind of girl are you?" he asked with an accusatory tone.

I wasn't sure how to answer. He asked me if I had breast implants. His questions were making me uncomfortable, and I told him so. When he pressed the issue about implants, I assured him I didn't.

"What you got between them skinny little legs of yours?" Mr. Dietz stepped into my personal space, his clenched fists looking like blacksmithing hammers. "A cunt or a cock?"

"I think I should call my folks." I backed away along the sidewalk toward the house party.

He stalked toward me. "You think my son's a cocksucker?"

"What? No! Of course not."

"You must. You're not a girl. You're just a little faggot in a dress, aren't you?"

I never saw the first blow coming. I just realized I was on my back on the sidewalk with my head throbbing. A thunderstorm of punches and kicks rained down on me. Somewhere in the blackness, Peyton shouted for his dad to stop. Or maybe I imagined it. I never saw him after that to confirm.

I woke up in the hospital days later with a fractured skull, a ruptured spleen, broken ribs, bruised kidneys, and a punctured lung. Barclay Dietz, I learned, was charged with aggravated assault but had jumped bail and hadn't been seen since.

It had been years since I'd even thought about that night. I'd been in countless fights with fugitives and their associates since then. Never fazed me. But Conor's slap brought it all back and shook me to my core. So much so that I found myself shivering in the shower, the water having turned cold.

Wrapped in a towel, I stumbled out of the bathroom, trying to stop the trembling. My lip was still swollen. My jaw hurt. My chest and wrists were sore.

Conor lay on his bed in a pair of camo boxers, reading a Lawrence Block paperback. Concern shot across his face. "You all right, love?"

"I'll survive." I sat on the bed next to him. "What was I thinking? Busting into Volkov's warehouse?"

"Don't be batterin' yourself. You held your own."

"And what did we accomplish? We're no closer to finding Holly." I lay next to him, drawn to his warmth. "This crazy theory about Holly getting kidnapped. Maybe Hardin's right.

Maybe she did kill her mother. Maybe someone's hiding her, trying to keep her from going to jail. I just don't know."

"Maybe the aunt. We can have another go at her tomorrow if ya'd like."

"There's something she's not telling, but I didn't get the feeling she was hiding Holly. Why would Morton risk losing her house over a girl she barely knows? She'd be better off taking her chances in court."

Fatigue was dragging me under like a powerful current. "I'm too tired to think."

Conor kissed me on my temple. "Let's get some rest, love, and reassess in the morning."

24

My head and body still ached when I woke the next morning to the sound of my phone ringing. Sunlight peeked through the vertical blinds in Conor's bedroom. I picked up my phone from the nightstand. It was a few minutes after seven. "Hi, Mom."

"Sweetie, you didn't return my call yesterday. You okay?"

"I'm fine. Sorry I didn't call back. I was busy till late last night."

"Ever since that awful newspaper outed you, I've been so worried. Your brother says it's all over the Twitter."

"I'm okay. Really." And even if I wasn't, I didn't need her worrying about me.

"The people at your work. They know?"

"I'm working for a different bail bond agent now. She knows, and she's fine with it."

"Maybe this is your chance to do something less dangerous. I don't like you chasing criminals all the time."

"Mom, relax! Most fugitives I pick up are good folks who simply forgot their court date. Nothing to be concerned about."

"But what about the dangerous criminals, sweetie? I saw on the news there was a big shoot-out in Buckeye between bounty hunters and human smugglers."

"Really? Huh. Well, I was nowhere near that warehouse. Just out searching for a young woman. No danger whatsoever."

What was I going to tell her? Yeah, Mom, I stabbed a guy in the neck, then shot two other guys while covered in the first guy's blood. So not going to happen.

"You coming over tomorrow morning for brunch?"

"Wouldn't miss it. Conor too."

"Perhaps you could come to Mass with me."

"Mom, we talked about this."

"I worry for your soul."

"My soul is fine." *Would God send me to hell for killing a murderous human smuggler? Do I even believe in God?* "I have to go, Mom. I have work to do. Love you."

"Okay, sweetie. See you tomorrow. I have some pretty dresses I'd like you to try on, so don't be late."

I rolled over and sighed. Conor leaned up on one arm, smiling at me. "Lying to your mother again?"

"What am I gonna do? Tell her I was going all Lisbeth Salander on a bunch of scumbags? She's already worried about me."

"So what's our game plan, Ms. Salander?"

"I honestly have no clue. I've been through the possible scenarios. Scenario A, she was kidnapped for ransom."

Conor nodded. "Except no one's received a ransom note as far as we know."

"True. Scenario B, she was kidnapped by human traffickers. Problem is, she wasn't at Volkov's warehouse last night. Agent Velasco said a paraplegic girl was there a week ago but assured me she wasn't Holly Schwartz."

"Which brings us to Scenario C—she's hiding voluntarily, most likely with some help."

"But help from who? And why?" I thought about it. "Maybe Detective Hardin was on to something. He claimed Holly wasn't as mentally disabled as everyone thinks she is. Her aunt hinted at the same thing. Maybe this whole thing about her being sick and disabled is just a scam."

"To what end?"

"Money. Attention. She's been on all of these telethons. Charities and individuals are sending her money."

"But according to her aunt, Holly's been sick since she was a baby. You yourself found a bunch of doctors' bills in their home, plus all those pill bottles at her aunt's house. Doesn't sound like a scam to me."

"According to Hardin, Bonnie was forcing Holly to get a feeding tube she claimed she didn't need. Maybe Mommy Dearest had that syndrome where parents make their kids sick to get attention."

"Munchausen by proxy?" Conor cocked an eyebrow. "Honestly, how could the mother fool the doctors for so long? Something would've shown up in the tests, right?"

I pondered his point. "I don't know. If she is disabled, who would take her? And why? And who killed her mother?"

"Maybe someone thought she was being abused."

"Possible. But then why not call the cops? Or report it to the Department of Child Safety?" I thought about it some more. "Unless someone did report it, and no one did anything about it."

I grabbed my phone and dialed Becca.

"Hey, Jinx! You been on social media lately?" She sounded better but concerned.

"No, why?"

"Girl, that story in *Phoenix Living* about you went viral."

"Shit. Just what I need."

"It'll pass. How's the hunt for Holly Schwartz going?"

"Not so great. Chasing a bunch of leads and coming up with zero. How are you doing?"

"Surprisingly well. Don't know how long that will last, but I'm down here at the Hub while I still have the energy to do so. By the way, I discovered something interesting."

"What's that?"

"Those donation checks that Bonnie Schwartz deposited over the past year? I took a look at the thumbnails of the checks on the bank statements. She only deposited about a third of each check's value. The rest she got in cash. Just a few thousand a month, but it struck me as odd. Not sure if that has any connection to Holly's disappearance."

"I'll look into it from my end. Maybe a substance abuse issue? Or something else she wanted to keep off the books."

"Kinda what I was thinking."

"Could you check to see if there were any abuse complaints filed against Bonnie Schwartz? Either with Phoenix PD or the Department of Child Safety."

"You think the mom was abusing Holly?"

"Just a theory I'm exploring. Right now I'm grasping at every thread to see what shakes loose."

"I'll check and call you back."

"Thanks, Becks."

"Just do yourself a favor and stay off social media for a while."

"Of course." I hung up and nervously checked Twitter. Because I was an idiot.

At the top of the trending topics list was the hashtag #TransBountyHunter. I pulled up the latest tweets. A lot of them were supportive, saying I was a hero and an inspiration. One mother of a trans teen called me a lifesaver. Others were outright vicious, misgendering me and threatening to rape and murder me. Some were creepy solicitations from men with a trans fetish, which some in the trans community called "chasers." Ugh.

I clicked to check my email and found it similarly filled with messages from grateful fans, violent haters, and nasty stalkers. Most of the hateful stuff, I deleted after reading the subject line.

One email looked like a possible job offer, with the subject line "I Want To Hire You." I opened it.

My Dearest Jinx,

Thank you for your recent visit to my warehouse. So sorry I wasn't there to greet you in person.

Despite the disruption you caused, you managed to root

out a couple of rats in my organization. For this I am in your debt. I am simultaneously impressed by your fighting skills and intrigued by your background. The article in Phoenix Living was very enlightening, though it left me with questions.

For example, do you still have a cock? I find the idea of a beautiful, sexy woman such as yourself having a cock quite a turn-on. I long to drizzle vodka over your nubile body and lick it off. I ache to fuck you till your ears bleed. Oh the fun we could have together. The pleasure and the pain, the agony and the ecstasy.

I would very much like the opportunity to thank you in person for your assistance and perhaps offer you a position on my staff, both literally and figuratively.

Please reply and let's meet.

Warmest Regards,

Milo

Holy fuck! Fuck, fuck, fuck, fuck! That psycho piece of shit, Milo fucking Volkov, knew who I was. He knew *what* I was. And he had my email address.

Bile rose in my throat. *Is this just a creepy invitation? Or a threat?* I closed the email app and tossed the phone on the bed. I didn't need this shit distracting me from my work.

"Ya all right, love?"

I jumped at Conor's voice. "What? Oh yeah. Just some assholes posting nasty shit about me on Twitter." I couldn't bring myself to show him the email from Volkov. Just too damn humiliating.

"Don't let the cheeky bastards get to ya. They're just jealous."

"Yeah, you're right. Listen, I need to work out the kinks from last night. Thinking of going for a run. Care to come with?"

He did. I put on some workout clothes I kept in one of Conor's dresser drawers.

We jogged north on Third Avenue to St. Joseph's Hospital, then hooked a left on Thomas and again on Fifth Avenue. When we got back to his place, my body felt charged and alive. He apparently felt the same, and soon we were engaged in a more intimate workout.

The gentleness of his lips on my body and the power of his body moving with mine left me gasping with pleasure. I let my mind go blank in a whirlwind of bliss until the words from Volkov's email crept into my consciousness.

My body went rigid, and I scrambled out from under Conor and curled into a trembling ball, perched on the edge of the bed.

"What's wrong? Did I hurt you?"

I sat with my back to him, trying to clear my mind and get my shit together. "I ... I'm fine. Just ... I don't know."

He slid next to me but thankfully didn't put his arm on me. "Something's got ya spooked. Is this about what happened at the warehouse?"

I looked up at him, struggling to maintain eye contact. "No, that was ... doesn't matter. I'm just in a weird space is all. Pissed off at being outed. Pissed at missing Comicon. Frustrated at not finding Holly. I'll be all right. Just need a shower."

"Ya want company?"

"Not really."

I took a shower and did some breathing exercises my father had taught me to deal with panic attacks. They seemed to help. Afterward, I got dressed and ate a bagel.

With food in my stomach and a clearer head, I printed out the docs Becca had sent me. I laid them out on the floor in Conor's spare bedroom, along with the photocopies from the murder book, and the bills and fan mail I'd picked up at the Schwartzes' house.

Conor walked in. "Feeling better?"

"A bit."

"That's a shite-load of paperwork," Conor said.

"Just trying to get an overview of the situation and figure out where she might be. My mind keeps going back to the description her lawyer gave of her mother's alleged attacker."

"Aye, it sounded familiar to me too. Hold on a sec." He

disappeared down the hall and returned moments later holding a *Sports Illustrated*. "How did Swearingen say Holly described the attacker?"

"Six-eight, medium-dark skin, long hair, black wing tattoo on one arm. Gold earring and an orange shirt."

"Like a Phoenix Suns jersey?" He held the magazine open to an article. On the page was a photo of Cedric Wilson, the Suns player who'd injured himself a while back in an accident. The description matched the photo exactly.

"There was an *Arizona Republic* article on Wilson in the Schwartzes' house. Must've made up the attacker's description based on Wilson's photo."

"Interesting." Conor tossed the magazine to the side.

"Still doesn't tell us where she is or who's helping her." I studied the paperwork laid out before me.

The bank statements had thumbnails of checks deposited. As Becca had pointed out, there was a distinct difference between check values and the amounts deposited. Nothing illegal in that. But highly suspicious under the circumstances. The question was, what was she doing with all of that cash?

It was nearly lunchtime when Becca called back.

"Hey, Becks! What'd you find?"

"According to the Department of Child Safety, there've been three complaints filed against Bonnie Schwartz. All cases were closed after social workers found no abuse."

"Who filed the complaints?"

"The first one was eight years ago by a doctor. The second a couple years later by Kimberly Morton, the aunt."

"That's interesting. She didn't mention that when Conor and I talked to her. What about the last one?"

Becca chuckled. "The last complaint was filed a year ago by a George Peavey."

"Why does that name ring a bell?"

"He was on both Holly and Bonnie's call logs. That's where things get interesting. Apparently, Peavey filed a request for a paternity hearing, claiming he's Holly's biological father. But he withdrew the request after Bonnie's murder."

"Wow, this just keeps getting weirder and weirder. So what do we know about this guy?"

"He's a mechanical engineer in Mesa, no criminal record. I can keep digging if you want."

"No, just text me his address and phone number."

"Will do. I also followed up on this Richard Delgado. He's a visiting nurse working for Compassionate Care and assigned to Holly. So no real surprise there."

"Thanks. Anything else?"

"Yeah, one thing. I rechecked Bonnie's cellphone account. There have been some recent phone calls. All local."

"How's that possible? Detective Hardin has both phones in evidence. And according to the evidence report, Bonnie's was smashed beyond repair. How could anyone be using it?"

"Could have pulled the SIM card before the police arrived," Becca said.

"She's a mentally disabled girl. How would she think to do that? *I* wouldn't think of that."

"Maybe she had help."

I looked at the array of paper in front of me. "Maybe she did. Question is from who?"

"Whom," Becca corrected.

"Whatever," I said. "So who's she calling?"

"The most frequent calls appear to be to prepaid phones. Burners. Not getting names on them. The rest of the calls are mostly food delivery. Jade Palace. Sub Barn. Tony and Maria's Trattoria."

"Tratto-what?"

"It's an Italian restaurant."

"Do we know where these deliveries are going?"

"I tried to look it up but came up empty."

"Damn." I pondered what we had so far. Nothing was gelling. Nothing made sense.

"I could try to trace the phone's location."

I felt a glimmer of hope. "How long will that take?"

"Hold on a moment." There was the tapping of computer keys in the background. "No luck. I can't ping the phone. It must be off with the battery removed."

"Crap. Okay, send me the info on Peavey. If he really is her father, maybe he has her. That would explain why he dropped the paternity suit. Keep checking that phone number every so often. See if you can get a location. Whoever has the phone with Bonnie's SIM card must be connected to Holly's disappearance."

"Will do."

I hung up. Moments later, I got a text from Becca with Peavey's information.

I found Conor on the phone with his team. When he hung up, I asked, "How are Deez and the boys doing up in Salt Lake City?"

"Zeroing in on their defendant. Almost had him at one point, but he managed to sneak out before they arrived. What'd Becca say?"

I filled him in on what Becca had told me. "You up for an outing? I want to talk to Daddy Dearest."

"As long as it doesn't involve shootouts with human smugglers, I'm game."

25

Before we left, I called George Peavey's phone. I didn't want to drive all the way to Mesa only to discover he was spending his Saturday elsewhere. At the same time, I didn't want to risk spooking him.

"This George Peavey?" I asked when he answered.

"It is. To whom am I speaking?"

"Oh, hi, I'm Liz Windsor. I live a couple streets over from you," I said in an overfriendly voice. "For some reason the post office delivered a box addressed to you."

"Again? They're always misdelivering my packages. Probably a book I ordered."

I decided to play along. "Yeah, judging from the size, that'd be my guess. You gonna be home for the next hour or so? I gotta dry my hair, and then I can drop it by."

"Yeah, I'll be around."

"Great. Toodles!"

"Liz Windsor?" Conor guffawed. "So now you're the bloody queen of England?"

"Could be. Never know what a girl can accomplish when she puts her mind to it," I said with a smirk.

What would have normally taken us thirty minutes ended up taking closer to an hour because ADOT had closed Highway 60 at the I-10 interchange. After twenty grueling minutes of slow-and-go traffic, we exited onto Baseline along with everyone and their brother. The traffic eased up once we crossed over the Loop 101and turned in to the Dobson Ranch area.

George Peavey's house was a white brick two-story with brown trim, set behind a three-car garage. We geared up with vest and weapons and walked up to the front door. After two quick doorbell rings followed by a good door pounding, I yelled, "Open up! Bail Enforcement!"

The door opened. George Peavey was a dumpy guy in his late thirties with a receding hairline. But his upturned nose, large eyes, and dark hair bore a strong resemblance to Holly Schwartz. The tangerine polo shirt he wore clashed with his mustard-colored cargo shorts.

"What's all this about? Who are you?"

"You're George Peavey?" I asked. "Holly Schwartz's father?"

His eyes narrowed. "Who wants to know?"

I held up my bail enforcement badge. "Jinx Ballou. Assurity Bail Bonds hired us to return Holly Schwartz to custody after she missed her court date."

"Geez, you people! She's a little girl who's lost her mother. Why can't you leave her alone, for God's sake?"

He turned to shut the door, but Conor held it open. "If she's here, mate, or ya know where she is, ya need to tell us now, or we can arrest you for obstruction. Ya could also be charged with conspiracy to commit murder after the fact."

Conor's words did their job. Peavey looked at us, clearly frustrated with the situation. "Look, she's not here. I haven't seen her in months."

"You filed a request for a paternity test?" I asked.

"Yes, I believe she's my daughter. I saw her and her mother interviewed on TV about a year ago. She looks just like me, and Bonnie and I had a thing about eighteen, nineteen years ago. I reached out to the two of them and was starting to get to know Holly. We bonded instantly, Holly and me. Then Bonnie got killed."

His face darkened. "I feel bad about talking ill of the dead, but I believe Bonnie was hurting Holly. In the brief time I spent with them, I realized Bonnie was obsessed with taking Holly to the doctor and the hospital for one thing after another. To the point of being abusive. Holly thought her mother was poisoning her. I reported her to DCS. Not that they listened."

"So Holly wasn't really disabled?" I asked.

"Holly insisted it was all a lie."

"How could Bonnie fool the doctors? Didn't they run tests?"

"I don't understand it all myself. Holly was so skinny from malnutrition and all the drugs the doctors were prescribing. The people from the charities simply never questioned them about it. The whole thing was nothing more than a twisted scam. Bonnie was obsessed with playing the saintly mother when she was closer to the devil incarnate."

"Un-fucking-believable," I said.

"She can walk. Can you believe that? Her mother threatened that if she spent too much time out of the wheelchair, her legs would become infected and have to be amputated."

"And Holly believed her?"

"She'd been manipulated by her mother since she was an infant. She was terrified of Bonnie. That's why I wanted to establish paternity and gain custody. Holly hated living in that house."

Conor narrowed his gaze. "Yet ya dropped the paternity claim after Bonnie was murdered? Having second thoughts about keeping a murderer under your roof? Or are ya hiding her from the law?"

"I don't know who killed Bonnie. If it was Holly, then she had a damned good reason, what with all she's endured." Peavey leaned against the door and stared out past us. "But I dropped the case temporarily until this whole mess got cleared up. I've talked to Bonnie's sister, Kim. Let her know I was willing to help in any way I can. Once all of this is behind us, I intend to file for custody. Holly wants to live with me."

So Morton did know about Peavey. What else was she hiding?

"Where's Holly?" I pressed. "We need to find her now, or the court will declare the bail bond forfeited, and Ms. Morton loses her house."

"I wish I knew where Holly was. Truly." He frowned. "I hoped Kim was hiding her, but I don't think she is. I keep expecting her to turn up. Somehow."

"Look, mate," Conor said. "We'd like to believe ya. But we're gonna have to take a look inside to confirm the girl's not here."

"Fine, be my guest." He stepped aside and let us in.

The place was simple, Scandinavian modern. Peavey was clearly a man who appreciated furniture that could be assembled with an Allen wrench. An entertainment center featured a fifty-inch flat screen surrounded by models of spaceships from a laundry list of sci-fi franchises. A copy of *Phoenix Living* with me on the cover lay on a coffee table. I did my best to ignore it.

In the master bedroom, there was an entire wall of DVDs. Mostly sci-fi and fantasy titles, with some westerns and action flicks thrown in for balance. But nowhere was there any indication of Holly's ever having been there.

No teenager-sized clothing or accessories in the spare bedroom. No meds except for a prescription bottle for statins, written for him, not Holly.

As we were leaving, Peavey stopped me. "Do I know you? You look so familiar for some reason."

My eyes instantly darted to the *Phoenix Living* on the table behind him. "I have no idea, sir."

I watched the wheels in his mind turning, then his eyes lit up. "Wait, I got it! Didn't I see you at Comicon last year? Wonder Woman, right?"

I breathed a sigh of relief. "Yeah, you caught me."

He grabbed a framed photo off the entertainment center and showed it to Conor and me. It was Peavey with his arm around me, in full superhero costumed glory. "I had no idea you were a bounty hunter. That's seriously rad!"

"Look at that, love," Conor said, chucking me on the shoulder. "You're a celebrity."

I forced a smile. Doing cosplay at Comicon was one thing. Getting recognized in my day job by grown-up fanboys felt a little surreal. My hunting his daughter made it more so. "Lucky me."

"I'd really love it if you could sign the photo." He popped it out of the frame.

"Sure. Why not?" I said as he scrambled for a permanent marker. "How should I sign it?"

"How about, 'To George, with all my love.' And your name, of course."

"Of course." *Because signing it "Your daughter's bounty hunter" would be really awkward,* I thought.

I signed it, and he put it back on the shelf. "Holly'll be thrilled to see that." His face grew somber. "Please, find her before anything bad happens to her."

I put a hand on his shoulder. "I'll do my superhero best." *Where the hell'd that come from?*

He escorted us out the front door and waved at us as we climbed into the Gray Ghost.

"See there, love," Conor said as I pulled out of Peavey's driveway. "You thought you were going to miss all those gushing fanboys at Comicon."

"I guess today's my lucky day. Let's hope we luck out and find Holly."

I was threading my way back onto the I-10 freeway, pondering Holly's possible whereabouts, when my phone rang. "Please let that be Becca with another lead!"

It wasn't. I didn't recognize the caller ID. "Jinx Ballou."

"Yeah, this is Edie Miller. You put up posters in my neighborhood, looking for Artie Renzelli."

Renzelli was one of Liberty Bail Bonds's fugitives wanted for dealing dope. I'd put up flyers asking for leads—on my dime, no less, because Big Bobby could be a real tightwad. Bobby had reassigned the case to Fiddler, but screw them both.

"Thanks so much for calling. Edie, is it? So you saw Renzelli?"

"He and Li'l Mike were out partying with some skank last night a couple doors down. I'm pretty sure they still there."

I had no idea who Li'l Mike was, nor did I care. But I took down the address Edie gave me.

"The poster didn't say nothing 'bout no reward. But I should get something for turning him in, right? I'm on a fixed income."

Nothing came free in this business. "Tell you what. If I catch him based on this tip, I'll give you twenty."

"Twenty dollars? Shit! Silent Witness pay a whole lot more than that."

"All right, I'll see what I can do. I'll be there shortly."

"You got a lead on our girl?" Conor asked.

"Nope. A tip on Artie Renzelli, one of Liberty's skips. I'm going after him."

Conor guffawed. "D'ya miss the part where Big Bobby sacked ya, love? What's the point if he's not gonna pay?"

I grinned mischievously. "Trust me. I'll make him pay, one way or another. You're down for this, right?"

"I was actually hoping we could grab lunch. I'm famished, and there's a new Irish pub near Thomas and the 51 I been meanin' to try."

"Come on! You help me bring this guy in, and I'll treat for lunch once we're done."

"Okay, fine! Let's get this guy."

"Oh, by the way, you got any more cash?" I asked.

26

I passed the address to Conor, who navigated us north to a neighborhood in Peoria with roundabouts and speed bumps every hundred yards. They called them traffic-calming devices, but they made me anything but calm. Maybe if I slowed down for them, but who had time for that?

We stopped in front of a small ash-gray house with wooden siding and a patchy yellowing lawn, littered with empty beer cans, liquor bottles, and a child's overturned tricycle. A line of scraggly Texas sage shrubs stood vigil in front of the iron-barred windows.

"Charming place." I switched on the walkie-talkie on my belt, slipped on my shades, and stepped out of the truck. "I'll take the front door. You take the back."

Conor pulled a shotgun loaded with beanbag rounds from the back of the Gray Ghost. "Copy that." He walked around the east side of the house, where there was a gate to the backyard.

I gave him a minute to get into position then pounded on the front door. "Bail enforcement! Open up!" I followed it up with more pounding. "Open the door now."

"I'm coming, I'm coming," an unhurried male voice said from inside the house. A heavyset guy with a mess of wild hair opened the door, wearing a rumpled T-shirt and plaid boxers, which revealed a lot more than I wanted to see. This was not Renzelli.

"I'm looking for Arthur Renzelli. I'm told he's here."

"Arthur who?" He scratched his belly.

From the other side of the house, I heard loud barking, followed by Conor shouting and cursing. *Aw, shit!*

I keyed my walkie. "Conor, you all right?"

The belly scratcher chuckled. "That your guy trespassing in my backyard? Guess he met Bert and Ernie."

I tried to push past the guy, but he held his ground. "Get out of my way, asshole!"

"Not a chance, little lady."

I planted my heel in his instep, and he fell forward onto the porch, howling. I flipped him on his belly, one arm twisted behind his back.

A shotgun blast thundered from the backyard and then another, followed by what I guessed were Bert and Ernie whimpering after getting hit with beanbags.

"Sumbitch shot my dogs!" Bellyscratcher yelped.

"Conor!" I called again into the walkie. "What's your status?"

"Just teaching a couple of mutts who's top dog around here."

Out of the corner of my eye, I caught movement on the west side of the house. A skinny guy with long black hair and wearing only jeans and flip-flops had slipped out the side window. This was my guy, Artie Renzelli. He took off running down the street.

"Fugitive's on the run westbound out the side window!" I yelled.

I chased after him, since Conor had a handle on the dogs and their owner. Renzelli sprinted across lawns and, with his long legs, was making good time. I may have been shorter, but I was in better shape and had proper footwear. After a couple of houses, I was gaining on him. I caught snippets of Conor trying to call me on the walkie, but I was running too fast to make out what he was saying.

I was almost on Renzelli with my Taser drawn when the neighborhood street we were running down emptied onto

Seventy-Fifth Avenue, thick with traffic. Renzelli charged full bore into the street, dodging vehicles amid squealing tires and angry honking.

I hesitated to follow, not wanting to get pancaked under someone's truck. When he reached the center turn lane, I decided to risk it. I didn't want to lose him. Not after chasing him for half a mile already.

With a quick glance at the oncoming vehicles, I threw myself into the street, hoping my mother's prayers for my safety would pay off. I reached the center turn lane just as Renzelli disappeared into a shopping center parking lot on the other side. I wanted to rush after him but had to wait on a dump truck to pass, followed by a slow-moving landscaper with a trailer.

When I finally reached the parking lot, I looked for Renzelli among the rows of cars. He was nowhere to be seen. I was about to tell Conor on my walkie that I'd lost him when I spotted my quarry ducking between a Corolla and a Jeep a hundred feet away. "Gotcha!"

I poured on maximum speed, angling through the maze of cars, narrowly missing a Caddy pulling out of a space. When I was almost on him, I raised the Taser and fired. A rapid whapp-whapp-whapp was followed by Renzelli howling and face-planting onto the hood of a Buick. I cuffed him and called Conor on my walkie.

"Yo, Conor!" I said between gulping breaths. "You still alive?"

"Aye! Doing better than those bloody hounds and their owner. Where the hell are ya?"

"Shopping center parking lot. In front of the Fry's Foods. Other side of Seventy-Fifth Avenue. Guess our guy wanted to do a little shopping before we hauled him back to jail. That right, Renzelli?"

"Kiss my ass!" Renzelli said.

"I'll be right over."

A few minutes later, Conor pulled up in the Gray Ghost. I secured Renzelli in the backseat, and Conor drove us toward the Peoria Police Department. I had one thing to do before returning our fugitive to custody.

I dialed the number I'd almost deleted from my contacts list. It rang four times before a familiar voice answered.

"Liberty Bail Bonds. Sara Jean speaking."

"Sara Jean, how the hell are you?" I asked.

"What do you want, pervert?"

"Now, Sara Jean. Don't be rude. I have something you want. Or rather someone."

"Who?"

"Your buddy Artie Renzelli. Dope peddler extraordinaire."

"That case was reassigned to Fiddler. I told you."

"So even if I turn him in and get the body receipt, you're not going to pay me?"

"I will not!" I could picture the self-righteous expression on her face.

"Huh." I turned to my prisoner in the backseat. "Hey, Renzelli, you want me to let you go?"

"Hell, yeah!" Renzelli had a confused but hopeful look.

"No!" Sara Jean shouted. "His bond comes due on Wednesday."

"But it's only Saturday," I teased. "I'm sure if I drop Artie back where he was hiding out, Fiddler'll find him in a week or three. Maybe."

"Don't you do it!"

"What's it going to be, Sara Jean? You going to pay me, or do I let this guy go?"

"Fine, I'll pay you," she grumbled.

I couldn't help smiling. "See you Monday morning around ten. Be a doll and have the check waiting for me. Wouldn't want to sully your office too much with my transgender cooties."

She hung up. I turned to the bare-chested man in my backseat. "Bad news, dude. Got to take you to Peoria PD to get this mess sorted out."

"Fuck you, bitch!"

"Aw, Renzelli darling, don't be cross. It's been kind of fun. We both got some sunshine and exercise. Almost got killed by crazy Arizona drivers. Maybe they'll reset your bail and we can do this all over again. "

He glared. Ugh, so much hostility. Oh well. At least I was getting paid. And at the end of the day, that was what really mattered as far as I was concerned.

A little while later, Renzelli was back in custody. I had my body receipt. I'd called Edie, my tipster, and sent her forty dollars via PayPal. Meanwhile, Conor and I were drinking ice-cold beers at McGowan's Pub, waiting on our lunch order.

Just as our server showed up with our food, my phone rang. It was Becca.

"What's up, Becks?" I asked between bites of my bangers and mash.

"Bonnie Schwartz's phone pinged. I got an address."

"Awesome! Where is it?"

"The phone's at the Desert View Inn. It's off the I-17 southbound access road just past Thunderbird."

"What room?"

"The information isn't that detailed. Sorry. I did call the motel, but they don't have any rooms rented to a Holly Schwartz."

"No problem. It's a start. Thanks!" I was about to hang up when an idea occurred to me. "Oh, one more thing! Get locations on the prepaid burner phones called by Bonnie's phone."

"Gimme a sec," Becca said. "Nope. Uh, no. And ... damn. No luck on any of them. All three burner phones must be turned off."

"I'll start with the motel. Thanks!"

I hung up and turned to Conor. "Pack it up. We gotta go."

"What? I'm still eating my bloody fish and chips." Conor gave me a what-the-hell look.

"Grab a box. We have a girl to rescue and a bounty to collect. On your feet, soldier."

Conor grunted. He tossed our lunches into a take-out box and left a couple of twenties on the table. Such a generous tipper. "Bloody hell, you're so bossy sometimes."

"Bitch, bitch, bitch," I mocked as I pushed him toward the front door.

27

As I drove us north on I-17, Conor's phone rang.

"'Ello? What? Now? I know I promised, but I'm busy at the moment." He paused with a frustrated and annoyed expression on his face. "Oy! Not *that* kind of busy." He blushed and glanced at me.

I mouthed, "Who is it?" He shook his head.

"Fine. I'll be there in half an hour." He hung up. "Sorry, love. I have an errand to run. I'll need ya to drop me off at my place."

"An errand? Who was that?"

He shook his head. "One of my mates needs my help moving a dresser." Something about his voice was off.

"Oh really?" I asked, not bothering to hide my suspicions. "Which one of your mates?"

"Jody. Not even his dresser, really. Just some girl he's shagging."

"Jody, huh? Sounds like a woman's name."

"Stop it! He's a bloke I know from work."

"Yeah, whatever," I grumbled. *Him and his damned secrets.* "But if I bag this chick without your help, I'm cutting your share in half."

"However ya want to split the bounty's fine with me. Just don't be mad." He reached for my hand, but I pulled it away. "Ah, love, I'm not runnin' 'round on ya. Ya know me better than that."

"Now you just sound guilty."

"I'm not guilty of anything 'cept wanting to help a mate."

"What about helping me? Aren't I your mate? Who knows what I could be walking into at this motel."

"You, darling, are my one true love. It's just that I owe this bloke a favor. If ya want to wait till I'm done, then wait. It won't take that long."

"Maybe I should come give you a hand?"

"What?" He shook his head vigorously. "No, that won't be necessary. You're on a deadline. Maybe Rodeo can be your backup."

"Screw Rodeo, and screw you. I can handle this myself." I rolled my eyes. "I'll drop you off at your place so you can help your so-called mate with his so-called girlfriend's so-called dresser."

We drove the rest of the way back to his place in awkward silence. I wasn't normally the jealous type. But after this thing with Levinson and now him obviously lying about this errand, I couldn't help going there.

When I pulled up in front of his house, I stared at the dash without a word.

"Jinxie, love." He lifted my hand from the steering wheel and gently placed three kisses on my knuckles. I felt my anger soften, which still kind of pissed me off. His chivalrous nature was my Achilles' heel, and he knew it. Damn him!

"I swear to the good Lord above, I've always been faithful to ya, and I always will. No one can steal my heart away."

I looked at him, fighting the angry tears pressing at the back of my eyes. My jaw felt tight, my stomach flip-flopping. I had no fear when it came to charging assholes with AK-47s. But this relationship shit could turn me into a whimpering child. "For reals?" I managed to squeak out.

"For reals."

Our eyes locked, and the tears flowed. I felt myself clinging to his words but terrified of believing them. "Go on. Help this Jody person. Call me when you're done."

He kissed me, cradling my face. My insides turned to custard. No one could kiss like that and cheat, could they?

When I opened my eyes, the passenger door was closed, and he was strolling across his yard, digging his keys out of his pocket.

I slid the Pink Trinket's album *TERF Whores* into my CD player and cranked it up to full blast before putting the Gray Ghost in Drive and slamming the accelerator.

It was one o'clock when I pulled in front of the Desert View Inn, a locally owned motel geared toward traveling families. The plaster walls outside the automatic doors showed their years, but the flowers in the planters were in full bloom in a rainbow of colors. I grabbed my paperwork and strode inside.

The woman behind the desk was fortyish and smelled of menthol cigarettes. She smiled as I approached. "Checking in?"

"Actually, I'm wondering if you've seen this person?" I showed her Holly's photo. "She might have been in a wheelchair. Or not."

She studied it for a second, then shook her head. "She doesn't look familiar. 'Course, I was off all last week. Today's my first day back."

"Anyone here who was working the past few days?"

"My coworker's on his lunch break. Should be back in an hour."

"All right, thanks." I started to walk away, then turned back. "You have security cameras?"

Her face grew less friendly and accommodating. "We're not allowed to show the security feeds to anyone without a manager present. And even then, only with a warrant."

I pulled out the authorization for me to apprehend Holly Schwartz. "I'm here on legal business. This person missed her court hearing, and I have reason to believe she may have been kidnapped."

"I'm sorry, but that's not a warrant for the security video."

"So you're just going to let this girl be raped, maybe even

killed, just because I have the wrong paperwork? What kind of person are you?" I was laying the guilt on a bit thick, but I'd learned from the best—my mother.

The woman raised her eyebrows in an apologetic fashion. "Even if I wanted to, I don't have a key to that room. You'll have to talk to my head manager."

"When's your head manager get here?"

"Six tonight."

Crap! I waltzed outside and sat in the Gray Ghost to figure out the best strategy. What did I know? I knew someone had a phone with the SIM card for Bonnie Schwartz's mobile account. Maybe it was Holly or an accomplice.

It could be a kidnapper, but even then they would have to have switched the SIM card between the murder and the time the police showed up. Why would they do that and not take Holly with them? In any case, it followed that if the phone was here, Holly probably was too.

I could stake out the parking lot, but there was no guarantee Holly would leave the room anytime soon. I could go knocking on doors. There were about a hundred rooms in the motel, all of them opened to the outside rather than a central hallway. It was too freaking hot to knock on that many doors. I'd die of heat stroke before I found her.

Searching on my phone, I found a Sub Barn sandwich shop a mile west on Thunderbird. I drove over and ordered a couple of sandwiches. While I was waiting on the order, I asked the freckle-faced kid at the counter, "How much for your hat?"

He looked confused. "I don't think they're for sale."

"Aw, come on. Five bucks. Ten?" I pulled out some of the cash I got off Conor.

A middle-aged man in a white button-down shirt wandered behind the counter. I called out to him. "Excuse me, are you the manager?"

Freckles blushed as the guy in the white shirt turned. "Yes, I'm Craig. Is there a problem?"

"No problem at all." I turned on my gushing fangirl charm. "In fact, I'm a die-hard Sub Barn fan. Love your sandwiches, especially the Barn Burner. So great! And that new ad with the talking horse is hilarious."

"Well, thank you. We're rather proud of it."

"I was wondering if I could purchase one of your hats." I batted my eyelashes and pushed out my chest.

His eyes dropped to my breasts. "Anything for a loyal customer."

Gushing smile turned up to eleven. "Oh, you're so sweet. How much?"

"For you, it's on the house. Call it a promotional investment."

"Aw, thanks so much, Craig."

"In fact," he said, leaning over the counter, "give me your number, and I'll throw in a shirt too. Bet you'd look hot in it."

Oh great. My flirting is working a little too well. Still, a shirt might help me get inside Holly's room. "Ya got a pen?" I replied coyly.

He popped one out of his pocket.

"Hand?" I asked with a wink.

He held out his palm, and I scribbled down the phone number for the local sex offenders' registry. Seemed appropriate.

He beamed. "I'll be right back." A moment later, he reappeared with a polo shirt and a cap, each wrapped in clear plastic. "You free for dinner?"

"I think so. Call me in an hour to confirm."

I trotted out with my bag of subs and my Sub Barn bling. A quick change in the back of the Gray Ghost, and I could have passed for a Sub Barn delivery girl.

When I pulled into the Desert View Inn's parking lot, I called the number for Bonnie's phone. A young female voice answered. "Hello?"

Was this Holly? I couldn't be sure. She didn't sound as fragile as she had on those telethons.

"Hi, someone placed a delivery order from Sub Barn. I'm

here at the motel, but I don't know your room number."

"Oh, that's strange. I guess Richie ordered lunch while he was out. Okay, we're in room 278. Second floor on the back side of the motel."

"Fabulous! I'll be there shortly."

I used to think stunts like this worked only in the movies, but I'd seen Conor pull the same deal time after time. Bottom line, people were gullible. And most criminals were downright stupid. Good for me, bad for them.

I drove around to the back of the motel and parked the SUV. I pulled my snazzy new polo shirt over my ballistic vest, but it bulged too much. I could see the words Bail Enforcement Agent through the thin fabric. If they looked out the door's peephole, I'd be made before I could grab her.

Reluctantly, I ditched the vest but pulled the shirt over my Taser. It peeked out only a little. I donned the Sub Barn cap, grabbed the bag of sandwiches, and hustled up the outside stairs to room 278, paying little attention to the people coming and going along the walkway. Apparently everyone staying at the motel was either headed to lunch or coming back.

"Who is it?" the same girl asked after I knocked.

"Sub Barn delivery."

A girl who looked to be in her early teens opened the door. She stood about four foot ten with an upturned nose and eyes that were hard and dark. Her hair was dark and extremely short, as if recently buzzed.

"Holly Schwartz?"

Her gaze locked with mine for a moment, then to something behind me. I turned to see what she was staring at and caught a blur of motion and then stars.

Next thing I knew, I was lying faceup on the motel bed with my hands cuffed to the headboard above me. Something soft had been stuffed in my mouth, with a strip of duct tape across my face. I was in trouble.

28

My head hurt with the fury of a hangover after a bender of well drinks and cheap wine. My stomach threatened to erupt like Vesuvius. I couldn't remember why I was hungover.

No memories of a wild night at the bars. Nothing to explain the handcuffs or the improvised gag.

"Who the heck are you?" a male voice asked.

My vision was a bit doubled as my eyes fluttered open. I managed to make out a man with long, straight black hair and tan skin. I guessed he was Native American or Latino. He stood above me, a nervous look on his face, pointing the Taser at my chest.

"I'm sorry I hit you. But ..." He glanced at the girl with the bristly hair who was standing beside him. "So who are you?"

I gave them an incredulous look and a muffled grunt. Like, how was I supposed to answer with a gag in my mouth?

The guy ripped off the duct tape. He must have mashed it on good because it felt as if half my face were coming off with it. He then pulled a sock out of my mouth.

"Jesus Christ on a cracker, that hurt!" I took a breath to clear my head. "I'm looking for Holly Schwartz."

The girl's gaze narrowed. "Why?"

"Holly?"

Her mouth was a thin line.

"Your aunt's worried about you. She asked me to find you. Your father too." Technically true, even if they didn't hire me.

"I'm fine."

"She's about to lose her house because of you. You missed your court date."

"Aw, crap, Holly. She's a bounty hunter."

"A bounty hunter? What do we do, Richie?"

The guy again jammed the sock in my mouth and slapped the duct tape back in place. "Look, I'm sorry, but I can't let you take her to jail. She's been through enough already."

I gave them an angry, muffled grunt through the gag. The guy pulled the trigger on my Taser, and my body convulsed in agony. Everything went black.

When I came to again, they were gone. My phone was ringing in my left back pocket. My mind was fuzzy, and the sick feeling in my stomach was worse. I steeled myself. Throwing up with a gag in my mouth could prove fatal. I wasn't going out like this. No freakin' way.

I took some slow, steadying breaths, trying to picture myself with Conor, but that made things worse as I thought about the fight we'd had. So I focused on my parents and my brother, Jake. The world was still swirling and unsettled, but I didn't feel as though I was going to puke and asphyxiate myself. By that time, my phone had quit ringing.

Okay, think, girl. You can get out of this. You have handcuff keys. I kept three keys on my person at all times. One was on my key chain in my front pocket but wasn't accessible since my hands were cuffed to a vertical metal bar attached to the headboard.

My second key was in my back jeans pocket. Also not accessible.

That left the one on a ball chain around my neck. I grabbed the chain at the back of my neck and pulled it up until I had the key in hand. Grateful laughter rumbled in my chest. I would get out of here. With a frustrating amount of effort, I released one hand, then the other.

When I sat up, the room started spinning. Bile rose in my throat. I ripped the duct tape off my raw lips and cheeks and pulled out the sock, trying not to puke. Wincing at the pain, I focused on my breathing until the vertigo lessened.

I pulled my phone out of my pocket. Three missed calls from Conor. One each from my mother and Becca. "Geez, how long have I been out?" The clock on my phone said it was nearly five o'clock. I rang Conor first.

"Jesus! Ya been dodgin' my calls? Ya treat me like a bloody tosser an' then ignore me."

"Con, listen." Another wave of nausea hit me. "I'm … something happened."

"Wha'? You all right, love?"

"I'm …" I hurled all over the floral polyester bedspread and thanked the stars I was no longer gagged. I continued heaving until nothing came up. By the time I was able to put the phone back to my ear, I was afraid he'd hung up. "You there, Conor?"

"Jinxie! Where the hell are ya?"

"I … I don't remember. Some motel room."

"Hang on, love. I'll track your phone. I'm on my way."

I shuffled unsteadily into the bathroom and splashed water on my face. The back of my head ached from where I'd been hit, and my hair was tacky with blood. Probably explained the nausea. I checked myself and found no other serious injuries, just chafed wrists from the cuffs and facial abrasions from the duct tape.

As for my weapons, my Ruger was locked in the Gray Ghost's glove box. I still had the revolver in my ankle holster. An expended cartridge was all that remained of my Taser. Still, it could have been worse.

I was still feeling nauseated when Conor pounded on the door.

"Jinxie, open up!"

Keeping a hand on the wall, I made my way to the door and opened it. The glaring afternoon sun and triple-digit heat hit me like a semi truck. Conor caught me before I lost my balance and helped me sit in a chair.

"What the bloody hell happened? Ya look like ya been battered."

"Holly. She's … not disabled. The whole thing. Must've been a con."

"She did this to you?"

"Some guy with her. Ambushed me from behind. Knocked me out. Then Tased me after I came to. Ugh, God, my head hurts so much."

Conor's hands gently touched the side of my head. "Cheeky bastards. Certainly gave you a knock, didn't they? Ya wanna call the cops?"

"No. My job's to catch Holly. Don't need the cops. How bad's it look?"

"There's a shite-load of blood, but I think ya stopped bleedin'. Oughta get ya checked out, though. Could have a concussion."

"Ugh, last thing I want to do is sit in some ER for the rest of the night."

"This yours?" Conor was pointing at the puke on the bed and floor.

I felt my face warm. "Yeah."

"Come on, love. We gotta get ya looked at. Your ma would have my arse if you up and died on me."

He helped me into his Charger and drove me to the entrance to John C. Lincoln's Emergency Department. I knew he wasn't coming in. For all his toughness and bravado, Conor had an extreme phobia of hospitals. He said it started after his sister was killed in a bombing in Northern Ireland.

I could see the ambivalence on his face as I gathered my strength to open the door. "I know. You can't go in."

"Gah! I feel like such a tosser, but …"

"I understand. Go grab some coffee. I'll call you when I know something. It may be a few hours, though."

"Ya want me to call someone to sit with ya?"

My eyes met his. He looked liked a wounded puppy. "I'll be okay. You got me this far."

A man in teal scrubs knocked on the door. "Are you okay, miss?"

I opened the door and pulled myself shakily to my feet. "I'll need help getting inside."

A woman in matching scrubs showed up with a wheelchair, and they whisked me inside. Four hours, one MRI, two Tylenol tablets with codeine, and a fourteen-hundred-dollar copay later, a young doctor with a South Asian name and a Brooklyn accent determined I did not have a skull fracture but did have a mild concussion. They treated my facial abrasions, cleaned out the wound on my scalp, and wrapped the top of my head with gauze.

The doctor pulled up my medical information on the hospital laptop near the bed. "It says here you take estradiol. What's that for?"

I hated answering that question. But I was too young to be menopausal and didn't feel right about lying and saying I'd had a hysterectomy. "I'm transgender," I said with all the confidence I could muster.

"I see. I suggest you stop taking the estrogen for a week or so."

"A week? Why?"

"Estradiol is a blood thinner. Because of your concussion, it puts you at risk for a brain bleed."

"Okay, you're the doc."

"We're also going to admit you for a twenty-four-hour observation. Just to be on the safe side."

"I don't think so. This job's already cost me enough. I can't afford an overnight stay. Thanks, but no thanks."

The doc looked concerned. "I hate to see money be the deciding factor on you getting proper medical care."

"You and me both. But you want to get paid, and I like to eat."

He waited with his arms crossed, perhaps expecting me to change my mind. When I didn't, he said, "I understand. I'll print out your release and some aftercare instructions, and you'll be on your way."

"Thanks for patching me up."

"No problem."

Twenty minutes later, they handed me my release papers, including a prescription for Tylenol with codeine for the headache. I texted Conor, and by the time they wheeled me outside, he was waiting for me. The nausea lingered, but I didn't think I would hurl again anytime soon.

"As if you aren't hormonal enough as it is," Conor said after I told him about going off the estrogen for a week. He meant it as a joke, trying to get me to laugh. It didn't work. Why did guys always think that was funny?

"Watch your step, buddy," I told him. "Or I may just cut off your balls with a dull knife and feed them to you. How'd you like that, funny man?"

"Aw, love, don't get your knickers in a twist. I'm sorry. Just trying to cheer you up."

"Doing a piss-poor job of it."

"I'm an arsehole. Let's get you home."

"I still need to pick up my truck."

"You sure you're okay to drive? You had quite a knock. And the doctor said you shouldn't be operating heavy machinery."

"Then I promise not to run the dishwasher when I get home." When he grimaced at my poor attempt at a joke, I continued. "I'm fine. I'm not woozy at all. You can follow me back home if you'd like."

Of course, there was another reason I wanted to go back to the motel.

29

When Conor pulled up to the Gray Ghost, I said, "There's one more thing I have to do here."

"Aw, love, you're hurt, and I'm knackered. Whaddya say we pack it in for the night?"

"I need to check with the front desk."

"Why? Ya getting a room for the night?"

"No, I want to see who rented Holly's room."

"Can't it wait till morning?"

"I'm here. I'm getting answers. Won't take long. If you don't want to stay, go on home."

He groaned as I climbed into the Gray Ghost. The codeine was taking the edge off the pain, but I still hurt. I couldn't keep this up for much longer.

I drove around to the lobby. A bald Latino dressed in a suit and tie stood behind the counter. His name tag read Miguel, Head Manager. Just the man I wanted to see.

When Miguel looked up, his professional smile was replaced with a concerned expression. "Are you okay, ma'am?" It was no doubt a reaction to my battered face and the bandage around my head.

"I'm fine, but I need your help."

Conor sidled up beside me as I handed the manager my authorization to apprehend Holly. "I've been hired by the court to rearrest Holly Schwartz, a fugitive charged with murder. She and an accomplice were staying in room 278 when they did this to me." I pointed at my head.

"A murderer's staying here?" His concern turned to panic. "Is she here now?"

"I suspect they bugged out after they ambushed me. I need to know who rented the room and to review your security footage."

"I'm sorry, but those records are private. I'd need a court order."

"Listen, mate," Conor said, leaning over the counter and tapping the paperwork. "This *is* a bloody court order. But if you'd prefer we call the cops and have them arrest ya for obstructing the apprehension of a fugitive, we can play it that way."

Most of what Conor said was bullshit, but I wasn't going to argue. "We can call the media too," I added. "I'm sure your guests would love to know they're staying in a motel with a murderer."

"That won't be necessary. Let me check our records." Miguel typed on a terminal behind the counter. "Okay, room 278 was rented to a Mr. Jablomi. Heywood Jablomi. Oh, crap."

"Heywood Jablomi?" Conor burst into laughter. "Cheeky bastard's got a sense of humor, I'll give 'im that."

I started to laugh too, but it made my head hurt, codeine or no. "Shit."

"I don't know why no one noticed this until now," Miguel mumbled.

"How did they pay?" I asked.

"They paid cash for a week, which would have brought them through next Wednesday. But we do have a credit card on file."

"What name's on the card?" Conor asked. "Ben Dover? Connie Lingus?"

"No, it belongs to Kimberly Morton."

"My fugitive's aunt." I thought about it. "Maybe Auntie Kim's helping her con-artist niece to escape."

"Unless they pinched it from her wallet," Conor suggested.

"Okay, Miguel," I said. "Let's see the security footage."

Miguel looked at me then Conor and nodded. "I really shouldn't, but considering the circumstances. Melissa!" he called.

A young woman came from the adjoining office. "You bellowed?"

"Watch the counter for me. I need to escort these people to the security room."

"I'm still on my break."

He gave her a look, and she threw up her hands. "All right. You're the boss."

He led us down a hallway, then turned left into a room the size of a broom closet. Four monitors and a keyboard were set up on a desk. Miguel sat and began typing. Conor offered me the remaining chair.

"Okay, you're looking for room 278. That's on the west side." Miguel pulled up a video showing camera footage along the walkway near the northwest stairs I'd used. He scanned backward through the footage until we reached the five o'clock mark. I spotted Holly's companion dragging a large suitcase out of the room and toward the elevator. He was too far away to get a good look at his face, but it was definitely him.

"Can we get a closer shot?" I hoped to get a printout of his photo to show around.

Miguel pulled up a different camera, this one by the elevator. He zoomed through the footage until we spotted our guy on the feed.

"There," I said. "That's him." He was wearing shades, but at least we got the shape of his face and his overall look. "Any way we can put this on a thumb drive?"

"I'm going to have to charge you. These flash drives aren't free, you know." Miguel pulled out a small black thumb drive from the desk drawer and slipped it into the USB port.

"Bill me." I dropped my business card on the desk. "Cost you a lot more if guests found out you're renting rooms to murderers with bogus names and stolen credit cards."

"So where's our girl, Holly?" Conor asked, pointing at the security video.

"Good question," I said.

Miguel scanned more footage, going back over the past couple of days. But despite all of the cameras, Holly didn't appear in a single frame. "You sure there was a girl with him? According to our records, he was staying alone in the room."

"Trust me, she was there."

"No offense, love," Conor said, "but ya got a rather nasty knock on your noggin. Maybe your memory's a bit dodgy."

"I know what I saw, Conor. Hell, I called her phone and spoke with her. That's how I found out which room number it was."

"So where is she?" he asked.

I stared at the monitor, remembering the petite girl with the hard eyes and bristly hair. "She's in the suitcase."

"Wha?" Conor asked. "No way! How'd she fit in that trunk?"

"It'd be a tight fit," I admitted, "but I bet she could do it. It's the only explanation."

"Why not use a disguise? Gives me claustrophobia just thinking about it."

"I don't know." I rubbed my face. The codeine was making it hard to concentrate. "What about the parking lot?"

"The parking lot?" Miguel asked.

"I want to see what they're driving."

Miguel pulled up the list of camera footage files and selected one of them that gave a view of the back parking lot. He scrolled until we saw our mystery man dragging the suitcase and approaching a minivan. The camera gave us only a shot of the driver's side.

The man disappeared around the passenger side, then reappeared moments later empty handed, climbed into the driver's seat, and drove off.

"Stop!" I said.

Miguel paused the feed.

"There!" I pointed at the screen with a hazy glimpse of

the inside of the minivan. A shadow was visible in the front passenger seat. "That's got to be her. She must have gotten out of the suitcase. Can we get a license plate on that vehicle?"

"Not from this angle." Miguel pulled up another camera feed and queued it up to the minivan pulling out of the parking lot.

Once the footage was enhanced, I managed to get the plate number and put it in my phone. "Gotcha, you son of a bitch."

"Come on, love." Conor put a hand on my shoulder. "Let's pack it in. You need to rest and recuperate."

I hated to admit defeat, but he was right. I was hanging on with little more than adrenaline and spite. "Okay, Miguel, put the footage on the drive, and we'll be out of your hair."

30

I was feeling no pain, thanks to the codeine, when I climbed back into the Gray Ghost. Conor followed me back to his place. I would've preferred my own bed, but Conor insisted on keeping an eye on me in case my condition worsened.

In his bedroom, I pulled off my clothes. I thought about taking a shower but was too tired. I didn't want to risk passing out and giving myself another concussion. So I stashed my gear next to his nightstand and crawled into bed. "Good night, babe," I said.

"Hey, I know you're tired, but aren't ya supposed to stay awake? You having a concussion and all?"

"Doctor said as long as I don't start puking again or go into a coma, I'll be fine."

He eyed me suspiciously. "You're not having me on, are ya?"

"Jake fell off a roof a couple years ago. The doctors told him the same thing. It's cool. Now let me go to sleep."

He didn't argue, and I drifted off.

Around two in the morning, I felt myself being shaken awake. "Jinxie, love, wake up."

"Huh? What's wrong?" My head was throbbing again.

"Wanted to make sure ya weren't in a coma."

"A coma? For fuck's sake. Let me sleep, or I'll put *you* in a coma."

"Couldn't see ya breathing. I got worried." His eyes glinted in the dim light. "How's your head?"

"Hurts."

"Ya don't feel sick?"

"Sick of these damned questions." I put a hand to my temple. "I'm not going to puke, if that's what you're worried about."

"Okay. G'night, love."

I huffed and turned my back to him. "Thanks for checking on me," I mumbled before falling back into a troubled sleep.

I woke to the sound of water running. Light filtered through the vertical blinds, and it took me a moment to realize where I was. Conor's side of the bed was empty. I sighed and took inventory of my injuries.

My head felt as if someone had been using it for a soccer ball. I thought about getting the codeine prescription filled. Damned good stuff once it kicked in. But I needed a clear head to track down Holly.

Conor emerged from the bathroom, his lower half wrapped in a towel. The sight of his ripped chest took my breath away. "Goddamn, I want you inside me."

He laughed and sat next to me on the bed. His hair was a wild mess of wet ginger curls. Beads of water on his chest glistened in the morning sunlight. "Much as I'd love a ride, I think we should take it easy till ya heal up a bit." He kissed me deep, and I felt it all the way to my groin.

I held his head in my hands, his green eyes shining like emeralds flecked with gold. "I'm fine. Really."

He stood up and pulled on a shirt. "Aren't ya supposed to be at your folks' place for brunch?"

"What time is it?"

"Ten o'clock."

"Ten? Oh shit! Why didn't you wake me sooner?" I bolted upright and fell into a wild ride of room spins, unsettling my stomach. I nearly fell over.

"Easy there, love. This is a strict no-floor-diving zone." He held me until the vertigo passed.

"I'm all right. Shit. I gotta get to my parents' place."

"I thought you were hell-bent on finding Holly Schwartz?"

"Oh, trust me, I am. But I could use a decent meal to get my head working right. Besides, if I miss Sunday brunch, losing out on this bounty will be the least of my worries. My mother will guilt me to death."

As if on cue, my phone rang. I answered it.

"Sweetie, where are you?"

"Sorry, Mom, I overslept. Late night."

"Food's getting cold," she said. "I was worried you weren't coming."

"I'll be there shortly."

I hung up and grabbed a quick shower, careful to avoid wetting the bandage around my head. From my drawer in Conor's dresser, I pulled out a white peasant blouse and jeans to wear with a pair of dressy sandals. I tossed a T-shirt, boots, and my gear in a bag for later.

"After brunch," I said as I attempted to cover the abrasions on my face with makeup, "I'll see if Becca can get a current location for that phone again or the burners she'd called with it."

"Ya think they're still using it? If it were me, I'd've ditched it soon as I learned it was compromised."

"It's possible. But Holly's just a girl, not a brilliant criminal tactician."

"Aside from them staying somewhere while using her mother's SIM card and her aunt's stolen Visa. And this guy she's with smuggled her out of the hotel in a suitcase."

"Allegedly stolen Visa. I'm still not convinced Morton's not in on it." I sighed and tried to recall anything useful Holly and the guy had said. "What was it she called him?" I couldn't remember.

I gingerly placed my Sub Barn ball cap over my bandaged head. "Okay, let's go have some brunch."

31

The neighborhood in Mesa, where I grew up, was a mishmash of Mexican, Native American, and Anglo cultures. Brightly colored murals, old redbrick buildings, *panaderías* next to New York–style delis next to stores selling Navajo and Hopi artwork. The Usery Mountains rose up in the east, where my father would take my brother and me on hikes.

The place had a smell all its own, a mixture of chiles and sweat and hope. Mexican pop music and American classic rock echoed from passing pickup trucks in equal measure. Most everyone spoke at least some Spanish. Even my dad, a Cajun from Lake Charles, Louisiana.

Things had deteriorated since I was a kid. Street gangs had moved in, bringing with them graffiti, drugs, and violence. The sheriff's department frequently rounded up innocent residents in its relentless hunt for the undocumented. Even my mother had been picked up twice for the crime of having tan skin and black hair, despite being a second-generation Italian-American.

Nevertheless, my folks' neighborhood held a sacred place in my heart. It felt safe in a way that defied explanation. As I drove the Gray Ghost down East Broadway Road, the sights, sounds, and aromas of my childhood flooded my mind. I was home.

My parents' house was easy to spot. It was the only pink one on the block. My mother always insisted it was Mediterranean rose, not pink. But everyone in the neighborhood called it the pink house on the street.

When I stepped into the kitchen, rich aromas caused my saliva glands to kick into overdrive. The table was filled with bagels with lox and cream cheese, French toast, stacks of bacon, Cajun-style eggs Benedict, and a bowlful of shrimp and grits.

Around this mouthwatering feast sat my family. My petite mother, Gianna, was clearing empty plates while my lanky father, Edward, chatted animatedly with my brother, Jake, about football.

"Morning, everyone!" I called as we walked in. "Something smells good."

My father caught one look at my bruised face and gasped. "Jenna! What in heavens happened to you?"

My mother nearly dropped the dishes she was carrying. She rushed over and peeled off my cap to reveal the bandage around my head. "Oh, my baby girl! Who did this to you?"

Jake gave me a concerned look. "Damn, sis, you lose a fight with a bulldozer?"

"Relax, people. I'm fine."

"Is this from you chasing after criminals?" my mother asked.

I shook my head. "No, just slipped in the shower." I didn't need another lecture from my mother about my chosen profession. I took a seat next to my brother while Conor sat on my other side.

"You sure you're okay?" Jake asked with a concerned look on his face.

"I'm fine." I loaded my plate with French toast and bacon. "Just starving is all."

"I don't think you slipped in the shower," my mother said. "You've used that line too many times before."

"Just don't want you to worry, Mom. I'm okay."

She didn't look convinced. "By the way, I have some new dresses I want you to try on."

I rolled my eyes. "Maybe after breakfast."

"Hey, Jinx, think you could give me a hand this afternoon? I'm replacing an RO system on a house in Glendale, but I need someone with small hands to reach the unit."

My brother had a thriving business restoring and flipping houses. I helped out on the renovations when my schedule allowed it.

"Sorry, I got plans." I made a sympathetic face. "What about Bosco? He's a little guy."

"Unfortunately, he threw his back out last week. And Torres and his husband are at Disneyland for their honeymoon. Everyone else on my crew has big hands."

"Wish I could help, but I'm on a tight deadline."

"Lemme guess. Chasing criminals."

"A girl's got to make a living."

"You know, Jake," my mother said, "Virginia Gottlieb has long, slender fingers. Bet she could help you with your problem."

"Mom, please." Jake cast a wary glance at her. "Is this another one of your setups?"

"What setup?" She shrugged, trying to look innocent. "She's a concert pianist. Very talented. Good strong fingers. I think she could help, all I'm saying."

I laughed so hard I almost choked on my food. Our mother was always trying to set him up with girls. Problem was, Jake was gay, though he was afraid to tell our folks. Despite my urging him to come out to them, he refused, afraid of dashing their hopes for grandkids. It was a bullshit reason, and I'd told him so on numerous occasions.

"Thanks, Mom," he said. "But I'm sure she's got better things to do."

"Plus she'd probably want to get paid," I added as a playful jab.

"Hey, that's not fair. I'd pay her!" Jake insisted.

"Oh good." My mother's face split into a grin. "I'll call her mother."

"Wait a minute, I've been snookered." Jake turned to Conor. "Help me out here, man."

Conor held up his hands in surrender. "Oh no, you're not pulling me into this."

"She's a nice girl, son," my father chimed in. "Smart, beautiful, and a laugh sweet as bread pudding. You could do worse."

Jake rolled his eyes. "Whatever. Fine. Call her."

My mother finished clearing dishes with a satisfied grin on her face. "Good. 'Cause I need some grandbabies running around this house."

My father, Conor, and I guffawed, while Jake hung his head over his plate.

When I was bursting at the seams from way too much food, I got up to help clear the last of the dishes.

"Jenna," my father said. He and Mom preferred my chosen first name over the moniker Juanita had given me. "Let the others clear the table. I've got something to show you."

I gave Conor a curious look, and he said, "Go with your da. We got it handled here."

I shrugged and followed my father down the hall to my old bedroom, now used for visiting family members. Only a few framed photos on the wall and an abstract floral mural remained from my childhood.

"What's up, Dad?"

He sat on the bed and patted the quilt beside him. "Just wanted to talk is all."

Uh-oh, one of those father-daughter talks. "What about?"

He put a hand on my shoulder and met my gaze. "I know you love what you do, Jenna."

"Dad, please don't start on this again."

"Just hear me out. I've always encouraged you to follow your heart. I supported you when you came out as trans. Cheered when you graduated from the police academy. And I still want you to enjoy your current line of work."

"But …"

He took a deep breath and let it out slowly. "But it's killing your mother. Every time there's a violent story on the news, she frets. She wakes up with panic attacks. A few nights ago, there was a report about several people shot in a raid on a human trafficking operation."

"What's that have to do with me?" I asked, trying to act innocent. "I'm not a cop."

"The reporter mentioned a couple of bounty hunters were involved."

"Oh." Busted.

"You still going to tell me this fist-shaped bruise on your face was from a slip in the shower?" He touched my cheek, and I winced.

"I don't know what to tell you, Dad. What I do is important."

"This is because of what happened with Barclay Dietz, isn't it?"

"No!" I insisted without conviction.

He gave me a don't-bullshit-me look.

"Okay, maybe a little. But it's more than that. I love what I do. It's hard and even scary sometimes, but it makes me happy. I was miserable as a cop."

"But there's so many things you could do with your education and experience. You could still go to law school. Your mother and I would pay for it."

"I have zero interest in being a lawyer. *So* not a part of the suit-and-tie crowd."

He chuckled. "Yeah, you've got that Lafitte blood in you. You're a rebellious soul just like Grandma Marie."

Marie Lafitte, my paternal grandmother, was the great-great-great-granddaughter of Captain Jean Lafitte, a pirate who helped the American army defeat the Brits in the Battle of New Orleans. When I was a kid, Grandma Lafitte delighted me with tales of her own mischief and rebellion, which included being a rumrunner and gun smuggler during Prohibition.

"Dad, you always told me to follow my own star, not to let anyone else get in the way. I'm sorry Mom worries. But I'm a big girl. I can take care of myself."

"This is taking care of yourself?" he asked. "Bandaged head and bruised jaw?"

"When Jake fell off a roof, I didn't hear anyone demand he stop renovating houses and become an architect."

"What can I say? You're my baby girl." My father shrugged. "Maybe it's sexist to hold you to a different standard or worry about you more than Jake. But it's only because we love you."

"Yes, it *is* sexist." I kissed him on the forehead. "But I love you too."

"Any trouble from that article in *Phoenix Living*?"

"Nothing I can't handle."

"Just be careful out there. People can be so mean and ugly. And I'm here, if you ever need to talk."

"I know, Dad."

32

After spending more time with my family, I stepped back into my old bedroom to change into my work clothes and call Becca.

The phone rang five times before she answered.

"Hey, Jinx. Wondered when you'd call back." She sounded as though she was having a rough day.

"Sorry, things got a little complicated yesterday. Listen, I need an updated location on Bonnie's phone. Also was wondering if any of those burners popped back up on the radar."

She huffed. "Okay, give me half an hour, all right? Did you not find her at that motel?"

"I did. She and some guy. Unfortunately, they got the jump on me. Get this. She's not disabled. At least not as far as I could tell."

"Some disabilities aren't as obvious as others, Jinx."

"All I know is that the 'mentally disabled girl in a wheel-chair' bit was all an act. Presumably as a way to make money."

"Are you serious? I hate people who do that. Makes those of us with real issues look bad."

"I hear you. I got a plate number I need you to look up and some surveillance footage from the motel I need facial recognition run on. You at the Hub?"

"Working from home, actually. Not up for the Hub's craziness today." Members of the Hub could be found working there around the clock. On weekends, the music and noise were often cranked up from the usual business routine.

"You mind if I drop off this thumb drive? I need to identify this dude Holly's with."

She groaned. "Yeah, I guess. The place is a mess."

"Doesn't matter to me. All I care about is finding this bitch and taking her back to lockup."

"Damn, girl. What exactly happened at that motel?"

"I'll fill you in later."

I hung up and checked my email and found another email from Volkov.

My dearest Jinx,

It saddens me I have not heard back from you. I'm not used to being ignored. Perhaps you mistook my previous correspondence as the confessions of a lovesick schoolboy. But let me assure you that my feelings for you are quite genuine. And I have an urgent need for someone like you. I am determined to make this a solid partnership. Perhaps a demonstration of my feelings will convince you.

Most sincerely,
Milo

There was an anonymized hyperlink at the bottom. I knew I shouldn't click on it. Most likely it led to some malware or porn site. But I couldn't stop myself from hitting the link. My YouTube app opened and began playing an old rock song from the 1980s—"I'll Be Watching You" by The Police. What a creepy fucking fuck!

I took a deep breath and focused on my mantra—WWWWD. What Would Wonder Woman Do? I wasn't going to let this sick bastard get to me. So he knew my email address. Big whoop. I was always careful to keep my home address and other personal information off the web. So he could pine away to his heart's content. I wasn't going to let him live rent free in my head any longer. And if he dared cross my path in person, I'd put him in the ground the same as I did his men at the warehouse.

I stepped back into the kitchen and found Conor and Jake arguing about soccer.

"You ready to go?" I asked.

Conor nodded.

"Leaving already, sis?" Jake gave me a hug.

I kissed his cheek. "Sorry, bro, got fugitives to catch."

"Keep her out of trouble, man," Jake said.

He and Conor gave each other a fist bump. I said goodbye to my folks and Jake.

When we stepped outside the front door, a full-sized black Hummer idled on the other side of the Gray Ghost. A hissing sound came from between the trucks, like air leaking out in short bursts. "What the hell?"

I ran behind the Gray Ghost and spotted a heavyset figure in a black hoodie between the vehicles. He ducked into the Hummer and shouted, "Go, man! Go!"

The Hummer's wheels squealed as it peeled out down the road. I chased after it for half a block, but it was gone. I put my hands on my knees, sucking air into my oxygen-starved lungs. Was this Volkov? Had he tracked me down somehow? My body shook with anger and fear in equal measure.

When a hand pressed on my back, I whirled around with fists flying and caught Conor on the side of the head. I stopped myself before driving my knee into his groin.

"Oy! At ease, soldier!" he joked, rubbing his temple.

"Sorry, I ..." I took a deep breath, trying to slow the pounding in my chest.

"It's all right. Ya get a plate number?"

"I ... yeah, it was LZ6 ... um ..." I struggled to picture it, but my mind went blank. "Crap, can't remember the last three."

He put an arm around me. "Don't worry, love. You all right?"

"Just winded." And pissed. And worried. "What were they doing?"

Conor looked at me, grim faced. "You're not gonna like it."

We walked back to my folks' place, and I saw it in bloodred paint. The words Trany Faggit were spray-painted across the side of the Gray Ghost. The two driver's-side tires were flat. "What the hell? Geez!"

"So disappointing," Conor said, shaking his head. "Ya'd think if they were going to vandalize someone's ride, the silly buggers would learn how to spell."

"So not funny." I glared at him.

Jake came running out of the house. "Everything all right? I heard shouting and tires squealing."

I pointed at the side of my Pathfinder. "I'm okay. Can't say the same for my truck."

"Damn! Who did this?"

"Probably someone who read that damn article," I said. *Someone like Milo fucking Volkov.* "Not sure how they tracked me to Mom and Dad's."

"You want me to call the cops?"

I thought about it. I needed to get to Becca's. It was already Sunday afternoon. I only had another two days to find Holly. At the same time, I was worried the vandals might come back and do something serious to our folks. "Yeah, I guess so. It's just that I got someplace to be."

"Leave it with me. I got a friend with a paint-and-body shop near Fifty-Ninth Avenue and Bethany Home Road," Jake said. "I'm sure he can fix this for you. He owes me a favor for some work I did for him last year when a monsoon damaged his roof."

"What do I drive in the meantime?"

Jake held out his keys. "Take mine."

"Yours? How will you haul lumber and equipment?"

"I can handle being without it for a few days. Worse comes to worst, I'll borrow Dad's truck."

I gave him a squeeze. "Thanks, man."

"'Course, you'll owe me."

A twisted smile spread across my face. "I knew there'd be a catch. Look, I'll pay you when I get paid on this next job."

"I don't need your money. You're gonna work it off." He smirked. "By the way, what ever happened to that Diamondbacks jersey I loaned you?"

"Um, didn't I give it back to you?" I asked. If I returned it with the collar sliced open, he'd never do me another favor.

"No, you definitely did not."

"Huh, I'll check around my place." A serious concern chased away my levity. "Jake, when the cops get here, see if they can keep close watch on Mom and Dad, will ya? I'm worried whoever tagged my truck might come back."

"I'll see what I can do. Don't worry."

"Thanks, bro." I hugged him. "And for God's sake, tell them you're gay. Before they set up poor Virginia Gottlieb, whoever she is, on a date that leads to nowhere land."

"I'll think about it."

"Don't think. Just do."

"Let me get my stuff out of my truck, and you two can head out." He hustled off toward his Dodge Ram pickup. I grabbed my gear from the Gray Ghost.

Moments later we swapped keys, and Conor and I drove to Becca's.

Becca answered the door a moment before I touched the doorbell. "Wow! Somebody really did a number on you." Her energy level sounded low.

"Yeah, you could say that. How'd you know we were here?"

Becca offered a weak grin and pointed at a small white device mounted above the door. "Camera sends a feed to my tablet when the motion sensors are tripped."

"I should get something like that for my folks."

"They having problems with prowlers?" She led Conor

and me to her dining room table on which sat three computer screens surrounded by a debris field of computer parts, empty cardboard boxes, dirty dishes, and discarded snack wrappers.

I cleared off a chair and handed her the surveillance video thumb drive from the motel. "Just some asshole stalking me and spray-painting bigoted graffiti on my truck. I'm worried they may go after my folks."

"Boy, you pissed someone off."

"Tell me something I don't know. Say, listen, you think you can run these plate numbers for me?"

"Plates numbers, plural?"

"One for the van Holly's riding in. Another for the asshole who vandalized my truck."

"Sure." She opened an app on her computer and went through a series of mouse clicks and keystrokes. "Damn."

"What's wrong?"

"Motor Vehicle's server is down for maintenance right now. I'll try them later."

I gave her the license plate information I had for the two vehicles. "Any luck with the phones?"

"I tried pinging Bonnie's phone, but it's off the grid for now. But not before calling one of those burners, which popped back up." She pulled up a map on her computer, showing a red blinking dot at the Burton Barr Central Library, north of downtown Phoenix.

"Is it near the library or in the library?" I asked. The last thing I needed was to have to go scouting around five floors.

Becca zoomed in. "Hard to tell. Here, give me your phone."

"My phone?" I unlocked the screen and handed it to her.

She clicked away, then handed it back to me. "It's installing a locator app."

"Like the one you put on Conor's and my phones before?"

"The one I put on before will let you track each other's phones. This new app will locate any phone based on a number. It's accurate to within about five feet."

"Damn, I'm glad you're on my team."

"Don't get caught with that on your phone. Its legality is questionable."

"Good to know. Can we take a look at the surveillance footage?"

Becca inserted the thumb drive into her desktop and pulled up a listing of six video files Miguel had saved on it. "Which one should I start with?"

"The one called Elevator," I replied.

She opened the file, and the video began playing.

"Go to sixteen hundred hours."

She zoomed ahead, and there was our guy, staring up into the camera in his shades. "Hello, Moto!" Becca said with a tired grin. "He's kinda cute."

"Any chance you can run facial recognition on this bloke?" Conor asked.

"The sunglasses don't help, but we might get some partial matches that could narrow it down. It'll take some time." She did a screen capture and uploaded the image to an online app.

"How much time?" I asked.

"This app compares the image against the major federal databases and Interpol. Should have results by tonight or tomorrow."

I sighed. "Becks, I need it right away."

"What do you want me to do, Jinx? Pull the answers out of my ass? It'll take as long as it takes. I should be in bed. I really don't have the spoons for this."

"Sorry. Get me what you can when you can. I'm sorry I got upset."

"No worries. I'll call you when I have something else."

"Thanks, Becks! You're the best." I hugged her and turned to Conor. "All right, let's go track down that burner at the library. See what we can find out."

33

I t was a short hop from Becca's house to the Burton Barr Central Library, a five-story building of glass and steel. The parking lot was filled with vehicles, as it often was on weekends. I breathed a sigh of relief when I spotted someone pulling out of a space. The truck's dash said it was a hundred and five degrees outside. The less I had to walk in this heat, the better.

I checked the app Becca had installed on my phone. "The burner shows as being on the library's east side. Guess we'll have to go floor by floor until we find it. Let's gear up."

"Just leave the weapons behind," Conor said.

"Aw, you're no fun," I said with a smirk. I pulled the revolver from my ankle holster and locked it in the glove box along with my Ruger.

When we reached the courtyard in front of the library's entrance, I checked the locator app again. According to the map, the burner phone wasn't in the building but about ten feet from it in the courtyard.

"It's right here," I whispered to Conor, comparing the map to my surroundings.

A dozen or so people sat on the low retaining walls on either side of the front door—a mixture of homeless people, college students, and skaters. Behind them, lantana, cacti, and other desert-tolerant plants grew in a xeriscape garden.

"So where is it?" Conor asked, looking over my shoulder.

I zoomed in as much as possible, then glanced at the people sitting along the north wall. "It appears to be one of them." I nodded in that direction.

We approached cautiously. Several people looked up, including one guy in his twenties with a hipster haircut, wearing a torn black hoodie. How he wasn't melting from the heat in that hoodie, I'd never know.

As soon as my gaze met his, he charged us and knocked me on my butt, sending my phone clattering to the ground. I regained my feet and hauled ass after the hipster. I had no idea who this wiseass was, but clearly he was involved. I wasn't going to let him get away.

He ran east past the employee lot and cut south toward Margaret T. Hance Park. I chased him over a small decorative wall lined with shrubs, then over a field of sun-scorched grass, turned west, and followed a paved walk toward the Central Avenue overpass.

I was starting to lose steam when he tripped and tumbled onto the hard surface. I grabbed hold of his hoodie, pinned him on his stomach, and cuffed him. "Gotcha!" I said between gulps of air.

"Get off me, you bitch. I ain't done nothing." He struggled to escape.

"Where's Holly?"

"Jinx! Jinxie, stop!" Conor came up panting.

"I don't know anyone named Holly."

"Jinx, let the lad go. He's not our guy." He held up my phone. There was no red dot where we were. The red dot was still back by the library's entrance.

"Aw, crap." I uncuffed the guy. "How come you ran?"

"None of your damn business." He stood up, examining a bloody hole in the elbow of his hoodie. "Shit. See what you did?"

"Sorry." *God, I hate being wrong.*

The kid flipped me a double bird as he backed away. "Kiss my ass, you stupid bitch."

"Well, that could have gone better." I fanned my face on our walk to the library. "Geez Louise, could it get any damn hotter?" My head was throbbing again.

Conor handed me my phone when we reached the library courtyard. The people sitting on the walls had cleared out. I guessed our little stunt was too much drama for them. But the burner phone was still showing here. "This doesn't make any sense. Where's the goddamn burner? No one's here."

I looked on the other side of the north wall into the flower bed and caught a reflection of something shiny. I reached down and picked up a black-and-silver flip phone.

"Clever girl!" Conor clapped me on the back.

"Yeah, but who had it?" I tried to recall the faces of the people sitting on the wall, but it was a blur.

"No tellin'."

I opened the phone and pulled up the call history. I recognized Bonnie's phone number on some earlier calls, but there were different numbers on the more recent ones. I was tempted to punch the numbers in the locator app, but I had no idea who they might belong to. Wouldn't do us any good to go chasing after dead ends.

"Maybe Becca can get something off the call history that can point us in the right direction."

We returned to my brother's pickup, and I cranked up the AC full blast. As I put the truck in gear, my phone rang. I put it back in Park and checked the caller ID, hoping it was Becca with more leads.

Instead, it was my friend Izzie Quiñones, owner of a women's bar called L Street on Camelback, just east of Twelfth Street. Izzie's wife, Chelsea, was a friend of mine from the Phoenix Gender Alliance.

"What's up, Izzie?"

"Remember those flyers you dropped off a week or so ago, looking for Mandy Tipton?"

Another one of Liberty's fugitives. She'd jumped bail on

charges of theft and trafficking in stolen property. "You know where she is?"

"Sitting at my bar, throwing back tequila shots, and getting uglier by the minute. You want this chick, come get her. Otherwise I'm cutting her off and calling her a cab."

"I'll be there in fifteen."

"Good, 'cause she's chasing away all my regulars. Sunday afternoons are slow enough as is."

"Be right there. And thanks for calling." I hung up and tossed the phone to Conor. "Change in plans, babe. One of Liberty's fugitives is getting shit-faced at my friend Izzie's bar."

Conor chuckled. "That makes two so far. Big Bobby's going to have a shite fit. Ya sure he'll pay ya?"

"He better. Even if he doesn't, I doubt he'll pay Fiddler, and that's its own reward. Because screw Fiddler."

"Aye! Screw Fiddler!"

34

I pulled up to L Street's front door. "Wait here," I told Conor. "I'll be right back."

"Ya don't want me to come in with ya?"

"Izzie's not too fond of men in her bar." I shrugged. "Besides, I think I can handle a drunk. You can cuff her once we get outside, if you like."

"Yeah, yeah."

I walked inside past a rack of queer-friendly magazines by the door. The Pink Trinket's "Singing Mammogram" played on the sound system, and the hoppy scent of beer filled the air.

Izzie stood behind the bar with a blond mullet haircut showing darker roots, particularly on the shaved sides. Her black cutoff T-shirt read I Kiss Girls in lavender letters. I figured she was in her mid-to-late forties.

"'Sup?" she asked.

"Someone called for an Uber ride?"

Izzie grinned. We'd played this game before. She pointed at the hunched-over brunette a couple of seats over. "Hey, Mandy, your ride's here."

Mandy raised her head. She had a drawn face and track marks on the inside of both elbows. She opened her eyes to a squint. "I didn't call for no ride."

"Sorry, chica," Izzie said. "Gotta cut you off, and you're too drunk to drive. I want you to get home safe."

"Cut me off? Shit! I ain't drunk. Goddamn, bulldagger." She started to slide off her barstool.

I caught her. "Easy there, princess. Let me get you home. I won't even charge you for the ride."

Her face was inches from mine. She looked up at me and smiled. "You won't? You're kinda cute, you know it?"

I forced a smile despite the wave of tequila breath and the cigarette smoke assaulting my nostrils. "Thanks. Come on. I'll help you into my truck." I gave a quick glance to Izzie and mouthed "Thank you."

I pushed open the door, and the furious summer heat rushed us like a flash fire.

"Damn!" Mandy flinched and almost slipped out of my grip. "So hot."

"Don't worry. I left the AC running."

She turned to me, giving me a drunken seductive look. "No, I mean you, sweetie. You're hot. I wanna take you to bed." She put an arm on my shoulder and leaned in, or fell, to kiss me.

"Sorry, sweet cheeks, I'm taken." I spun her around and opened the back door of Jake's pickup truck. Conor slipped behind her and snapped the cuffs on.

"What the hell?"

"Mandy Tipton, you failed to appear at your court date. Your bail bond agent hired me to return you to custody." I tried to help her into the truck, but she started to buck and kick away at the step.

"I ain't going back to jail. You said you were taking me home." She snapped her head back and caught me on the nose. I once again saw stars as a shock wave of pain traveled through my skull.

"Fuck!" I grabbed a fistful of her hair and slammed her face against the side of the truck.

"Ow! You're burning me."

I pulled her away from the hot metal, slightly, but kept my grip on her. "Settle down, or I'll put you face-first on the pavement. You understand me?"

She stopped struggling and hung her head and sobbed. "Please don't send me back to jail. I didn't do nothing. I just needed money."

"Not for me to decide. You missed your court date, you go back to jail. That's the rules. But if you're nice on the way back, maybe you can get your bail reset. Okay?"

She nodded without saying anything. Just sniffling and ugly crying.

Conor and I helped her into the truck and got her seat belted in without any problems. I handed Conor my keys. "You drive."

I hopped into the passenger seat and used a packet of tissues to stop my nose from bleeding. I didn't think it was broken, but it wasn't helping my headache.

"It was all a misunderstanding," Mandy mumbled from the backseat. "My girlfriend just overreacted. Next thing I know, cops show up at my door."

"You steal her stuff?" I asked.

"Technically it was her grandma's. But I told her I'd pay her back."

"Uh-huh." *That's what they all say,* I thought as I dabbed at my nose with the bloody tissue.

"My public defender ain't done shit for me. Fucking loser!"

I ignored her and punched Sara Jean's number on my phone's contacts list.

"Gosh darn it, Jinx. Now what do you want? It's Sunday afternoon for crying out loud. I'm at a church picnic."

I wanted to taunt her, but my head hurt too much to be cute. "Just wanted to get a verbal acknowledgment that you'll pay me for Mandy Tipton."

"Mandy Tipton? I told you Renzelli was the last one. I'm not paying you for Tipton. That case belongs to Fiddler."

"And yet I have her and Fiddler doesn't. Found her in one of the valley's many gay bars. Guess it pays sometimes to be a part of the queer community after all. If I let her go, Fiddler will never find her. I guarantee that. Liberty will be on the hook for the entire amount of her bail. What was it? Twenty grand?"

"You think you're so smart, don'tcha?"

"Five seconds, girlfriend. Four. Three. Two."

"Oh, all right! I'll pay you for Tipton too."

"Pleasure doing business with you." I hung up.

"You can still let me go." Mandy looked like a puppy begging for table scraps.

"Yeah, right. I'd rather get paid."

When we turned south on Central, Tipton groaned. "I don't feel so good."

I turned around in my seat and looked at her. "Aw, crap. Conor, pull over. She's going to puke."

"Hold on. I'm in the left lane. Gotta let this bloke on my arse get past me."

"Hurry, she's—"

The woman leaned forward and unleashed what looked like gallons of vomit all over the back of Conor's seat and the floor.

"Aw, shit." The smell hit my nose and made me gag.

By the time Conor pulled into the parking lot of the Park Central shopping center, Tipton was down to dry heaving and spitting into the mess on the floor of my brother's truck. He was going to kill me.

"I ... I feel better now," Tipton said.

35

After turning Tipton over to the fine folks at the Madison Street Jail's intake, we stopped at a do-it-yourself car wash on McDowell and rinsed out the backseat of the truck as best we could. Still, the stink of vomit lingered. I figured I could get the truck detailed in the next day or so before I returned it to Jake.

It was dark when I dropped off Conor at his place.

"Ya coming in?" he asked as he handed me the truck keys by the driver's door.

"I feel like sleeping in my own bed tonight."

"Ya don't look well, love. Ya okay to drive?"

"Just got a headache, and my nose hurts. I'll survive." I hugged him and gave him a peck on the lips.

"I could follow ya back to your place."

"Up to you. I won't be much company."

When we walked in my front door, I made a beeline to my kitchen for a couple of acetaminophen. I chased them down with a cold beer Conor handed me as I flopped down in a chair and rested my head on the table.

"You all right, love? Ya look like shite warmed over."

I pressed the bottle against my temple. "Should've stopped to fill that pain meds prescription."

"Ya want me to go fill it for ya?"

"No, thanks."

"Ya want something to eat?"

"No!" The thought of food turned my stomach.

"Ya feelin' nauseous? Should I take ya back to hospital?"

"The word's nauseated. Even if I were, I'm not spending another night in the ER."

"Nauseous, nauseated. Same difference to me."

"Just leave me alone."

"Feelin' hormonal, huh?"

I raised my head and gave him a death stare. "First of all, fuck you. Second, I only missed one dose, so no, I'm not hormonal. I've got a busted nose and a headache, a fugitive that I can't find, and your endless questions are annoying the hell out of me. So for the love of all things holy, shut the fuck up."

"Sorry, love. I'm a tosser for saying you're hormonal," he said in an appeasing tone. "Whaddya say we go back into your bedroom for a ride, eh? Get your mind off work stuff."

"What fucking part of 'I've got a fucking headache' did you fucking not under-fucking-stand?"

"Fine. Then what do you want?"

"I want you to shut the fuck up."

He folded his arms and glared at me. "Look, love, I'm sorry ya've got a headache. And I'm sorry you're in a pissy mood. And I'm sorry ya haven't caught your fugitive. But I'll not be treated like a bloody bastard when I'm tryin' to help ya feel better. I'm outta here."

He stormed out and slammed the front door so hard the windows rattled. I buried my head in my arms. "Fuck."

An hour later, the acetaminophen had taken the edge off my headache. I called up Becca, hoping for some help and more than a little BFF sympathy.

"Hello?" She sounded worse than I felt.

"I need you to research some phone numbers for me."

"It'll have to wait until morning, Jinx. I'm not able to handle anything tonight."

"Crap." I was tempted to press her, but even in my mood,

I knew it would be wrong. "All right. Hope you feel better tomorrow." I hung up.

I made myself a bowl of cereal just to have something in my stomach. I felt like shit. I no doubt looked like shit. Shit. Shit. Shit.

I pulled out the burner phone we found and grabbed a yellow legal pad and a pen. I created a written log of the recent calls, then started dialing the numbers I didn't recognize. Three were no longer in service. One rang at the motel where I'd found Holly and her boy toy. And two more had a male voice saying, "I'm not here. Leave a message." No names. I wasn't sure if it was the same voice on both numbers.

I dialed the first number again and forced myself to sound chipper but professional, which in my condition took considerable effort.

"Hi, my name's Liz Windsor with the Arizona Foundation for People with Disabilities. I'm not sure if I have the right number, but I'm looking for either Holly or Bonnie Schwartz. I have a check made out to them for nine thousand dollars. Please call me back so I can send you your money." I left my phone number and hung up, then did the same on the other mystery number.

I poured myself a hot bubble bath and played one of Selena's albums on my old iPod. When I was a teenager longing to be a girl, listening to her music always made me feel better. I popped in my earbuds as I eased into the water. My phone was on the floor within arm's reach, in case Holly called looking for her imaginary check.

I had only a couple of days left to locate Holly Schwartz and very few leads. If I didn't find her in time, chances were Sadie Levinson wouldn't hire me to locate any more of her skips. And then what would I do? No one else wanted to hire me. What would I do for income? Working a nine-to-five was not an option. Not for a pirate girl like me. Too much Lafitte blood coursing through my veins.

Selena's song "Dreaming of You" got me thinking about how I treated Conor. I was a bitch. Totally. Sure, I was off my hormones, and my body felt like shit. My head still hadn't completely stopped hurting. But those were just excuses. If he'd treated me that way, I would've walked away too. I felt awful.

I turned off the music and called him. It went straight to voicemail.

"Uh, hi, Conor. Sorry I was such a bitch tonight. I, uh, call me when you get this. Thanks."

Did I apologize enough? Should I call him back and apologize some more? Have I already screwed up everything beyond repair? Is he avoiding my calls? Is he talking to someone else? Is he cheating on me?

Pressure built up behind my eyes. Tears streaked down my face until I was full-on ugly crying in the tub. *Just soap in my eyes,* I told myself. That and I felt utterly alone, worthless, and miserable.

36

As I was drying off, my phone pinged. I prayed it was Conor sending me a text saying he was sorry too and he would be over to make everything okay. Underneath all the badass was a princess who sometimes just wanted to be taken care of.

I picked up the phone. It was a text but from an unfamiliar number.

I'm hoping the gift I left on your doorstep will convey my true feelings for you.

Was this Volkov again? And what the hell was left on my doorstep?

I pulled on some shorts and a shirt, flung open my front door, and gasped. A six-foot-long bundle of clear plastic stretched on the floor of my front porch. I didn't have to unwrap it to know it was a body. I could see smears of blood on the inside of the plastic. What I didn't know was whose body it was or who had left it.

Panic blazed in my mind as I rushed to unwrap the body. *Please don't be Conor!* My hands grew slick with blood from pulling at the slippery plastic in my furtive attempts to reveal the body in front of me. *Please, please, no!*

When the last layer of plastic was peeled away, I didn't

immediately recognize the body. The face was a battered, pulpy mess. I dug into the victim's pockets and pulled out a wallet. The driver's license read Thom Hensley.

I barked out a laugh of relief as I realized it wasn't Conor. One laugh turned into a series of guffaws that abruptly devolved into uncontrollable sobs. My mind struggled to make sense of the situation. I hated Thom Hensley for what he did to me, but I never wished him dead.

Under the golden glow of my porch light, I sat on the wooden bench, staring at the carnage. An envelope underneath the layers of plastic caught my eye. I snatched it up and tore it open, smearing it with blood. A computer-printed note read:

My dearest Jinx,
I'm told this man outed you without your permission. Truly a tawdry, cruel, and invasive thing to do to such a lovely and gifted woman as yourself. A man like that does not deserve to live. Please take this gift as a token of my affection.
Warmest regards,
Milo

I felt numb. Why was this sick fucker so obsessed with me? Was this revenge for raiding his warehouse? Or did he really have a twisted crush on me? I'd hoped if I ignored him, he'd give up and leave me alone. Clearly, that wasn't working. And now he knew where I lived.

I was in way over my head. It was time to bring in reinforcements. I called Conor, my hand shaking as I held the phone. The call again went to voicemail. "C-Conor, please call me. It's … it's an emergency."

Why wasn't he answering? Was he punishing me? Or had something happened to him too? I tried not to think about it. I punched his number into the locator app on my phone. It showed his phone was at his house. I was tempted to drive over, but I couldn't leave Hensley's body on my porch. Sooner or later the cops would show up. It would look worse for me if it was someone else who called them.

I made one more call before bringing in my former brothers in blue.

"Somebody better be dead or on fire," Kirsten Pasternak's groggy voice said.

"S-Someone's dead."

"Jinx? What happened?"

I took a deep breath to get a hold on my emotions. "Someone killed Thom Hensley. Dumped his body at my place."

"Thom Hensley, the reporter?"

"Yeah."

"Where are you?"

"At home. On my front porch with the body."

"Are the cops there?"

"No."

"Call 911, but do not answer any questions until I get there. You hear me? Just tell them you found a body on your porch. Nothing else."

"Copy that."

Within minutes of my call to 911, patrol cars had cordoned off the street. Curious neighbors stood outside their homes and peeked from windows, drawn like moths to the flashing lights. When the first officer on the scene, an Officer McAfee, started his battery of questions, I told him I'd found the body and would answer the rest of his questions when my attorney arrived.

By the time Kirsten walked up my driveway, yellow crime scene tape stretched across the wrought-iron supports holding up the roof of my porch. Crime scene techs scoured the scene for evidence, including Volkov's note.

I breathed a sigh of relief. "Thank God you're here."

"What happened to your face?" she asked.

"Drunk fugitive head butted me. Nothing to do with this mess."

She eyed me suspiciously. "If you say so. Let's step inside, and you tell me what happened."

I led her to my kitchen table, afraid I'd get blood from my clothes on anything else. I gave her a complete rundown of events, showing her the emails and text I'd received from Volkov. "Will I have to surrender my phone as evidence?" I asked. "I rely on this for work." Also, I still had that locator app that I didn't want them to find.

"We'll see what we can work out."

I heard a knock on my front door, followed by a familiar voice. "Hello? Anyone home?"

"In here." I gave Kirsten a look.

Detective Hardin shuffled into my kitchen. "Gotta say, Ballou, you're the last person I expected to be talking to this evening."

"Feeling's mutual."

"Then again, bounty hunters do like to push legal boundaries." He nodded at Kirsten and pulled out a pen and a notepad. "Good evening, Counselor."

"Evening, Detective."

"I didn't do this, Hardin, if that's what you're thinking."

"If you say so. Why don't we start with a statement."

I provided a brief explanation of my infiltration of the warehouse, leaving out the part about Conor and me killing Volkov's men. I brought up the disruption of the FBI sting and the release of the kidnapped women being held at the warehouse, giving retaliation as a possible motive for Volkov. Finally, I mentioned the note left with the body.

"If Volkov's mad at you for disrupting his human trafficking operation, why would he murder Hensley?"

"How should I know? I've never met Volkov. But judging from the note he left, he seems to have some weird fascination with me."

Hardin nodded, taking notes. "When's the last time you saw Hensley?"

I took a breath and shared a glance with Kirsten. She nodded. "The day that article came out. He and I had a heated discussion about it after he outed me without my permission. But it was just an argument. I let it go."

"So you were angry at him."

"Yeah, but not enough to kill him. He's an asshole. But so what? The world's full of assholes."

"You never threatened him?"

I tried to remember what I'd said to him in his office. "I threatened to sue him. That's it."

"Tell me, Jinx, why's your face all black and blue? You and the victim get in a fight?"

"No, a drunken fugitive head butted me this afternoon."

"Really? Where were you earlier this evening?"

"Conor and I dropped a fugitive off at the Madison Street Jail around seven. Got back here around eight o'clock. Been home alone ever since."

"Last time I checked, it didn't take an hour to get from the jail to here. Maybe fifteen minutes in heavy traffic."

"We had to rinse out the backseat of my truck after a fugitive got sick." I ignored Hardin's chuckles and continued. "Then I dropped off Conor at his place and came home."

"And the body wasn't here when you got home?"

"Sure, it was here," I said sardonically. "I thought I'd wait until the middle of the night to call you guys. What, do you think I'm crazy?"

"You didn't ask Volkov to kill him?"

"I have never talked to Volkov. Nor do I ever want to." I just wanted to put a few bullets into the sleazeball's skull.

"We're going to need your clothes for evidence. And we'll need to swab your hands for GSR."

"Fine, whatever."

37

Hardin promised to have Patrol keep an eye on the house in case Volkov or one of his goons showed up. He made me swear to let his team handle it. I was too tired to argue. It was nearly dawn by the time the last of the officers left.

When I was finally alone, I showered and collapsed in my bed, only to wake what felt like minutes later to the sound of my phone ringing. "Conor?"

"Sorry, girl, no. It's Becca."

It took a second for my brain to focus. Right. Becca. Plate numbers. "Hey, Becks, what's up? What time is it?"

"Eight twenty-one. Too early?"

"Late night. Someone murdered Thom Hensley and dumped his body on my doorstep."

"Seriously? Holy crap! Are you okay?"

"I'm fine. Just exhausted."

"Any idea who did it?"

"Milo Volkov."

I heard her gasp. "Are you serious? Girl, you should get someplace safe till they catch him."

"I'm not worried, just pissed off." I swung out of bed and shuffled into the kitchen. I'd forgotten to put coffee grounds in the coffeemaker, so there was a lovely carafe of hot water waiting for me. Shit. I popped in a fresh filter and some grounds, dumped the water into the reservoir, and pressed the brew button.

While it ran, I grabbed my file on the Holly Schwartz case. "What've you got for me on those license plates?"

"The one from the hotel is a rental from Cheap Ride Rentals."

It was a national chain. "Do you know which office?" I asked.

"Northwest corner of Tatum and Shea."

I wrote down the address, which wasn't far from Kim Morton's house. "That's a start. What about the Hummer that tagged the Gray Ghost?"

"You only gave me a partial plate, so I was able to narrow it down to three vehicles. One belongs to a Dmitri Gorkov."

"Never heard of him." I wondered if he was an associate of Volkov's.

"The other two possible matches are Yvonne McKinley and Robert Dixon."

"Wait, did you say Robert Dixon?"

"Yeah, full name is Robert Lee Dixon. You know him?"

I sighed. "Fiddler. It was motherfuckin' Fiddler. I swear, next time I see him, I'll kick his ass."

"You know him?"

"Old bounty hunter for Liberty Bail Bonds who was on my team until a few days ago. The one Big Bobby gave my outstanding cases to." I managed a smile. "He also was looking for Holly Schwartz, until Sadie Levinson turned the case over to me. Thanks for the 411."

"Glad I could help."

"Do me a favor, though. Don't tell Conor it was Fiddler, if you happen to talk to him."

"Why not?"

"I want to handle it myself."

"You got it. Anything else?"

I thought about it. I hadn't heard back from my charity check scam on those two phone numbers. "Yeah, I located that burner that had been calling Bonnie Schwartz's number. Got some other phone numbers I want you to reach." I gave them to her.

"I'll run them and let you know what I find out."

I poured myself a cup of coffee. Despite my lack of sleep, I actually felt better than I had the day before. My nose was still tender, but my headache was gone. After some eggs and coffee, I was actually feeling almost human. I still felt a bit emotional, especially when I thought about Conor. *Why the hell hasn't he called me back?*

After throwing on some clothes, I decided it was time to get paid. I hopped into Jake's truck, which still stank faintly of vomit, and zipped downtown to Liberty Bail Bonds with body receipts in hand.

Big Bobby was talking with Sara Jean when I walked in through their glass doors. They did not look happy to see me, which made the situation all the sweeter. Assuming I actually got paid, that was.

"Good morning, assholes! How the hell are you?" I said with a smug grin.

Big Bobby stood up tall and crossed his arms. Damn, he was a big man. "What the hell you doing here? We fired you last week."

"Maybe so, but you still owe me for these two." I waved the body receipts.

Sara Jean looked as if she'd just eaten a cockroach. Big Bobby got a confused look on his face.

"We ain't paying you for those!" Big Bobby insisted. "We gave your cases to Fiddler." He reached for the body receipts, but I pulled them out of his grasp.

"*Au contraire, monsieur.* Sara Jean and I already discussed it. I even recorded our conversation."

"What?" He turned to Sara Jean. "What the hell's she yammering about?"

Sara Jean harrumphed. "What was I supposed to do, Bobby?

We were running out of time on those two. She grabbed Renzelli on Saturday. Said she'd release him if we didn't agree to pay her."

"What about the other one?"

"Mandy Tipton?" I asked with a smirk. "Grabbed her yesterday."

"She was at one of them lezzie bars," Sara Jean said with a sneer. "Fiddler never woulda found her."

"Aw, why all the sour faces? This is good news. I found your skips, turned them in, and saved you good people a ton of money and hassle."

Big Bobby still didn't seem grateful. Oh well, not my problem.

"Enough chitchat." I set the body receipts on Sara Jean's desk. "Time to pay for services rendered."

"I don't care what Sara Jean told you." Big Bobby stepped between me and Sara Jean's desk. "I'm the owner of this here outfit. And I say, I ain't paying you nothin', ya little pervert."

"Seriously? I'm the pervert?" This was getting old. Time for a change of tactics. "From what Fiddler told me, Bobby, you've been spending a lot of time with a young thing you met at Chasing Tails, that strip club near Grand Avenue and Indian School. The one that dresses up like a Catholic schoolgirl? Not that I judge."

"You what?" Sara Jean glared at him.

Big Bobby muttered incoherently, no doubt trying to come up with an explanation. "I, uh, she don't know what she's talking about."

"Big Bobby, are you seriously going to deny it? You want me to show Sara Jean your credit card receipts? I mean, seriously, who puts lap dances on a credit card? Honestly, I think you wanted to get caught."

Sara Jean slapped him. "You filthy pig. You said you was on a stakeout."

"I was, sugar pie, honest."

"Don't get so high and mighty, Miss Sara Jean."

Sara Jean turned back to me with a confused look on her face. "Me? What did I do?"

"Gee, let me think. How about the money you've been slipping some of the defense attorneys under the table. I wonder what the Department of Insurance would say to that if they found out you were paying referrals to lawyers. They could shut you down."

Her fleshy face turned a lovely shade of fuchsia. "You wouldn't?"

"Hey, I understand. Cost of doing business. And as long as I get paid for these body receipts, it'll just be our little secret."

"That's extortion," Big Bobby exclaimed.

"Naw, extortion would be if I demanded another ten grand to keep my mouth shut. I just want what I would have earned if you two weren't such backwoods bigots."

"All right, all right. Pay the woman, Sara Jean!" Big Bobby glared at me. "But this is it, ya hear? All your other cases have been reassigned."

Sara Jean scribbled out a check and handed it to me without a word.

"Thanks!" I said, slipping the check in my back pocket. "You two hypocrites have yourselves a fabulous fucking day."

The office door squeaked open behind me. I turned, and Fiddler was walking in. The image of my spray-painted truck popped into my head. My blood boiled. "There you are!"

Fiddler's eyes went wide. "Aw, shit!" He turned tail and dashed out the door with me on his heels. I maneuvered through a trail of toppled pedestrians left in Fiddler's wake as he barreled down the sidewalk. He didn't get more than half a block before I grabbed him and threw him against a building.

"Whatcha running from, Fiddler?"

He was gasping, trying to catch his breath. "I ... I don't know ... what ... you're talking 'bout," he huffed. "Just seemed ... nice day for ... a run."

"Cut the shit, Fiddler. I know you vandalized my ride." I popped open my phone and showed him the photo.

"Not me."

"Had a friend of mine trace your license plate, douchebag." A small crowd of people started to gather around us, holding up their phones, no doubt recording the excitement.

"So what?" He got a smug look on his face. "You *are* a faggot, right? Heard you even got your dick cut off. Fucking tranny faggot."

Suddenly Fiddler was on the ground, moaning. Blood dribbled from his nose and a cut below his left eye. I didn't remember hitting him, despite the throbbing in my fist.

"Stay away from me, Fiddler, or I will kick the ever-loving shit out of you. Got it?" I turned away, cradling my hand. I glared at the lookie-loos recording me. "What are you looking at?"

As I was on the way back to the parking garage, my phone rang. "Yeah?"

"Jinxie? You okay?"

I felt all the bluster go out of me like a deflating balloon. "Conor."

I collapsed onto a nearby bus stop bench. Memories of the night before flooded my mind. The acrid smell of blood, death, and plastic. Hardin's never-ending questions.

"Hensley's dead."

"Aye. Heard about that on the news. Recognized your house on the telly."

"It's Volkov. He's … " I wasn't sure how to explain it. "He's been stalking me. Sending creepy emails. Then this."

"Jesus Christ, I'll kill the fucker before he lays a hand on ya."

"Honestly, I think he's got a creepy crush on me. I promised to let Hardin's guys handle it. I need to focus on finding Holly Schwartz."

"Where are ya?"

"Downtown. Just picked up a check from Liberty. Had a run-in with Fiddler."

"Fiddler? What about?"

"He's the one who vandalized the Gray Ghost."

"That bloody wanker! Ya give him what for?"

"I punched him in the face." I actually felt bad about it, which made me wonder what the hell was wrong with me. Was I going soft?

"Good for you, lass." I heard him chuckle.

"Conor, I'm sorry for getting all pissy with you yesterday."

"Aw, Jinxie, I understand. Been a rough couple of days."

"Thanks, you're the best."

"So ya want some company?"

"Yeah. I'm heading to a rental car place at Tatum and Shea. Seems our girl and her boyfriend rented that minivan from Cheap Rides."

"Cheap Rides?" Conor guffawed. "Sounds like a low-cost hooker."

"Yeah, yeah. Very funny. You in?"

"Aye! I'll meet ya there."

38

onor was already sitting in his Charger in the parking lot when I pulled in. I parked and stepped out into the heat, wearing my gear. He hugged me, and it honestly felt good to be held.

"I'm sorry for yelling at you," I said, trying not to tear up. If I had to go much longer without my hormones, I was going to fucking kill someone. I only hoped it wasn't him.

"Don't give it a second thought, love." He kissed me on the forehead. "You doing okay?"

I shrugged. "I'll feel better once we apprehend Schwartz."

"You said Volkov's been stalking you?"

I showed him the emails and the text.

"Jesus, Mary, and Joseph! Why didn't ya mention this earlier? He could've killed ya."

"Hoped he'd give up when I didn't respond."

"Bloody good that did."

"So this is my fault?" I glared at him incredulously.

"Not saying that. This is all on him. But we have to watch our backs."

"Fuck Volkov! I hope Hardin kills him," I said, getting control of my runaway emotions. "I have more important things to worry about than some twisted, lovesick Chechen gangster."

"Aye. Let's go see what the good folks at Cheap Rides can tell us about who rented that vehicle."

We stepped into the small office with cheap carpeting and even cheaper-looking cubicles on the other side of the scratched-up counter. A clean-cut man a few years younger than me, wearing a clip-on tie and a white dress shirt, stepped up to the counter with a car salesman smile. "Hi, my name is Chad. How can I help you folks?"

I flashed my Bail Enforcement Agent badge. "One of our fugitives was seen with a man who rented a car from your office. We need to find out who he is and where he lives."

"I'm sorry, but I can't give that information out to just anyone."

Conor pointed at my bruised and battered face. "See this, lad? The people we're looking for did that. Nearly killed her. They're wanted for murder."

"Trust me," I said, "you want us to get them off the streets. We might even get your minivan back for you."

"You don't think they'll return our van?"

I raised an eyebrow. "They're wanted for murdering a woman and jumping bail. You think they're worried about stealing your van?"

Chad went pale and stepped up to one of the computer terminals at the counter. "What are their names?"

"I'm not sure what name they rented under. Here's the license plate." I slid him the paper I'd written the plate number on.

He did his magic on the computer. "That car was rented a month or so ago by a Richard Delgado."

Holly's nurse. "He got an address, mate?" Conor asked.

"Komatke, Arizona. Diamondback Drive." Chad wrote down the exact address.

"Where's Komatke?" Conor gave me a quizzical look.

"Down on the Gila River Indian Reservation south of town. You have a phone number for him?" I asked the guy.

"I'll print out the file for you."

He tapped on the keyboard, and a nearby laser printer spit

out a few pages. Chad handed them to Conor, who passed them to me. "He look familiar?"

The printout had a copy of Delgado's driver's license picture. "Yeah, that's the guy who roughed me up. The one with Holly."

"Anything else?" Chad asked.

"No, that'll do. Thanks." I gave him a smile and turned to leave. "Guess we're taking a trip south of the city."

"You will call, won't you?" he said as Conor and I walked out. "Let us know if you find the van."

"Sure," I lied.

I climbed into Jake's truck with Conor following behind in his Charger. On the way to Komatke, I called Becca.

"The guy who rented the car's named Richard Delgado."

"Delgado? Holly's nurse."

"Conor and I are headed to his house in Komatke now. Pull up everything you can on him. Phone logs, bank records, the works."

"Will do."

"Thanks, Becks."

I hung up and breathed a sigh of relief. I was back in the hunt. With a little luck, we'd find Holly hiding out at Delgado's place, and with Conor there, I wasn't going to get ambushed like before. Maybe I'd even get my Taser back.

Still, something nagged me. Why hadn't Conor answered his phone when I called to apologize last night? Did he not feel like talking to me after I'd been so awful to him? I couldn't shake the feeling that something else was going on.

He'd disappeared a couple of times the past few days without explanation. When I'd pressed him, he lied. Or maybe the lack of hormones was making me paranoid. Ugh. I hated this.

I decided when I got home, I'd take a double dose of estradiol. I didn't care what that doctor at the ER said. The mood swings and the fucking crying was worse than dying. If I didn't get relief soon, I'd be the one going on a murderous rampage. Could I plead temporary insanity?

39

Komatke was a sparsely populated town in the Gila River Indian Community, in the open desert south of Phoenix. I'd occasionally passed through Komatke in an attempt to bypass rush hour traffic when I had to get from west Phoenix to the southeast valley and beyond.

We parked on the street in front of Delgado's place, a small wooden frame house coated in a layer of desert dust so thick it was difficult to tell what color it'd been painted. The yard was natural desert. No lawn. No crushed rock. Just bare ground littered with wild grass, creosote, brittlebush, and other plants I saw all the time but didn't know the names of. One of them might have been a Mormon tea bush. But what did I know? I was no botanist. I wasn't Mormon. And I didn't even like tea all that much.

No cars were parked in front in Delgado's dirt driveway. The curtains were drawn. Not a sign of life anywhere. The nearest house was a quarter mile away.

"Think they're in there?" I asked Conor as we met between our vehicles. I donned my shades and racked the slide of my Ruger. If Delgado tried to ambush me again, he'd find me rather unforgiving.

"No vehicles, but those tire tracks in the driveway look recent."

"Maybe they had someone drop them off so it would look like no one was home."

It was flimsy, and we both knew it. Technically, we could force our way in only if we had reason to believe our fugitive was inside. It was a gray area. If we were right, we were golden. If we were wrong, we could be in a whole lot of trouble, especially on the reservation.

Several years back, a team of bounty hunters was given bogus information. They stormed a house while looking for a fugitive, only to discover the address they'd been given belonged to the Phoenix chief of police. Several innocent people were hurt in the process. The bounty hunters were sentenced to serious time in federal prison.

I didn't want to face the same fate. Trans people didn't do well in prison. But I wasn't going to let Holly slip through my fingers again. This was about more than the fifty-thousand-dollar bounty. I had a grudge to settle.

I looked around. The street was empty in all directions. "Let's do it."

Conor nodded. "Suits me, love. Ya want the front or the back?"

"I'll take the back this time. I'll wait for your signal." I turned on my walkie.

"Suits me fine."

I hustled around to the back. Under a small porch, a ceramic chiminea sat next to a couple of dust-covered plastic lawn chairs. The back door looked weathered, the outer laminate peeling at the bottom. I put my back against the wall next to the door, my Ruger ready.

Conor pounded on the front. "Open up! Bail enforcement." He pounded again. There was no response.

"Looks like no one's home," Conor said over the walkie.

A crash came from inside, like a box of something being knocked over. "Someone's in there. I'm going in."

"Jinx, hold on."

I gave the back door a good kick with my boot. The frame shattered, and the door snapped inward. I rushed in, pivoting right and left as I advanced into a dark room. A flurry of dust motes swirled in the air lit up by the midafternoon sun pouring through the back windows. I whipped off my shades to better assess my surroundings. I was in the kitchen. The scent of cooking oil hung in the air.

I checked under the small kitchen table and opened every cabinet. I'd had fugitives hide on closet shelves and even in a chimney once. After Delgado spirited Schwartz away in the suitcase, I wasn't making any assumptions. But after a thorough search of the kitchen, I'd turned up nothing but a drying rack full of dishes.

I continued into the living room, modestly furnished with an aging Barcalounger and a bulky TV that looked about twenty years old. An entertainment center held a stereo, turntable, and a stack of LPs. Photos of Delgado and lots of family members covered the wall. On another hung several awards from the Komatke High School Rifle Club recognizing Richie Delgado as their top marksman. Unopened mail lay in a basket on an end table.

Warily, I unlocked the front door and let Conor in.

"A tribal police car drove past but didn't stop. I think we're in the clear," he said.

"Good to know."

We continued down a short hallway and verified that the two cozy bedrooms and only bathroom were unoccupied, as was a utility room with a stacked washer and dryer.

"I swear, I heard somebody knock something over," I said, rechecking one of the bedrooms. "Wait a minute."

I found a bowl of kibble on the floor.

"Looks like Delgado has a cat," Conor called from the bathroom. "Found a litter box."

I rechecked under the bed and noticed a pair of eyes, like glowing coals. "Hello, kitty."

I met Conor in the hallway.

"Also found this," he said, holding up my Taser.

I holstered my Ruger and tucked the Taser into my waist-band. "So they were here."

"Aye, but it looks like they bugged out."

"Now what?"

"Nothing of interest here," he replied. "We could conduct a stakeout."

"Doesn't seem promising. Let me see if Becca's got anything else on Delgado."

I called and updated her on our situation. From the noise in the background, I could tell she was working at the Hub today.

"I've done some digging around. He goes by Richie. He posts a lot on Facebook and Twitter, but nothing significant. He's got a brother named Christopher Delgado. Nothing of interest on his bank statements. The only recent transaction on his bank card was an authorization for a car rental. No recent activity on his cell phone account."

My phone buzzed. "I got another call coming in, Becks. Let me know what else you find out."

"Will do."

I clicked over to the other call, hoping my little phishing expedition from the night before was finally paying off. "Hello?"

"Ms. Ballou? This is Sadie Levinson. Where are you on the Schwartz case?"

"Sadie! How the hell are you? Good news, I'm closing in, hoping to have her in custody by the end of the day."

"Really?" She didn't sound convinced. "Sounds like one of Fiddler's cock-and-bull stories."

"Ouch! Sadie, you wound me."

"Cut the theatrics, Ms. Ballou. Schwartz's bond goes up for summary judgment first thing Wednesday. I can't afford to lose this. I'll be out of business, and so will you."

I sighed. "We'll find her. Don't worry."

"Hold on, love. Looks like we got company." Conor spun me around and lifted the corner of the living room curtain. A tribal police patrol car had pulled up behind Conor's Charger.

"Who's we?" Sadie asked. "Is that Conor Doyle I hear?"

Aw, shit. Shit, shit, shit. "Oh, that? Naw, just the TV."

"That was Conor. I'd know that Irish brogue anywhere."

I made crackling sounds with my mouth. "What's that? Can't … hear … breaking up."

"You're not fooling me. I told you that I specifically did not—"

"Gotta go … fugitives to catch." I ended the call. Because apparently I was an eight-year-old in a twenty-nine-year-old's body.

"Sadie?" Conor asked.

"Yeah," I said, keeping my eye on the police cruiser outside. "One of these days you're going to tell me what the hell happened between you two."

He grimaced. "Another time. Right now, we have more immediate concerns."

The officer stepped out of his cruiser and circled our vehicles, then turned toward us peering out the window. "Aw, crap."

40

There was a solid knock on the front door. I pushed Conor aside. "Let me handle it. People like me."

Conor cough-laughed. "Oh really? I've met sandpaper less abrasive than you."

I gave him an eat-shit look. "Don't push me, Doyle." I pulled off my ballistic vest and tactical belt, tossed them to the side, and opened the door.

Officer Quiroz, whose name was on a brass name tag, was slender with a smallish face, wary eyes, and a pleasant smile, which I tried to return as convincingly as I could.

"Hi," I said. "What's up?" Mentally, I kicked myself. Could I sound more like a vapid teenager?

"Afternoon, ma'am. Are you the owner of the house?"

I thought about saying yes but didn't figure I could pull it off. "No, I'm afraid the owner of the house isn't here right now. I'm house-sitting. Is something wrong?"

"When will the owner be back?"

I shrugged. "Hard to say. He's out of town on family business." Sounded vague enough to be reasonable.

"The owner is Richie Delgado, is that correct?" He took out his notepad and started writing.

My stomach sank. Conor approached as if to "handle the situation," but I was in no mood. I gave him a back-off glare. "Oh yeah, good ol' Richie. We go way back."

"Really? That's interesting. Is he up at his brother's cabin in Payson?" Clearly, Officer Quiroz knew more than he was letting on. How long before this guy was slapping the cuffs on me for B&E?

"You know, I think he did mention Payson. Yeah."

"That so? Because his brother's cabin is in Prescott."

Crap. "Prescott. Payson. I get them confused sometimes."

"Tell me something, ma'am. What happened to your face?"

Conor stepped between us and held up his bail enforcement agent shield. "Look, Officer Quiroz, the truth is we're looking for a fugitive named Holly Schwartz who is charged with the murder of her mother. Mr. Delgado has been actively interfering in her recapture."

"Really? You have any paperwork backing up these claims?"

"In my truck." I led him out to Jake's truck, with Conor shutting the front door behind us. I showed Quiroz the paperwork authorizing me to apprehend Holly Schwartz.

"You have proof that Richie is involved in this?"

I was done playing nice. "I found him hiding Schwartz in a Phoenix motel room under an assumed name and using a stolen credit card. When I attempted to apprehend my fugitive, Delgado assaulted me. I had reason to believe he might have brought her back here."

"You know," Quiroz said, gazing out at the very blue horizon, "Richie's my cousin. Known him my whole life. Sweetest, most gentle soul I've met. Can't imagine him doing anything like what you claim."

"Don't believe me? Call the Desert View Inn on Black Canyon Highway. Ask for the head manager."

Quiroz stared at me, then Conor for a few moments before saying, "I should charge you both with trespassing."

"We are authorized to …" I was about to launch into my speech about the historic court case authorizing bounty hunters to enter, when Quiroz held up his hand.

"But I'll let you go with a warning. And the warning is this.

If I ever catch either of you in this community, breaking into a home without the owner's permission, I will run you in. If you so much as drive one mile an hour over the speed limit, I will hit you with every violation I can. You understand?"

I considered our options. Clearly Schwartz wasn't here. Time to move on. "Yes, sir," I said.

"Now get out of my sight before I change my mind."

I climbed into Jake's truck, and Conor hopped into his Charger. I turned north on Fifty-First Avenue headed back to Phoenix and talked into my walkie. "Hey, Conor. You copy?"

"I copy, love. What's the plan?"

"I think we need to find this cabin in Prescott Officer Quiroz was talking about."

"Be a brilliant place to hide someone."

"Let's stop by the Hub and see if Becca can give us a location."

"Roger that."

As I turned east onto I-10, my phone rang again. "Jinx Ballou."

"Good news, sis," Jake said. "Your Pathfinder looks good as new. My friend squeezed you in right away."

"So soon? It's barely been a day." I took a sniff and was sure I could smell a hint of Mandy Tipton's vomit.

"Looks better than new, actually. Tell me where you are, and we can swap vehicles."

"You know, I should really get your truck detailed. It's the least I can do."

"Forget it. I use it for construction. Doesn't need to be clean. Just functional. Besides, how dirty could it be?"

"Okay." I sighed. Maybe he wouldn't notice. "I'm on my way to the Hub."

"I can be there in half an hour. Will that work?"

"Yeah, I guess so."

"Something wrong?"

"Not at all. I'll see you at the Hub." I took another sniff. It definitely still smelled like puke.

41

The Hub was located at the three-way intersection of Grand Avenue, Roosevelt Street, and Fifteenth Avenue. The old building reminded me of an inverted boat, with a keel that rose into the sky. It started out as a car dealership, later converted to a bank, then became the home for the Phoenix Council on the Arts.

For the past few years, it had served as a coworking space for solo entrepreneurs. Most members were in the tech industry, a few were artists, and then there was me, a bounty hunter.

The parking lot was small, but Conor and I managed to grab the last two spaces and hustled inside the glass doors to get out of the heat.

The interior was an open grungy industrial space with a cracked cement slab for a floor, pockmarked with divots from where they'd pulled out the walls. Dozens of collapsible tables served as desks with a wild assortment of secondhand chairs, from fancy super adjustable executive-style thrones to flimsy plastic folding numbers.

The hypnotic beat of electronic dance music thrummed from unseen speakers. Overhead lighting was subdued. Conor and I strolled across the room to where Becca stared vacantly at a pair of flat screens. "S'up?" Becca asked without a glance.

"I have a lead on where Delgado may have taken Holly Schwartz. His brother has a cabin up in Prescott somewhere."

"Interesting. I've done more digging on Delgado. No criminal record. Good credit. Worked as a nurse for much of his adult life. First at the Gila River Medical Center, then as a visiting nurse for Compassionate Care. As far as I can see, he's clean as a whistle."

"So why is he helping hide Schwartz?"

"Beats me." Becca went through a series of mouse clicks and keystrokes. "Christopher Delgado, age forty-two. Real estate developer. Owner of Stardust Properties Corporation. Makes good money too."

"Great. Where's the cabin?"

"Let me take a look." She cycled through a number of screens. "Aha! Yes, he owns a property in Prescott." She typed the address into a map. "Looks like it's down off of Senator Highway south of Prescott."

"Gotcha, you son of a bitch!" I shouted a little too loud. A half dozen people around us looked up. I flushed. "Sorry."

I returned to the task at hand. "So how exactly do we get there?"

"I'll print you out a map. You'll be taking some forest service roads, most of which aren't paved. Not all intersections are well marked, either."

"Thanks. I'm sure between Conor and me, we can figure it out."

My brother walked up. Becca sat up straighter, beaming at him. She'd never admit it, but she'd always had a crush on him, even when we were in high school. She was disappointed when she learned he was gay. Not that it stopped her from embarrassing herself whenever he was around.

"Hi, Jake," she said, gushing like a schoolgirl.

"Hi, Becca. Conor." He gave me a hug and handed me my keys. "Hey, sis. I parked your Gray Ghost on Thirteenth Avenue. Couldn't find a closer parking space."

"I'll manage. Thanks for doing this so quickly."

"You owe me big-time. And I intend to collect."

"How?" I asked warily.

"Just closed on a house near Northern and Thirty-Ninth. Needs some serious demo work. You're going to help me this coming Saturday."

"Fine. Just tell me the house has AC."

"Power's turned off, but I've got some portable swamp coolers I can bring in."

I sighed. "Fine. Fair's fair." I pulled his keys out of my pocket, hoping again he didn't notice the puke smell in his truck. "Thanks for the quick turnaround."

He gave me a mischievous grin. "See you Saturday. Bring lots of Gatorade."

What have I gotten myself into? I wondered. As he turned to leave, I asked, "You tell Mom and Dad about you know what?"

He sighed. "I'm working up to it. Talk to you later."

I turned to Conor when Jake left. "I don't think your Charger will do so well on the back roads of Prescott National Forest."

"Aye. I've been up there a few times. Lots of tranny rocks."

I raised an eyebrow. "Tranny rocks?"

"Aye, tranny rocks. They're rocks that stick up out of the road, waiting for some dumb bloke in a car. When he drives over the rock, it rips the tranny right out from the undercarriage."

I rolled my eyes. "Tranny as in transmission. Got it."

Conor flushed. "Oh, sorry. Didn't think about the other meaning."

"Let's just go before I decide to rip out your undercarriage." I pushed him toward the door. "Thanks for the info, Becks," I said over my shoulder.

"Hey, wait!" she called. "You need to see this."

"What? We're losing daylight." I returned to her desk. She had some news articles on her screen.

"There are rumors floating around that Christopher Delgado may be laundering money for the Sinaloa cartel. Watch your ass, Jinx."

"Thanks for the warning."

42

onor drove me to where the Gray Ghost was parked on Thirteenth Avenue. My brother was right. On the outside, it looked like a brand-new vehicle. The dented, scraped-up, dull-gray side panels were now gleaming silver, like a newly minted coin. Maybe a little too new. Not nearly as invisible as before. But at least Fiddler's spray-painted epithets were gone.

When we stopped at Conor's, we loaded up on a little extra firepower—his assault rifle, a shotgun, boxes of ammo, my trusty battering ram, plus a few flash bangs for good measure. We had no idea what we were walking into, so I wanted to be prepared.

The drive up Black Canyon Highway to Prescott took a few hours. I started out driving, then at Cortes Junction, we switched places. From there, we took Highway 69 through Prescott Valley and grabbed a quick bite to eat at a Tastee Freez.

My phone rang. It was my lawyer. "What's up, Kirsten?"

"Bad news. The FBI is looking like they want to press charges for your interference in their sting operation at Volkov's warehouse."

"We had every right to be there. We had good intel."

"If it was good intel, we wouldn't be talking, would we?"

I sighed. "Crap. So what do we do?"

"They want you in their office for further questioning tomorrow morning. I gave them my word you'd be there."

"Are they going to arrest us?"

"Possibly. Unless you can think of something to offer them. Intel on Volkov they don't have. Like where he's hiding out. He has been contacting you, right?"

"He's a sick chaser, but I have no idea where he is, nor do I want to."

"Be at their offices tomorrow at nine a.m. Dress professional. That goes for Conor too."

"I'm busy on a case. I'm almost out of time."

"You'll be cooling your heels in federal lockup if you don't show, Jinx."

I sighed. "Fine. We'll be there."

"What's up?" Conor asked. I filled him in. He was almost as overjoyed as I was. Damn feds!

The shadows were getting long and the sun was sitting on the mountains to the west when we pulled onto Gurley Street in Prescott and finally turned left onto South Senator Highway.

I'd always loved this part of Prescott. Older homes, some dating back to when Arizona was still a territory, were crowded on tiny lots under stately oaks and ponderosa pines.

I rolled down the windows and was treated to the cool mountain air scented with juniper and pine. The drone of cicadas brought back memories of childhood camping trips. The effect was hypnotic. I started to wish we could forget about chasing Holly and grab a room in one of the old hotels off Prescott's Courthouse Square.

"So where the hell are we going?" Conor asked as the road went from paved to gravel on the outskirts of town.

"Looks like stay on this road for another couple of miles, then bear sort of left onto Stone Mill Road." I flicked on the light from the visor's vanity mirror to get a better look at the map. "After that, the road winds around for about five miles and then we take another left—no, wait." I rotated the printout, trying to make sense of the twisty road. "No, it's a right onto Davis Homestead Trail. David or Davis, I'm not sure which. Can't read it in this light."

"Let me see that." Conor grabbed the map, and we hit a deep divot in the road. "Damn it!"

"Keep your eyes on the road, will you? Last thing we need to do is blow a tire or run off the side of a mountain."

The farther we went, the harder it became to negotiate. The last glimmers of twilight were fading. Deep ruts and large rocks troubled the road. Conor slowed to a snail's pace, making me all the more tense.

"There, turn there!" I pointed at a gap in the trees off to the left.

"Bloody hell! Is that even a road?"

I wasn't entirely convinced, but there appeared to be a parallel set of wheel ruts with tall weeds growing between them. "I think so," I replied. "Maybe."

We turned, and the road smoothed out for a mile before growing considerably more rocky and uneven. My headache was back, pounding out a primal beat of pain that ran from the top of my skull down my spine. I felt at any minute we'd blow the shocks.

Finally, we came to a clearing. Two trails branched off to our right, a third off to the left. I studied the map and surveyed the dark trails leading off into the night. I pointed at the one on the right that wasn't as sharp a turn.

"I think it's that way." I held up my crossed fingers as we inched our way along. Gullies appeared on either side of the trail.

"Christ, I hope you're right," Conor replied. "It'd be a bloody nightmare to turn around here."

"According to the map, the cabin should be a mile ahead on the left." Tree branches scraped the side of the Gray Ghost, like fingernails on a chalkboard. So much for my new paint job.

The trail grew narrower as it turned sharply uphill. Every bump sent a new shock wave of pain through my skull. I tried not to show how I was feeling, but after a glance in my direction, Conor asked, "You all right, love?"

"I'll survive. Just get us there in one piece."

I caught a glimpse of a light up in the distance on the left. "Hold on. Cut the lights."

Conor turned off the ignition. Darkness rushed in.

"That's gotta be it." I pointed at a cluster of lights, soft amber glowing in the pitch black of the forest. My pulse sped up as I anticipated catching my quarry.

Conor started the engine again and crept forward without the headlights until we reached a makeshift driveway where a large 4x4 pickup truck sat parked. No sign of the rented minivan. "I'm going to turn us around so we can make an easy getaway if we need to."

"Okay."

It took some maneuvering, but Conor managed to get the Gray Ghost turned around the way we came and pulled to the side. The truck lurched to the right, and the passenger-side tires dipped into the gully.

"Conor!" I yelled, holding on to the oh-shit handle above the door as the truck listed sharply.

Conor growled and turned the wheel. One of the wheels whined as it spun freely. "Bollocks!"

He put it in reverse and gave it a little gas. We slipped farther into the gully.

"We're never gonna get out of here, with or without Holly."

"Shut it. I got this." He turned the wheel again and eased on a little acceleration. Finally the truck lurched level again onto the trail.

I breathed a sigh of relief. "Thank God! Much as I wouldn't mind spending a night under the stars with you, this isn't exactly what I had in mind."

"No worries. Let's gear up and grab our girl."

43

When we stepped out of the Gray Ghost, my eyes were drawn to the sky. Stars blazed as if someone had scattered glitter across the black expanse of space. The full moon crested the tops of the trees. "Wow."

"Aye, it's a pretty sight. But we've got a job to do."

We opened up the back of the truck and put on our vests and walkie-talkies. Conor racked the slide on his Glock. I snagged the shotgun loaded with beanbag rounds. My Ruger was on my right hip, my revolver on my ankle, in case things went badly.

"You ready?" Conor whispered.

"Ready as I'll ever be. Let's go rock their world."

In the silver moonlight, I spotted a wooden sign along the gravel walk leading up to the cabin. The name Delgado was carved on it. At least we had the right place. Last thing I wanted to do was burst in on Ma and Pa Kettle and have them both drop dead of a heart attack. It'd look very bad on my report.

The two-story log cabin was sixty feet wide and solidly built. Three steps led up to a wraparound porch. We scouted the perimeter, making note of windows and the back door. Muffled voices drifted from inside, both male.

When we circled back to the front, Conor gestured that he'd cover the back door. A moment later his voice crackled in on the walkie. "Ready when you are."

"Roger that."

I checked the door. It was unlocked. I burst into a room the length of the building, filled with rustic furniture and with a large kitchen on my left. I leveled my shotgun at two men playing cards at a rough-hewn wooden table. One was Richie. The other man was older with similar facial features but a broader jaw and cropped hair—his brother, Christopher, no doubt, the one with ties to the Sinaloa cartel.

"Bail enforcement!" I shouted. "On the ground! On the ground now! Hands above your heads."

"What the hell's this?" Christopher remained sitting even as his brother complied with my commands. "This is a private residence."

Conor charged through the back door, his pistol trained on Christopher. "Bail enforcement. Get on the ground, or I'll put a hole in ya."

Christopher glared at Conor but lay on the floor next to Richie.

"Where's Holly Schwartz?" I demanded.

"We don't know anyone by that name," Christopher said matter-of-factly.

"This one does. He took her from her aunt's house." I kicked Richie hard in the ribs, and he cried out in pain. "You gave me a concussion, asshole."

"I'm sorry," Richie whimpered. "I was just trying to protect Holly."

"Where is she, ya little shite?" Conor asked.

Richie shook his head. "She's not here."

"Where. Is. She?" I pressed my boot into his side, making him wince.

He turned his head and shot daggers at me with his stare. "I'm not telling you. Holly's mother tortured her for years with countless unnecessary medical procedures. I'm not letting you or anyone else hurt her again."

"She murdered her mother, Richie," I said. "She has to answer for that."

"She did what she had to do to survive."

"Then she can plead self-defense. You have to tell me where she is, or you're guilty after the fact."

"We won't tell you shit," Christopher piped in.

Conor kicked Christopher. "Either ya start talking or we'll beat it outta ya."

A gunshot shook the cabin. Conor doubled over, groaning and holding his chest. I whipped around to see where the shot came from. Perched on the rail of the second-floor loft, Holly glared down at us, a deer rifle in hand. I fired a beanbag round at her, which hit her in the gut. She fell back, howling in pain.

Before I could race up the stairs after her, Christopher growled behind me. "Drop the shotgun, or I kill your boyfriend."

I turned. Christopher stood using Conor as a shield, with the Glock to my boyfriend's head. I couldn't get a clean shot. And even if I did, a beanbag round wouldn't prevent Christopher from pulling the trigger.

"You don't want to do this," I said, keeping the shotgun trained on him.

"You came into my home, assaulted me and my brother, and shot his friend. Don't tell me what I want."

"She'll be okay. It was just a beanbag round. Everyone can still walk away. Just put down the pistol."

Above us, Holly continued crying. Richie got to his feet, holding his side, and hobbled up the stairs. "Hang on, kiddo. I'm coming."

"The only way you're getting out of here alive is if you drop that shotgun." Christopher's eyes were cold. He wouldn't hesitate to pull the trigger.

"Not going to happen." I caught Conor's eyes. He was in pain, but there was no blood. His vest had stopped the bullet. "If it makes you feel better, you can point your gun at me, since I'm the one who shot Holly." It was a gamble, but it was the only move I had.

Christopher followed my suggestion, and I stared down

that cavernous .40-caliber barrel. I gave Conor the smallest of nods, and he drove his elbow into Christopher's rib cage. Pain exploded in my lower chest an instant before I heard the gunshot.

I dropped to one knee, struggling to bring in air. Pain engulfed my body, and it felt as though a rib was broken. I steeled myself and rose to my feet. Conor now had Christopher back on the ground, hands cuffed behind his back.

I tossed the shotgun on the kitchen table, drew my Ruger, and aimed it up at the loft. The top of Richie's head peeked above the loft floor with his eye to the scope of the deer rifle, now aimed at me. Distracted by the searing pain in my chest and struggling to breathe, I found my aim wobbling uncontrollably. I had no shot.

"Drop your weapons, both of you." Richie's voice was shaky, but that didn't mean he wouldn't pull the trigger, especially to defend his brother. I recalled the rifle club awards in his house. "Or I put a bullet through her head."

"Take it easy, man," I said, gritting my teeth against the pain. "We're not here to hurt anyone."

"Drop your guns."

I was tempted to shoot, but with so little of him exposed, the odds of me hitting my target were slim. If I missed, he wouldn't. Our best chance of getting out alive, much less with Holly in custody, was to de-escalate the situation. I laid my pistol on the table and raised my hands. Conor did the same.

"Happy now?" I asked.

"Uncuff my brother."

Conor huffed but obeyed. The elder Delgado brother got to his feet and snapped the cuffs on Conor. He then grabbed Conor's Glock as well as my Ruger. This night was so not going as planned.

"You busted into my home." Christopher pressed a pistol against my temple. "You shot Holly."

"With a beanbag round," I reiterated.

"You white trash bounty hunters are going to pay."

"Oy! We did what ya asked, lads," Conor said. "Let us go, and we'll be on our way."

"You think we're stupid?" Christopher asked. "You won't stop till you drag this poor girl back to jail, and us along with her. Time we ended this here and now."

If my chest hadn't been hurting so much, I could've disarmed Christopher and taken him out along with Richie. But every breath was a new experience in pain. I didn't have the speed or the strength required.

"Chris, don't." Richie and Holly gingerly descended the stairs. He looked a lot less threatening without the rifle. "Not in front of Holly."

"Fine, we take them outside and shoot them."

"Don't do this, guys. We can help Holly straighten things out. Get her bail reset." I locked gazes with Holly. "You want your aunt to lose her house? She paid your bail. Took you in. Paid for your lawyer. Is that how you repay her?"

"I'm not going back," she said, tears streaming down her face. "That lawyer was a joke, wanted me to pretend like I'm crazy. My mother was the crazy one! Not me. I did what I had to."

She wiped her face and pulled closer to Richie. "Richie and Chris are the only ones who care about me."

"Ya can't run away from it, lass," Conor said. "Sooner or later, someone'll track ya down. And now ya've got your mates involved too. Come along now, and we won't charge them."

"What do we do, Richie?" Holly begged. "I can't go to jail."

Richie took the Ruger from his brother. "Chris, you and Holly put our gear in the truck. I'll take our guests outside."

My heart thundered as I searched for a way out of the situation.

44

onor and I shuffled ahead of Richie out the front door into the yellow glow of the porch light. I bent down, reaching for the revolver in my ankle holster, and instantly felt Richie's foot kicking me in the same place I'd been shot. Stars exploded in my vision as I tumbled down the steps, rolling down the hill until I collided with a tree. I struggled to breathe, despite dizziness and chest-crushing pain.

"Jinxie, you okay, love?" Conor sounded as though he was next to me.

I reached out but felt only the bark of the pine tree I'd collided with. "Oh … okay." I dug deep and pulled myself shakily to my feet.

"Just don't know when to quit, do you?" Richie stood five feet away in the darkness.

"Yeah, I'm funny that way."

"Not so funny when you're dead." Richie pulled the cuffs out of the pouch on my tactical belt and snapped them around my wrists.

"Richie, ya don't have to do this, lad. You're a nurse. Ya have a duty to protect life, not take it."

"Shut up. Where are your keys?"

"My front pocket," Conor said.

Richie fished into Conor's jeans, pulled out the keys, and pitched them into the inky night.

"Bloody wanker."

"You rather I shot you?"

Is he going to let us live? I couldn't figure out his play. "Now what?"

"Keep walking down the hill."

Conor and I trudged down the hillside, past the road, trying not to trip over a root and pitch headlong into darkness. As the ground leveled out, I heard the gurgle of a stream. Moonlight flickered off the moving water.

"Sit down, back-to-back, against this tree," Richie said.

I could barely make out a foot-wide tree near the edge of the stream. I knelt down next to it, lost my balance on the uneven ground, and slammed my back into the trunk. "Fuck!"

By the time the pain and shock of the impact subsided, Richie had recuffed Conor and me to each other on opposite sides of the tree trunk. Richie stood silhouetted against the dim light of the cabin up the hill. He raised the Ruger. I glared at him, refusing to look away.

But instead of shooting us, he fired two shots straight up into the air, then tossed the pistol at my feet. Without a word, he disappeared up the hill.

"You okay, love?" Conor asked.

I groaned, wishing I had some of those pain pills from the ER. "I've had better days."

"Are ya hurt?" He sounded concerned.

"Cracked rib, I think. You?"

"Nothing that won't heal. Maybe we should call Richie back. He can do his nursing thing for your rib," Conor said with a chuckle.

I started to laugh and felt a sharp jab of pain. "Ow! Fuck! Don't make me laugh."

"Sorry, love."

"How the hell'd this happen? We're professionals."

Conor sighed. "We were outnumbered. It's why I prefer working in a team of three or more."

"I underestimated them. Again." I reached into my back pocket for the handcuff key I kept there and went to work finding the keyhole in one of the pairs of cuffs. It was trickier doing it one-handed with the tree in the way.

By the time the first pair of handcuffs ratcheted open, I heard the roar of a truck pulling away.

"At least they're gone," Conor said as I twisted around to release the other pair of cuffs.

"Yeah, but so is our bounty." Using the tree as support, I pulled myself to my feet. "I'm really tired of them getting the best of us."

"It's a pisser, no doubt. But we're alive to fight another day." He picked up my Ruger and handed it to me. I slipped it into my holster.

As we climbed the hill, he turned on the flashlight app on his phone. It cast harsh, dancing shadows among the underbrush along the hillside.

"What're you doing?" I mumbled as I plodded toward the cabin.

"Tryin' to find the keys to your lorry so we can get the hell out of here."

"You'll never find them in the dark."

"I can bloody well try. Maybe if ya helped, it'd go quicker."

I pulled mine out. "I got five percent power left. And no signal. We really are in the ass end of nowhere."

I left Conor searching the bushes and continued up the hill. When I reached the cabin, I tried to open the front door, but the knob didn't turn. "Fuck." I plopped down on the top step of the porch, wrapping my arms around my rib cage, trying not to breathe too deeply despite being winded from the climb.

Twenty minutes later, the step creaked beside me, and I felt Conor's presence.

"Jinxie?"

"Find the keys?" I didn't look up at him.

"'Fraid not. What say we go inside and grab some sleep."

"Door's locked."

"Oy! Bloody bastards." I heard him slam against the door a few times. "Jesus fuckin' Christ."

The clomp of his boots faded around the corner of the building. The muffled crack of shattering wood made me wince. Moments later, the front door creaked open. "Wankers made off with my shooter. But we have a place to sleep, at least. Back door wasn't nearly as solid."

"I hurt too much to sleep. I just want to kill those fucking guys and drag Holly's skinny white ass to jail."

His hand rested on my shoulder. I almost shrugged it off but didn't. "Jinxie, love, I know you're hurting."

"And pissed."

"And pissed. I am too. But we're not getting out of here till morning, and we need rest. Let's gets some ice on that cracked rib of yours. Maybe we can find something to wrap it with too."

"Whatever." He helped me up and led me inside, where I sat at the kitchen table while Conor rifled through the cabinets.

A few minutes later, I gasped as something cold pressed against my side. I took hold of the ice pack he offered. "Thanks."

"Found some ibuprofen and a wrap in the loo and a six-pack in the fridge." He deposited a rolled-up ACE bandage, two white pills, and an open beer bottle on the table.

Drops of condensation glistened on the brown glass. It was some microbrew whose name I didn't recognize. I popped the pills in my mouth and took a long pull on the beer to wash them down. It tasted rich and earthy with a hint of citrus. "Thanks, hon. Why do you put up with me?"

"Because you're hot as hell, wicked smart, and can kick ass with the best of them. And when I see ya in your Wonder Woman costume, it's all I can do not to jump your bones." He sat next to me.

"You're too good for me, you know that?" I clasped his hands and soon found myself kissing that sweet Irish face of his.

"Whaddya say we drink all their beer. Then I'll wrap your chest and we can catch some shut-eye."

"Works for me."

Midway through our third beer, Conor's face darkened. "I want to tell you about what happened between Sadie and me."

45

stared at him, not really interested in hearing the ugly details about his previous relationship with Sadie. "Look, you two had a bad breakup. I get it. Ancient history. No big deal."

"That's not it. We didn't have a bad breakup. In fact, we never dated."

"Then what?"

"For starters, my name wasn't always Conor Doyle."

"What was it?"

"Liam Patrick O'Callaghan."

"I don't understand. Why—"

"Because when I was seventeen, I did something stupid."

"We all do stupid shit when we're seventeen."

"Not like this."

I set down my beer and took his hand. "Conor ... er, Liam ... what should I call you?"

"Conor."

"Conor, what happened?"

Waves of anger and grief radiated from him so intensely I braced myself for what he might say or do. His hand was trembling so much I thought he'd drop his beer bottle.

I put my hand on his. "Does this have something to do with when your sister was killed?"

His eyes pricked with tears. His mouth opened, but no sound came out at first. "Yes." It was more of a croak than a word.

"Oh, sweetie, I'm so sorry."

"I was five when my da moved our family from Dublin to a small village in Northern Ireland called Gillygooley. He was a member of the Provisional IRA, using his skills as an electrician to wire bombs."

"Holy shit." My chest tightened. "Why?"

"Most people in the States think the Troubles were about claiming Northern Ireland for the Republic. But that was only a small part of it. Catholics in Northern Ireland faced a lot of brutality and oppression, much like trans people do today in this country. Bad enough the government treated us like second-class citizens, limiting our rights to vote. But loyalist paramilitary organizations like the UVF often attacked Catholics' homes, businesses, and individuals. Several of my childhood friends were murdered."

"Jesus! Couldn't the police do anything to stop the violence?"

"The RUC, which was the police force there, usually turned a blind eye to it. Sometimes they were behind it." He picked at a knot in the wooden table. "That was why the IRA turned to violence themselves. We were fighting for our survival."

"I had no idea."

"I was thirteen when I learned my da worked for the IRA. I wanted to get involved myself, to do my part to protect Catholics. But my father refused. Didn't want me getting hurt or going to prison."

"But you did, anyway."

"Eventually. In 1998, it was looking like the Troubles were coming to an end. The Provisional IRA signed an agreement with the Brits early that year ending discrimination against Catholics in Northern Ireland."

"That's good, right?"

"It was. But that summer, the Orange Order, an organization with loyalist paramilitary ties, staged one of their 'marches' through Catholic neighborhoods," he said with air quotes. "They weren't really marches. More like terrorist attacks on innocent people. The government tried to ban the march, but the Order rallied thousands of loyalist thugs armed with guns and petrol bombs. Three children were burned alive by loyalist bombs."

"Oh God."

"Many members of the Provisional IRA, including my da, broke off to form a new organization, the Real IRA. If the loyalists weren't going to abide by the cease-fire, neither would they. They stole a car, and my da wired it with five hundred pounds of explosives. Another volunteer drove it to Omagh, a town not far from where we lived. It was a Sunday afternoon, and there were a lot of people shopping along Market Street where the bomb car was parked."

His eyes grew distant, lost in the horror of his youth. My heart was breaking. I didn't want to hear more, but I had to know. And at some level, he needed to confess.

"Since I was seventeen, my da allowed me to get involved. My job was to call the media and give them a general location where the bomb was, supposedly to minimize civilian casualties. But somehow I was told the wrong intersection. As a result, the RUC unknowingly herded people toward the bomb car instead of away from it."

I instinctively released his hand and covered my mouth in shock. "Oh my God."

Like a piece of paper set alight, his face disintegrated into a knot of agony. "I showed up at the scene moments later, expecting a glorious victory. Instead, it was a bloody nightmare. Body parts strewn everywhere. The air was filled with screams and sirens. It was no victory. It was an abomination. And it was my fault. I had made this happen."

I didn't know how to respond. This was a man whom I loved, and yet I was repulsed by what he had done.

"As I walked through the carnage, I got a call from my mum telling me to come quick to the hospital. My sister, Bernie, had been in town, shopping for a friend who was ill."

He began bawling. "When I got there ... God almighty ... the floors were slick with blood. They were so overcapacity, people lay dying in hallways. And Bernadette, my sweet, generous big sister, who had a heart big as the moon … they'd tried to save her, but she'd lost too much blood. Her face was so mangled, I barely recognized her."

He buried his head in his arms and sobbed uncontrollably. I laid my head on his shoulders.

Over the next hour, he confessed that a friend of his father's had helped him get papers under the name Conor Doyle and get the money to travel to the States, where he started a new life.

"Sadie knew about this?"

Conor sighed. "I used to work for Aaron Levinson, Sadie's father. She was working as his office manager at the time. I learned he was giving kickbacks to attorneys who hired him to bail out their clients, which is, of course, illegal. When I confronted Aaron about it, he told me they knew about my past."

"How'd he find out?" I asked.

"Some documentary the BBC did on the bombing. Aaron recognized me in one of the photos they showed of potential suspects. He made it clear that if I turned him in over the kickbacks, he'd notify INS and have me deported. I would've been turned over to Scotland Yard to face charges. We made a pact to keep quiet about each other's crimes. I quit working for Aaron. A few days later, Sadie called and asked why I quit. I told her to ask her father. That was the last time I spoke to them."

I found myself wrestling with feelings of betrayal. And yet it was obvious he had suffered for his crimes. I didn't know whether to scream at him or comfort him. "So you and Sadie were never a couple, huh?"

"We shagged a few times. But she's a wee bit posh for my tastes."

"Why are you only telling me now after we've been dating a year? I told you I was trans before we were ever romantic."

"I should have. I'm sorry. I'd like to think I'm not that same person anymore. Liam O'Callaghan died the day I saw my sister's body in the hospital. He was a naïve kid, in the middle of a war he didn't understand."

"I don't know who you are," I confessed. "I thought I did, but this ..."

"I've worked hard to become a good man, the man who loves you." His gaze met mine. Our fingers intertwined.

"I love you too," I whispered, though the words felt empty. My mind struggled to wrap itself around the horrors of Conor's past and the fact that he'd waited until now to tell me. Could I love such a man? If I had grown up as he did, would I have done the same thing? I couldn't count the number of times I'd wanted to plant a bomb in some transphobic politician's office. But to kill innocent civilians? It was all so much to take in.

"Let's go to bed," I suggested when I'd drained the last drops of my beer. I wasn't feeling much pain. The ice in the pack was melted.

"I'll help ya up the stairs."

"That's okay. I can manage on my own."

I hobbled up to the loft, with Conor behind me, where we found a double bed. I stripped off my vest, wincing. The mushroomed .40-caliber slug was still embedded in the layers of Kevlar. I dug it out and pitched it across the room.

When Conor helped me off with my shirt, I found a bull's-eye-like bruise the size of a grapefruit under my left breast—a swirl of dark crimson around a black, fingernail-sized spot of dried blood.

"Oy, that's a nasty bruise," Conor said, kneeling down shirtless in front of me. A similar bruise darkened his upper chest. "How's mine?"

"Ugly. How's it feel?"

"Hurts, but don't think it broke anything. A twenty-two doesn't do near the damage of a forty cal at point-blank range."

"Tell me about it."

He held out the rolled ACE bandage. "Ya want me to wrap your chest?"

I shook my head. "Rather not."

"Suit yourself." He set it on a nearby table. "If ya change your mind, let me know."

"Good thing it was a twenty-two rifle," I mumbled, remembering my shock when he'd been shot. "Most hunting rounds go through Kevlar like butter."

"Aye! Suppose we should count our lucky stars."

"Too tired to count. Just want sleep." I lay on the bed, my head swimming with the beer. Our confrontation with Holly and the Delgados played on a loop in my mind, mixed with horrific scenes from Conor's confession. I tried to will it all to turn out differently. It never did. Somewhere in the early hours, I drifted into a restless sleep.

46

I woke around nine the next morning to the aroma of fresh coffee drifting up from the kitchen. It took me a few minutes to get my bearings. Log cabin. Middle of fucking nowhere. I hated waking up in a strange bed.

My mouth was dry as cotton. My head felt achy and hung-over. My rib cage burned, but breathing seemed easier. Maybe I hadn't broken a rib after all. Still, it was another morning without my hormones. God help whoever got in my way. I was out for blood.

I pulled myself into a seated position. My clothes and gear lay in a pile in the corner of the dimly lit loft. I had only the vaguest memory of taking them off. Too much beer, no doubt. I remembered Conor's confession, and the empty, unsettled feelings returned.

I shuffled down the stairs, wearing only my shirt and underwear, following the savory aromas of breakfast. Conor stood over the stove, cooking.

"Morning, love. How ya feeling?"

"Like I lost a fight to a heavyweight champion." I leaned my head on his shoulder, clinging to the memory of the man I thought I knew.

"Hungry? Managed to scrounge some eggs and bacon. Coffee's by the sink."

"That'd be great. Thanks." I didn't have much of an appetite, but I needed the fuel if we were going to catch Holly. I kissed him on the ear and sat at the table. "Any ideas on getting out of this little prison in paradise?"

"Now that the sun's up, I'm hoping we can locate your keys. If not, we can break the window and hot-wire your lorry."

"It has a chipped key. Makes hot-wiring it a bit difficult."

"Ah, yeah. Not like the good old days, huh? When I was a lad in Ireland ... never mind."

He brought over a plate with a couple of over-easy eggs, their yolks a pale pink. The bacon wasn't as crisp as I liked it, but I didn't complain. The coffee was strong and helped pull me out of my funk.

"After breakfast, I'll climb the hill," I said. "Try to get a phone signal."

He nodded as he lay into his own breakfast. "Sounds like a plan."

Fifteen minutes later, I pulled on my gear and stepped outside. The air was chilly and damp with the scent of evergreens. It felt good. Climbing the hill helped warm me up.

By the time I reached the summit, my heart was hammering in my chest, and I was gasping for breath as if I had just run a sprint. At six thousand feet above sea level, the air was quite a bit thinner than the low desert in Phoenix. My rib cage burned as I tried to avoid breathing too deeply.

I checked my phone. I had one bar of connectivity. The battery was at two percent, enough for one call. I was about to dial Becca when the phone rang. I tried to push it off to voice-mail but hit the answer button by mistake. "Hello?"

"Ms. Ballou, I need an update," a very stern Sadie Levinson said. "We're down to the wire here. Do you have Holly Schwartz in custody?"

"Not exactly. We had her, but she gave us the slip."

"Again? I thought you were better than Fiddler."

"We are. I mean, I am. Unfortunately, she's got two guys

helping her. But we'll bring her in. I swear it." I had no idea where Holly was, but I wasn't going to tell Sadie that.

"You keep saying 'we.' You're working with Conor, aren't you?"

"Yes, I'm working with Conor."

"After I specifically told you not to."

"Look, lady, you want this girl brought in or not?"

"Yes."

"Then let me do my job and leave my personnel choices to me."

"You want to split your bounty with Mr. Doyle, so be it. But unless Ms. Schwartz is in custody by the end of the day, I will no longer require your services. Are we cl—?"

The call ended. My phone was powering down. Out of juice. I hoped Conor hadn't used up all of his phone's battery while looking for the keys last night. I slogged back down the hill, shivering from the chill. If we couldn't find my keys, it would be a long-ass walk back to civilization.

I found Conor sitting on the cabin's front steps, my keys dangling from his index finger.

"Where'd you find them?" I asked.

"They landed in a patch of prickly pear. Managed to fish them out with a twig."

"Thank God! Now for the love of Xena, can we get the hell out of here? We have a fugitive to catch and not a helluva lot of time to do it. Sadie's about to have kittens over us not having Holly in custody."

"She called?"

"Just as I got to the top of the hill. My phone died in the middle of the conversation."

"No worries, love. I think I know where Holly may be headed."

47

"So where are we going?" I asked once I was again behind the wheel of the Gray Ghost, my phone plugged into the charger. The narrow, rutted dirt road was much easier to navigate in the daylight.

"When I was walking around to the back door before we made entry, I caught bits of the Delgados' conversation. They were talking about getting new IDs."

"They mention where from?"

"Picardo." Conor beamed.

Picardo was the top producer of fake IDs in Phoenix. No matter what the state or federal governments did to try to make passports, drivers' licenses, and other identification hack proof, Picardo somehow had a way to duplicate them.

Over the years, Conor had developed an arrangement with Picardo. He'd help us track down our fugitives who used his services, and we wouldn't turn him in to the law. So far it had worked well for everyone involved except our bail jumpers.

When we got back into Prescott and within range of cell towers, my phone rang. Kirsten. Shit! The meeting with the FBI. I sent it to voicemail and looked over at Conor. "We're going to be in big shit, dude."

Conor nodded and placed a call of his own. When he hung up, he said, "Good news. Picardo says a woman and a man matching Holly and Richie's description showed up at his place this morning, asking for two complete sets of IDs. Passports, credit cards, birth certificates, drivers' licenses, and a digital paper trail to boot. New names are David and Olivia García. They're due to pick up the new IDs day after tomorrow."

"Day after tomorrow? That's no good. We need them today, or the bond defaults."

"That's what I told Picardo. He'll see if he can get them in this afternoon."

I stared out at the serene hilly grassland around us, which contrasted with the maelstrom of concerns and emotions battering my psyche. Losing out on this bounty now seemed the least of our worries. Missing this meeting with the feds could mean charges and prison. For a trans woman, that could easily be a death sentence. It could also mean they'd discover Conor's true identity and deport him overseas. While I was still wrestling with my thoughts on his past, I wasn't ready to lose him.

By one o'clock, we were hitting the outskirts of metro Phoenix. Conor's phone rang. He spoke to the caller for a few minutes and hung up.

"Picardo talked to Richie. Told them he bumped them up on the schedule. They'll be at Picardo's at three."

"Think they'll suspect a setup?"

Conor shrugged. "With these people, I don't know what to think. Holly's a clever girl, no doubt. But they're desperate. Ya heard them in the cabin."

I glanced at the clock. "Three o'clock gives us two hours. I could really use a shower and a change of clothes."

"You and me both."

Traffic was light coming down the Black Canyon Freeway, though it slowed when we reached Glendale Avenue. I turned off onto Thomas Road a few exits later. When I pulled up in front of my house, my phone rang. It was Becca.

"You get your fugitive?" she asked.

"Not yet," I replied. "But we're closing in."

"I've been tracking credit cards belonging to your buddy, Christopher Delgado."

"And?"

"He just bought a bunch of tickets."

"What kind of tickets?"

"Multiple plane tickets, train tickets, and bus tickets. Nearly twenty total. All in pairs in the name of David and Olivia García, each leaving from Phoenix but going to different destinations."

"Why different destinations?" I thought about it a second. "He's trying to throw us off the trail."

"That would be my guess. They're harder to catch if you don't know where they're going."

"What are the destinations?"

"Plane flights are headed to Honduras, New York, and Toronto. Train tickets show destinations as Dallas, Philly, and DC. Buses are headed to El Paso, Salt Lake City, and San Ysidro, California."

"Clever, but not clever enough. They're planning to pick up fake IDs at Picardo's at three. Conor and I will be there when they do."

"So my search was a waste of time."

"Not at all. It just confirms my suspicions. I was afraid they'd be on to us. But since they put the tickets in their fake names, it tells me that everything's going according to plan. Our plan, that is, not theirs. I'll be in touch soon."

After a shower, my head felt clearer than it had in days. Conor wrapped an ACE bandage around my chest after the pain worsened. As I watched him stretch the bandage around me, I decided that knowing his past didn't change anything for me. We were two imperfect people with past lives we'd rather forget. Sometimes we treated each other kinda shitty, even taking the other for granted. But I, for one, still wanted him in my life.

"That too tight?"

I took a breath and grimaced as my rib cage pressed against the bandage. "No, that's good. Thanks."

"We good?" He gave me that wounded-puppy-dog look.

I took him in my arms and kissed him. "We're good."

From my place, we headed over to Conor's bunker so he could replace the Glock he'd lost in Prescott. From the mini-arsenal in his walk-in closet, he opted for a Smith & Wesson .44 Magnum. He was always a Dirty Harry fan, and we were both in a Dirty Harry kind of mood. We then hit the road toward Picardo's.

Picardo lived in a nice house in east Phoenix, not far from the Papago Buttes, a cluster of wind-carved sandstone hills. We ran into a wall of traffic on the I-10 between the Deck Park Tunnel and the Loop 202 turnoff thanks to a four-car pileup blocking two lanes. It was three thirty by the time I parked the Gray Ghost a couple of doors down from Picardo's.

I grabbed the sawed-off shotgun, Conor the TEC-9, and we charged down the street, hoping not to draw too much attention from neighbors. I pounded on the door only to find it unlatched.

"That can't be good," I said.

"Picardo?" Conor pushed past me and stepped inside, his TEC-9 raised. I followed, ready for anything.

Picardo, a skinny Latino, lay on the dining room floor. The side of his face was smeared with blood. His bottle-thick glasses were askew.

Conor checked his pulse. "He's alive." Conor shook him. "Hey, Picardo. Wakey, wakey!"

The skinny man groaned and winced, straining his eyes to open. "What? Where am I?"

"You're at your place, mate. What happened?"

We helped Picardo into a chair. "Y'all are late." He glared at us.

"We got delayed," I said. "Major accident on the highway. Where's our fugitive?"

"Gone."

"Shit!" I grabbed a small towel from his kitchen and handed it to him. "How long ago did they leave?"

"I dunno." He pressed the towel to his head and glanced at his watch. "Maybe twenty minutes ago. When I told them their IDs weren't finished, they demanded their money back. They weren't thrilled about my no-refund policy. That was when the chick punched me. I swear, for a little thing, she packs a wallop."

"Any idea where they went from here?" I asked.

"How the hell should I know? You know, not being able to deliver as promised isn't good for business."

"Relax, mate. You got paid fifty percent on a job you didn't even have to deliver on. That's something."

Picardo didn't look pleased. He patted his back pocket. "Shit! Wallet's gone. I had nearly a grand in there. Dammit to hell."

My phone rang. It was Becca. "One of the phones you have me tracking? Just made a call to Tijuana."

"Any idea who in TJ they were calling?" I asked. "Or where they were when they called?"

"No idea who was on the other end. At the time of the call, they were on McDowell and Fifty-Second Street heading east, but then the phone went offline again."

"No worries. I know where they're heading. Thanks for the update, Becks!"

I hung up and grabbed Conor. "We got to get to the bus station."

"Hey, wait a minute!" Picardo grumbled. "What about me?"

"Oh, you want to come too?" Conor asked with a smirk as he and I rushed to the front door.

"I did y'all a solid, and your fugitives beat me up and robbed me. I think some compensation's in order."

"Have to settle up later, mate." Conor slammed the door behind him.

I could still hear Picardo shouting from inside his house as we scrambled into the Gray Ghost.

I had to hand it to the Delgados. Booking multiple tickets going to multiple destinations via multiple forms of transportation was clever. But calling someone down in Tijuana gave them away. One of the bus tickets was for San Ysidro, California, just this side of the border from Tijuana. If we could catch them at the Greyhound station before the bus left, we could grab Holly.

48

The Greyhound station was just the other side of Sky Harbor International Airport, which wasn't far from Picardo's. Unfortunately, when we reached the station, the parking lot was near capacity.

I pulled up to the passenger drop-off area and turned to Conor. "I'm running in. You find a parking space." I removed the Glocks and the shoulder rig as well as my Ruger and the Rossi revolver, as weapons were banned inside the bus station.

Conor didn't look pleased that I was leaving him with the job of finding a parking space, but he didn't argue, either. By the time he pulled away from the curb, I'd stepped inside the glass doors and surveyed the bustling terminal.

People swarmed in all directions, like ants after someone kicked their nest. Many wore sports jerseys I didn't recognize. I wondered if a soccer tournament was in town. I wasn't a fan myself, but the sport was very popular in the Latino community. Just my luck that Holly picked this time to get the hell out of Dodge.

I hustled to where an overhead schedule of departures was displayed near the ticket counter. The bus bound for San Ysidro was due to leave in ten minutes from Gate Four. Great. So where the hell was Gate Four?

As I glanced around looking for signs directing me to the right gate, I spotted a familiar petite figure with bristly dark hair walking down the corridor, dragging two large suitcases. I pushed my way through the press of people, getting angry glances and obscenities muttered in Spanish and English.

When she was in reach, I grabbed her by the back of the collar and drove her hard to the floor. "Gotcha this time. Holly Schwartz, you're under arrest."

She yelled and squirmed under me. "*¡Ayudeme!* Security! Help!"

As I reached for my handcuffs, I realized the voice was deeper and strongly accented. I turned her over. It wasn't Holly. The woman was Latina, probably in her midforties.

"Aw, shit." I was tempted to help her up, but two Phoenix police officers were working their way through the crowd, headed in my direction.

"Sorry," I muttered and took off running toward the gate.

I was just passing Gate Five when I spotted Chris Delgado leaning against the wall, talking on a cellphone. I grabbed him by the front of the collar. "Where is she, asshole?"

His eyes grew wide. "You're alive?"

I leaned into him. "Tell me where Holly is, or you won't be."

He pushed me away and straightened his shirt. "Gone where you can't reach her."

"She's a fugitive, wanted for murder. You realize helping a fugitive is a felony, right?"

"What are you going to do? Arrest me? You're not a cop. You're just a pathetic little bounty hunter."

Over the PA system came the announcement, "Last call for Bus Number 534 for San Ysidro, California, Gate Four."

The sign for Gate Four caught my eye. I was about to rush toward it when a hand gripped my shoulder. "Excuse me, ma'am."

I turned to see one of the uniforms with a stern expression on his face. "Did you assault this woman?"

The other uniform was standing with the woman I had mistaken for Holly. The two of them blocked my access to Gate Four.

Meanwhile, Chris Delgado nonchalantly disappeared into the crowd, giving me a little fuck-you wave and blowing me a kiss. I didn't have time for this. I had a skip to catch.

I pivoted out of the one cop's grip and bolted back toward the terminal's main entrance, ignoring all commands to stop. I bobbed and weaved through the swarm of people, using all of my parkour skills.

I vaulted over benches and leapt through the narrowest gaps between clusters of impatient passengers. Unfortunately, I was getting farther and farther from the gate. I dodged a heavyset man gazing at a map. Bounded over a cluster of toddlers herded by a frazzled-looking woman. Zipped down the railing of a short flight of stairs. Leapt atop a bank of pay phones and grabbed hold of the overhead sign to swing over a dozen or so people. Skidded underneath the zigzag queue lines of passengers waiting at the ticket counter and jumped over it, ricocheted off the back wall, then rolled to my right and into the back personnel area.

Uniformed employees gave me quizzical looks as I raced past offices, pushed through a door, and burst into the bright sunlight. I looked around. To my left were a string of buses side-by-side in various stages of boarding and unboarding. To my immediate right was a large green dumpster. Beyond that stood the fueling bays for the buses.

From the other side of the door came the sounds of shouting and leather soles slapping tile. I heaved the dumpster in front of the door, its wheels squealing in protest, then took off running toward the buses, in hopes of catching the one bound for San Ysidro.

I pushed past people waiting to board while also glancing at the digital destination signs on the front of the buses. Tucson. Los Angeles. Albuquerque. A bus slowly backed away from the building. It had to be the San Ysidro bus. Crap!

Behind me, I heard the cops shouting for me to stop. The dumpster must not have been much of an obstacle after all. I grabbed the side mirror of the nearest bus and swung onto its roof. From there, I vaulted across to the bus next to it and the two next to that one.

The San Ysidro bus was still pulling away from the gate. I poured on speed, sprinting the length of the bus I was on, and leapt with all my might across the twenty-foot gap. For an instant, I was soaring. And then the roof of the San Ysidro bus flew at me with blinding speed.

I landed hard on the roof, my legs smacking the side windows. My chest exploded in pain. I felt myself starting to slide off. I slapped my hands flat on the scorching-hot sheet metal. Somehow I got purchase in a ridge, while my boots pushed off the top edge of a window.

Ignoring the agony of my torso, I dragged my body onto the roof, even as the bus itself maneuvered out of the terminal lot and onto the surface streets.

As the wind speed blowing across my face increased, my eyes began to water. I shimmied to one of the roof hatches that served as both an emergency exit and a vent. Try as I might, I couldn't open it from the outside. I had nothing to use as a pry bar. What the hell was I thinking?

With one hand clinging to the hatch, I pulled out my phone with the other and called Conor.

"Where are ya, love? Ya sound like you're in a wind tunnel."

"On the San Ysidro bus," I said through clenched teeth, doing my best to ignore the pain.

"Ya got her in custody?"

"No, I'm on top of the bus. Pulling onto the I-10 as we speak."

"Did you say you're on top of the bus?"

"Yes. For the moment, anyway."

"Hold on, Jinxie! I'm on my way."

I put away my phone and began pounding on the roof with my free hand. Cars around me were honking. When the I-10 turned west near the Loop 202 interchange, my legs began to swing right toward the edge of the roof. I white-knuckled my two-handed grip on the roof hatch, desperately hoping not to slide off into early rush hour traffic.

When the bus straightened again, I resumed my pounding with my last remaining strength. As we approached the Deck Park Tunnel, I pressed myself flat against the roof of the bus, terrified I'd get swept off by the roof of the tunnel. I heard the whoosh of cross supports breezing past just above my head.

When we reemerged into daylight, the bus moved left into the carpool lane and began picking up speed. The wind became a roar in my ears. I wanted to continue pounding, but it was all I could do to hang on.

After what felt like an eternity, I heard the shrill scream of police sirens. At first I thought it might be just the wind whistling in my ears. But then the bus began to slow, changing lanes to the right until we pulled off onto the shoulder. In the distance I could see the signs for the Verrado Way exit. We were at the far reaches of the west valley, a few miles outside the Loop 303.

My heart thundered in my heaving chest. Sweat dripped down my forehead and burned my eyes. I was in a daze. I struggled to figure out a next move.

"What the hell you think you're doing, lady?" called a voice on the right side of the bus.

I crawled to the edge of the roof and swung down using the side mirror. The driver was an African-American woman with a name tag that read Flo.

"Trying to stop a murderer," I said between gulps of air. "My name is Jinx Ballou. Bail enforcement agent."

She raised an eyebrow. "A murderer? On my bus?"

I nodded. Flashing lights caught my eye. Two Phoenix PD cruisers had parked behind the bus. The unis emerged, weapons drawn. Flo pointed at me.

"Aw, shit."

I was grabbed by an officer a few years older than me with a cheesy Magnum PI mustache. He threw me to the ground and cuffed me. "You're under arrest for trespassing and assault."

"Get off me! I'm a bail enforcement agent! I have a fugitive who skipped bail on a murder charge on that bus." I pointed my head in the direction of the bus. "You really want to let a murderer escape justice?"

Officer Magnum lifted me to my feet and glanced at my Kevlar vest. "Do you have proof to back up your story?"

"If you uncuff me." I twisted around and held out my cuffed hands.

Magnum removed the handcuffs. I showed him my ID as a licensed bail enforcement agent.

"Who's your fugitive?"

"Holly Schwartz. Murdered her mother. She has an accomplice on board too—a guy named Richie Delgado."

Another uniform showed up just as I noticed the Gray Ghost pulling off behind the farthest patrol car.

49

"You know what she looks like?" Magnum asked.

I pulled out my phone and showed her photo. "Her hair's been buzzed short since this photo."

Conor walked up, and I introduced him to the two officers. Once we'd established our bona fides, the driver escorted us on board.

I'd never been on a cross-country bus before, and I was honestly impressed. It was a lot nicer than the rattling hunk of junk that used to take my classmates and me to elementary school.

I crept down the aisle, scanning the faces, but didn't see Holly or Richie. Had they actually boarded, or was this whole thing another ruse by Christopher to throw us off the trail? I was almost to the back of the bus when I noticed a couple of empty seats in the otherwise filled bus. I ducked down and spotted Holly trying to hide under the bench seat.

She darted out, quick as a bunny, slamming into the rear emergency exit. She was still fumbling with the mechanism to open it when I grabbed her.

"No!" she said, twisting and swinging and punching like a maniac. "No, you're not taking me back. No, no, no!"

There wasn't a lot of room to grapple. In the struggle, she kicked the back door open, and an alarm sounded. I wrapped her in a bear hug. She tried to bite me, and I spun her around, pinned her to the floor in the aisle, and cuffed her.

"Stop it, Holly. I don't want to hurt you."

"No, I can't go back to jail. Please don't do this to me."

I nearly lost my grip on Holly when someone grabbed my ponytail and started pulling. I turned and ducked just in time to dodge a blow from Richie. Conor grabbed him and tackled him to the floor, then turned him over to one of the officers.

Richie cried out as the cop dragged him to the front of the bus. "Leave her alone! It's not her fault."

"Get him out of here." I turned my attention back to Holly, who continued to scream and struggle. "Settle down!"

"Please, please don't send me back to jail. I'm just a kid. She was killing me." She bawled and howled like a toddler who'd been told that her beloved kitten was dead.

As mad as I was for all the shit she'd put me through, it got to me. She might have been almost eighteen, but in so many ways she was still a frightened kid, robbed of her childhood by a deranged mother.

"Settle down. I know you don't want to go back to jail. But maybe I can help you if you cooperate."

She stopped struggling. "How?"

"I got a really good lawyer. She's offered to help you. Maybe she'll let you plead self-defense." Hell, the girl had convinced me. Who was to say she couldn't sway a jury?

"I ain't got no money. Spent all I had on the fake IDs we never got."

"That the money that was stashed in your mom's bathroom?" I asked, remembering the money machine.

"How'd you know about that?"

"Call it an educated guess."

"She had about ten thousand. But it's gone now."

"Well, you're in luck. My lawyer's agreed to take your case pro bono." She certainly never did that with mine, unfortunately.

"What's that mean?"

"Means you don't have to pay. But only if you come along quietly back to jail."

She let out a deep breath, like a punctured tire. "All right. What about Richie?"

"I'm afraid Richie's got problems of his own. At the very least, for assaulting me in that hotel room. Possibly for harboring a fugitive."

"He was just trying to help me." She started bawling again.

"Hey! Enough with the waterworks. Nothing I can do. Now you coming along peacefully or not?"

She nodded.

I helped her to her feet while the passengers looked on among whispers of "Who is she?" "What'd she do?" and "She one of them illegals?"

Conor was waiting for me outside along with a cluster of Phoenix PD officers.

"Come on," I told her, nudging her toward the Gray Ghost. "It'll all work out."

I thanked the officers and got Holly buckled into the backseat of the Gray Ghost. I climbed behind the wheel with Conor in the passenger seat next to me and pulled onto the Verrado Way exit to get turned around toward Phoenix. Rush hour traffic was starting to pick up. Fortunately, the majority of vehicles were going the other way.

A few miles before we reached the Loop 101, I heard some honking and a roaring engine behind us. I noticed a familiar Hummer in my rearview mirror, bearing down on us and driving aggressively.

"What the hell?" At first I thought it was a typical aggressive Phoenix driver. Then it clicked. "Shit! It's Fiddler."

Conor whipped around and looked. "How the hell'd he find us?"

"Beats the hell out of me, and I don't intend to ask him." I pressed harder on the accelerator.

"Who's Fiddler?" a very nervous Holly asked.

"The bounty hunter originally assigned to pick you up."

"Him?" she whimpered. "He's a psycho."

"Won't argue with you on that." I spared a glance in the mirror. He was barreling into us from behind, apparently trying to ram us. "Everybody hold on."

I jammed the accelerator to the floor and started weaving through the traffic as best I could without rolling the Ghost. We had a lot of power but not the wide wheelbase that Fiddler's Hummer had. Our best chance was to outrun him. But even with the lighter inbound traffic, there were enough cars to make maneuvering around them tricky.

I got caught behind a slow-moving Caddy. All the other cars were maneuvering around it, making it impossible for me to pass. The Hummer slammed into the Gray Ghost's rear bumper. My seat belt grabbed hard, making me wince in pain.

"Fuck!" I cut off a Corvette trying to pass the Caddy. The Corvette driver flipped me off. I didn't care.

I squeezed through narrow gaps between vehicles until I reached the HOV lane, which was clear for the next mile or so. I slammed on the gas, and the speedometer rose. Ninety. A hundred. One ten. I prayed that no one in the lane to our right pulled in front of us. I continued to floor it. One twenty. One thirty. We were in the redline now, but the Hummer stayed on our tail.

We were rapidly closing in on a cluster of cars driving at a reasonable rate of speed.

"Jinx, you got cars coming up."

"I see them." I didn't slow down, too busy looking for a gap on the right to maneuver around them. But there wasn't one.

"Jinxie …"

"Yeah, yeah." At the last second, I jerked the Gray Ghost onto the shoulder, sending up a cloud of gravel and dust behind us, nearly tipping us. The right wheels slammed down again as we blew past the slower cars. When the HOV lane was clear again, I pulled back onto the road.

"Good God, woman, this isn't NASCAR."

"No, I call it survival. He still behind us?" I studied the

traffic ahead. We were approaching the I-17 interchange and an impenetrable wall of cars.

"Don't see him," Conor said.

I breathed a sigh of relief, mentally patting myself on my back for my fast and furious mad skills.

"No, wait. Shite! The bugger's still on our tail."

I spotted a gap in the cars in the regular lanes and pulled in, then I continued to push my way to the right, hoping he'd lose track of us. In the process of squeezing between cars, I swapped paint with a few of them.

We were in the center lane when the Hummer pulled alongside of us and rolled down the passenger window. I caught the black dot of a gun barrel and a flash just as I was showered in broken glass. I instinctively jerked the wheel right, then slammed on the brakes to avoid colliding with a semi stopped in front of us.

"Everybody okay?" I asked. I took a quick inventory of myself. I was in shock from the blast but wasn't shot. I glanced around us and didn't see the Hummer.

"I'm okay," Conor said. "You're bleeding on the side of your face."

I wiped my face, and my hand came away wet with blood. "It's from the glass. I'll live."

"Holly? You still with us?" I looked in the backseat. Holly was bent over at the waist, not making any sounds. "You okay?"

She didn't move or say anything. Since I had my seat belt on, I couldn't reach her. With the traffic at a standstill and no sign of Fiddler's Hummer, I hopped out and opened the back door. I shook Holly.

She groaned and sat up. "What happened?" Her eyes were dilated.

"Fiddler shot out my window. But he's gone." I searched her for signs of injury but didn't find any.

"She okay?" Conor asked, looking back at her.

"I think she may be in shock."

"We'll deal with it at the jail, love. Traffic's moving again."

A car honked and slipped past me. I closed Holly's door and found myself face-to-face with Fiddler pointing a .38-caliber revolver at me. "Give 'er to me, you goddamn freak."

50

"Oy! Ya bloody wanker!" Conor called from the passenger seat. "You hurt her, I'll fuckin' end ya!"

Fiddler pulled out a compact semiautomatic with his left hand and aimed it at Conor. "Keep talking, smart-ass! I'll put a hole in her head and then yours."

"You really are an asshole, Fiddler," I said, staring past the gaping barrel in my face, my pulse racing. I thought about trying to disarm him, but he was far enough away that he would pull the trigger before I reached him.

"Just want what's rightfully mine. This was my case."

"We apprehended her. She's ours."

His trigger finger tightened.

"Whoa!" I held up my hands. "Fine. You can have her."

"No funny business, Ballou."

I reopened Holly's door. "What's going on?" she asked in a terror-filled voice.

I released her seat belt and grimaced. "Sorry, kiddo, but looks like you're going with Fiddler."

"What? No."

"Don't worry. You'll be okay. He'll take you down to the jail instead of us. He won't hurt you." I hoped. At this point, anything was possible. But if Fiddler wanted to get paid, he'd have to get Holly checked into custody unharmed.

I helped Holly out of the truck and handed her over to

Fiddler. He holstered one of the pistols and grabbed her by the back of the collar.

I glared at him. "You're going to regret this, douchebag."

"Oooh, I'm trembling," he said with a sneer. "You two faggots think you're so clever. But no one beats Fiddler. Where's her paperwork?"

"It's in the console."

"Well, fucking hand it over. And so help me, if you try anything…"

"Just keep your pants on." I leaned inside the front seat. As I did, Conor showed me the gun in his hand. He offered it to me grip first.

"Not worth the risk," I whispered. "Best just to let him have her."

I grabbed the folder and handed it to Fiddler. "Holly, do as he says, and everything'll be fine. I'll call my lawyer and let her know where you are."

He aimed the compact pistol at the Gray Ghost's left front tire and fired off two rounds. Holly screamed and dropped to her knees.

Fiddler kicked her. "Get up, you little cunt."

Holly obeyed, giving me a final glance, as if she were going to her execution. The two of them disappeared into a shifting tableau of cars driven by rage-filled drivers.

"Jesus, Mary, and Joseph, I swear I'm gonna wreck that guy," Conor said as I climbed back into the driver's seat.

"Going to have to get in line behind me."

I started the engine and pulled off onto the shoulder. The front tire hissed as the last of the air escaped.

A half hour later, I had the spare on. It would've been too easy to forget about Holly and let her take her chances with the legal system and the lawyer her aunt hired, but I felt responsible for her. Maybe it was my lack of hormones. I would call Kirsten when I got home to let her know Holly was in custody.

Conor agreed to drive us back to his place, while I used the first aid kit in the glove box to treat the cuts on my face and arm from the broken glass. On the outside I appeared calm, but on the inside, a tempest was brewing. I was counting on that bounty.

What would Sadie say when she learned what happened? Would she believe me or Fiddler? Who would she hire in the future? Maybe it was time to get my PI license and expand my options. But the thought of taking photos of cheating spouses for a living was as appealing as eating a bowl of cat turds.

My father was always telling me to trust the process, but I never understood what he meant by that. Whenever I pressed him, he gave me a lot of abstract nonsense answers. What process? The process by which the rich and powerful screwed the rest of us?

As we pulled onto the Seventh Avenue exit into downtown Phoenix, my phone dinged from a text. I opened it.

Oh, my dearest Jinx,
I have a lovely surprise for you! One I know you will appre-
ciate. More soon.
Warmest regards,
Milo

Chills ran down my spine. "Fuck!"

"What's wrong, love?" Conor shot me a concerned look.

"Fucking Volkov's sending me messages again."

"Jesus Christ! Why doesn't that bloke just bugger off! What'd he say this time?"

"He's got another surprise for me." I noticed my hand was trembling as a chill ran down my spine. Holly! "Drive to the Madison Street Jail!"

"What? Why? You can't get a body receipt if Fiddler's returning her to custody."

"I have a bad feeling."

Conor turned around and drove to the garage next to the

jail. We walked in and showed our identification to Sergeant O'Brien, an old friend who was working the intake desk.

"Evening, Ms. Ballou, Mr. Doyle. How can I help you two this sultry summer evening?" the desk sergeant asked.

"I want to make sure Holly Schwartz was returned to custody. Fiddler ..." I resisted the urge to spit. "Fiddler should have brought her a little while ago."

He crinkled his brow and began typing on his computer keyboard. "I'm sorry. No Holly Schwartz here. And haven't seen Fiddler today."

My heart sank. "Are you sure?" *Why would Fiddler take her to Volkov instead of here? Would Volkov pay him more than the bounty was worth?*

"Sorry, Jinx. Maybe he took her to the detention facility up on Dunlap by mistake." O'Brien clicked a few times with his mouse. "Nope. Not there, either. Honestly, I think that Fiddler fella is starting to slip."

"Bollocks! I knew that bastard was up to no good," Conor said. "Ya shoulda plugged 'im when ya had the chance, love."

"Maybe he stopped for a bite on the way," O'Brien suggested.

"Thanks anyway, O'Brien."

"Y'all have a good night."

As we were crossing over the street to the parking garage, my phone rang. The number wasn't one I recognized. "This is Jinx Ballou. Can I help you?"

"Ah, Ms. Ballou. What a pleasure to hear your voice at last." The caller was male, his voice resonant and slightly accented. Eastern Europe by way of London, perhaps?

"Who the fuck is this?" But I knew the answer before I even asked.

"Someone who has a lovely surprise for you."

My heart leapt into my throat. "What the hell do you want, Volkov?"

51

"I believe you are acquainted with one of my associates. A gentleman who goes by the moniker Fiddler."

"Fiddler works for you?" I could have spit nails. Was this how he tracked me down? None of this was making sense.

"Over the years he's performed a number of tasks. But between you and me, I've been less than impressed with his performance of late. So unreliable. He takes that medical marijuana for his cancer. I think it has made his mind mush."

"Is there a fucking point to this phone call?"

"Why, yes, there is." He chuckled. The sound of it made my skin crawl. "I'd like to offer you a job."

"A job? Doing what? Working as one of your sex slaves? No, thanks!"

"Oh heavens, no! You are far too talented in other areas, though I do think you and I could have so much fun pleasuring each other. Tell me, do you still have your cock? You never did say."

"Fuck you! I'm hanging up now."

"Oh, I wouldn't if I were you." His voice became cold steel.

"What do you want?"

"By busting into my facility some nights ago, you exposed an FBI sting attempting to infiltrate my organization. For this, I am immensely grateful. I'm also impressed with how well you handle yourself. I could use someone with your skill set to handle certain tasks for me."

"What makes you think that I would consider working for a fucking flesh peddler like you?"

"A fair question. In a word, leverage. I understand you apprehended a fugitive by the name of Holly Schwartz earlier today."

"Yeah, what of it?" I grew from being annoyed to genuinely concerned.

"Except Fiddler took her from you. Such a dishonorable thing to do. Was your truck damaged much?"

"Never you mind."

"Since Fiddler works for me and I am very interested in meeting with you, I picked them both up. So now I have her for you to pick up and take to the jail and collect your bounty. Pretty hefty one, so I've heard. What was it? Fifty grand?"

"Yeah." My heart thundered in my chest.

"So here's my generous offer to you. You come to work for me, for which I will compensate you generously. And I turn this poor girl over to you, and you collect the fifty grand. And you're still free to do your bounty hunting so long as it doesn't interfere with any of my operations. It's a win-win."

"Not interested. And if you dare hurt one hair on Holly's head—"

"I'll even throw in a little signing bonus," he continued. "I understand those FBI agents who infiltrated my outfit are causing you some trouble. Something about interfering with a federal investigation or some nonsense."

"What about it?"

"Those charges hinge on the testimony of those two agents, yes?"

"Maybe. Why do you care?"

I heard muffled voices on the other end of the line, followed by two gunshots that nearly shattered my eardrum. "No more charges. "

My jaw dropped. "What the fuck did you do?"

"I made your problem go away. See how generous I can be?"

Bile rose in my throat. I didn't want to believe he'd just executed those agents, but in my gut I knew he had. Still, I was not going to let his violence turn me into one of his goons. "You're a sick fuck, you know that?"

"Oh, my dearest Jinx, can't you see I did you a favor?"

"I will never work for you. I will make it my mission to hunt you down and bury you in a hole where no one will ever find you."

I heard a girl's pleading voice in the background. It was Holly's. "You really do not want to test my temper." His voice turned icy once again. "If you won't work for me, then I must make you reconsider."

"Come and get me, motherfucker. Meaner assholes than you have tried to kill me and failed."

"Oh, I will not kill you. But I will kill everyone you love. Your boyfriend. Your family. And every one of your friends. Also I certainly won't have need to keep this poor girl Holly alive any longer." Holly's screams intensified.

"Wait. Stop!" I begged.

"Yes? I'm listening."

"Can we meet to discuss this further?"

"But of course, my dear." Once again the delightful entrepreneur. "Nothing would give me more pleasure. But just you. Your friend, what's his name, Doyle? I have no interest in him. I just want you, my delicious tranny."

"The word's transgender, you goddamn piece of shit."

"Apologies. I don't care what you call yourself, so long as you are working for me."

Every cell in my body told me to tell him no. But I couldn't. I couldn't put my family or Conor or Becca or even Holly at risk. I had to find a way out of this. And in order to do that, I had to stall for time. "Fine. Where are you?"

"I'll have a driver pick you up from the corner of Central and Thomas. Next to the Indian statue. Thirty minutes"

"I'll be there."

"And Jinxie dear, I want you there alone. If my driver sees your man Doyle anywhere around or attempting to follow, he has orders to shoot you. Is that understood?"

"I understand."

"Excellent. I so look forward to meeting you."

52

hung up, and Conor was giving me looks. "What the bloody hell was that about?"

"Volkov wants me to work for him."

"Fucking mother of Christ, Jinxie, you're not seriously considering working for that gobshite, are ya?"

"Not in a million years."

Relief washed over his face. "Thank the heavens above for that. I thought you'd lost your mind."

"But I am meeting with him."

"You what? Are you daft?"

"He's got Holly. And he just killed those two feds while I was on the phone with him."

"I don't care if he's about to shoot the bloody pope, you're not meeting with him. He'll put a bullet in you too. Or worse. The man's a complete nutter. I'm not letting you walk into that mess."

"If I don't at least meet with him, he'll go after my family and after you. I can't risk that." I sighed as I tried to formulate a strategy, but I had no idea where Volkov's driver would take me. "Maybe I'll get lucky and put him out of everyone's misery."

"Maybe ya hadn't noticed, love, but luck ain't been on our side lately."

"What do you expect me to do, Conor? Walk away? Pretend everything's hunky-dory? What happens when he goes after my family?"

"Why you?"

"Who knows? He's a sick fuck who apparently has a fetish for trans women. He also likes how I fight, supposedly. He thinks he's got me cowed. But he doesn't know the shit I've been through. I won't let him win."

"I can't let you walk into this shitstorm alone."

"His guy's picking me up from the corner of Thomas and Indian School by the code talker statue. If you try to tail him, he has orders to shoot me. But I've got a plan."

"What?"

"Track my phone. At a distance, so there's no way he can spot you. Stay at least a mile behind."

Conor and I stood there, our eyes locked. I understood his need to protect. But I couldn't let this go any further. I would save Holly if I could. I wouldn't give this asshole a chance to hurt my family.

"I don't like this, love. Too many things can go wrong."

"I know."

"But you're gonna do what you're gonna do regardless of what I say."

"Damn straight I am."

"Then I'll follow your plan, because I don't know what else to do. Just stay alive long enough for me to show up."

"So you can come riding up on your white horse and rescue me?" A sad grin curled the corners of my mouth. I patted his chest. "You're cute when you're trying to be noble."

Conor dropped me off at the corner of Thomas and Indian School with five minutes to spare.

I was grateful the sun had gone down, but even at seven o'clock in the evening, the temperature was still in the triple digits and would be until almost midnight. Especially around the center of town. The day's heat clung to the concrete jungle like water to a sponge.

Conor had wanted me to at least wear a ballistic vest, but I chose not to. Odds were Volkov or his driver would force me to remove it, anyway. It also made it tougher to move around as freely as I liked. I needed the flexibility if I was going to survive.

Right at seven, a black Escalade pulled up and stopped at the curb, much to the frustration of the drivers behind it. The back door opened, and a burly meathead of a guy stepped out.

"You Jinx Ballou?" he asked.

"Yeah."

He patted me down, getting a little friskier than I liked around my breasts and between my legs. I guess he couldn't be too careful. Surprisingly, he let me keep my phone and wallet. "Get in."

I did so and found myself wedged between him and another guy. They were all dressed in black suits. All sporting shoulder rigs with large pistols.

As soon as the Escalade was in motion again, the slab of beef on my right slapped a black hood over my head. I protested, but they insisted it was Volkov's orders.

"Dude, we're on the same team."

They didn't answer.

I sat back and tried to follow where we were based on the sensations of movement and the muffled sounds outside. Despite my best efforts, I soon had no idea where we were, much less where we were headed. We could have been in north Phoenix or still downtown, or we could have been in one of the outlying suburbs. I hoped Conor was keeping enough distance so as not to be noticed.

When the truck finally stopped, I expected the hood to be removed. No such luck.

"Get out," Meathead One said.

"Can I at least take this stupid bag off my head? It's embarrassing."

"No."

I started to take it off, anyway. A strong grip crushed my upper arm. Something hard and metallic pressed against my temple.

"Don't," Meathead One said.

I raised my hand in surrender. "Fine. No need to get physical."

I was pulled out of the vehicle and struggled to gain my footing on the concrete slab beneath my feet. From the echoey sounds, I guessed we were in an underground garage.

We stopped walking. A moment later, a ding sounded, followed by the whoosh of an elevator door opening. I was pushed forward, then spun around as the doors closed. Unlike some elevators, there was no audible indication of the floors we were passing. Even if Conor found the building, his chances of finding where I was in the building were slim to none. As were my chances of surviving without agreeing to be Volkov's new play toy.

Another ding, and the doors whooshed open. Meathead One led me out.

We traipsed down a carpeted hallway. One of the meatheads knocked on a very solid-sounding door. It squeaked open, and I was led through a series of turns. Another door opened, and the bag was removed.

The meatheads walked out and closed the door as my eyes adjusted to the brightly lit office.

Volkov sat behind an antique wooden desk with his hands tented as we assessed each other. He looked to be in his sixties, though rather physically fit. He had a certain Hollywood-leading-actor look about him. He was clean shaven and dressed in a coal-gray suit with his tie loosened and the top button of his shirt undone.

An automatic pistol fixed with a silencer lay on one side of the desktop, a stack of folders and a laptop on the other. A familiar metallic scent hung in the air—the smell of blood. Either Volkov had peculiar taste in cologne, or this was where he'd shot special agents Gleeson and Velasco.

Behind him, a wide collection of books, framed photos, and knickknacks occupied a floor-to-ceiling bookshelf. On the opposite side of the room was another door with a sign that read Private.

A floor-to-ceiling window revealed a view of the Central corridor with the red lights atop South Mountain twinkling in the distance. I judged we must be about seven or eight floors up.

"We meet at last, Jinx Ballou," Volkov said, a wicked grin curling the corners of his mouth.

53

"Funny, I thought you'd be taller." My mind was busy formulating a strategy. Assessing potential weapons, defenses, and tactics.

"Did you? And here I thought our first meeting would be more civil."

"Happy to disappoint."

A wry smile split his face. "My sweet, sweet Jinx, we could exchange barbs all evening. But I'd rather get down to business. And then later perhaps we can have some fun." The sudden zeal in his eyes unsettled me.

"Fine, let's talk business."

"You don't seem enthusiastic about my offer. Why?"

"For one, I don't like being threatened. Two, I don't like men who treat women like property. And three, I don't like your ugly face."

"Ah, back to exchanging insults. How droll." He picked up a folder from his desk. "Tell me, are you familiar with the name Liam Patrick O'Callaghan?"

I shrugged. "Should I be?" I wondered how much Volkov knew.

"I didn't think you were." He flipped through papers in the folder. "You see, you're not the only one I checked up on. I researched your Irish-born boyfriend as well. Very interesting history. Tragic, even. I think you'd be surprised."

I folded my arms. "If you brought me down here to annoy me with vague innuendos and boring conversation, maybe I should leave."

He slapped down the folder and picked up the pistol, aiming at me. "And how far do you think you'd get?"

I glared at him but held my tongue.

"I realize you think I'm a monster. But despite what you may have heard, the sex workers I bring into my employ are given a much better life than the abject poverty from whence they came."

"Oh really? So being endlessly raped and abused is better than being poor?"

"They are provided with excellent healthcare, for starters. Better than most laborers in this country of yours. Not to mention decent housing, fine clothing, and other niceties. All in all, it's a good life."

His tone and demeanor might have been convincing if I hadn't already known he was a lying sack of shit. But I played along, vying for my chance to turn the tables and successfully get Holly and myself to safety.

"So what exactly do you need me to do? What's the job?"

"For starters, I want you to help train my existing security personnel in some of those fancy moves you do. What is it? Taekwondo? Jujitsu?"

"Aikido and krav maga, actually. But I'm not an instructor."

"Considering what I'll be paying you, I'm sure you can come up with a training program. I also want you to consult with my director of security on how to better harden our holding locations. Like the one you and your colleague infiltrated. Clearly changes need to be made, and you are the ideal candidate."

I sat there holding his gaze, trying to appear to consider his offer. "Fine. I'm in."

He beamed. "Excellent. That's what I like to hear." He pressed a button on the phone. "Mr. Richardson, please bring in our other two guests."

The office door opened, and the meatheads shoved Holly and Fiddler into the room. Both had their hands bound behind them. The meatheads stood next to the door, their hands folded in front of them, clearly awaiting their boss's next order.

Holly's face was bruised and swollen. Her eyes were wild with fear. Fiddler just looked pissed.

"I assume you know these two people."

"Yeah."

"Then now is where the rubber meets the road." Volkov offered me the pistol grip-first. "If you are truly on the team, I want you to shoot Fiddler here. I know there's no love lost between the two of you. And honestly, he has outserved his usefulness."

Fiddler stepped forward. "Hey, now, I can still—"

"Silence!" Volkov barked.

"If I do as you ask, what happens to Holly?"

"Jinx, please, don't listen to him," Fiddler pleaded. Meathead One belted him in the gut. He doubled over, groaning.

"Holly will be put to work. Don't worry. No sex work. You have my word on that." An indulgent grin creased his face as he leered at her. "I wrote to you a while back. Saw you on the television with your mother. Everybody so inspired by this poor little crippled girl with the voice of an angel. But you were nothing but a fraud, weren't you? A fraud and now a murderer."

Holly just sobbed.

"Leave her alone."

"What? I'm just saying she has skills maybe we can put to use. Maybe she could be your apprentice, Ms. Ballou. Wouldn't that be a helluva thing. Two female assassins, taking out my enemies. Very sexy."

"I don't think so," I muttered. "Holly goes free to live her own life away from you."

"Your other option is to shoot Holly and let Fiddler live. But then if I keep him, I won't have much use for you, now will I?"

I held his gaze as I considered the pieces on the board.

Moves. Countermoves. Risks. Sacrifices. I waited a breath, hoping Conor would come busting through the door with an army of cops. Didn't happen. Not that I was a Prince-Charming-saving-the-day kind of girl. And I was no Cinderella. More leather boots than glass slipper.

I took the offered pistol and immediately confirmed what I suspected. It felt light. I pressed the magazine release, caught the magazine, and slapped it on his desk. I then racked the slide, which locked back, revealing no round in the chamber, either. "What game are you playing, Volkov?"

Volkov burst out laughing. "Clever girl. See that, Richardson? This girl knows her stuff."

Meathead One, aka Richardson, shrugged, apparently unimpressed.

As Volkov launched into some self-indulgent monologue, I spun around and nailed Richardson in the head with the butt of the pistol. As he fell like a domino onto Meathead Two, I snagged the pistol from Richardson's shoulder rig. Meathead Two got off a shot that zinged past my ear. I put a round under his left eye and a second one just above it.

Holly screamed, but it was in the background of my consciousness. I turned toward Volkov, ducking behind the desk. I caught a glimpse of a gun barrel an instant before a shock of white-hot pain erupted in my left arm. I fell back against the wall, raised my pistol, and fired twice but only hit the desk and the laptop.

A section of the bookshelf swung inward then slid back into place.

"What the ...?" I raced around the desk, forcing myself to ignore the pain in my arm. Volkov was gone. Asshole had a secret passage out of his office.

"Look out!" Holly screamed behind me. I turned and caught Richardson raising a gun toward me. I put two in his chest and a third in his forehead.

I looked around the room. Fiddler was on the floor, blood

pouring from a neck wound. His eyes were wide and glassy, his face pale. He wasn't moving or making any sounds. I turned to Holly, who was curled in a ball on the floor, shivering.

"Are you hit?" I searched her but saw no obvious wounds.

"I ... I ..." She dissolved into a sobbing mess.

I hugged her. "It's all right. You're safe."

I heard feet pounding on carpet, getting closer by the second. I was torn between fighting off these goons and going after Volkov. I stood up and opened the wooden door marked Private. It was a bathroom with a lock on it. "Holly, get in there and hide."

She remained on the floor, her arms wrapped around her legs, shaking like a leaf and moaning.

"Holly! Snap the hell out of it. Get in the goddamn bathroom!" She looked up at me. "Why?"

I didn't have time to explain. I picked her up by the arm and practically tossed her inside the bathroom. When she reached for the light switch, I batted her hand away. "Leave it off. Lock the door. Don't open it until I come for you. Got it?"

She stood there shivering. Footsteps and voices were getting louder.

"Do you understand?"

She nodded. I closed the door and rushed across the room. I pushed against the concealed door in the bookshelf. It was stiff, but it gave way. I wedged it open with a book. Better to have the goons chasing after me than looking in the bathroom for Holly.

I entered the dimly lit corridor lined with metal studs holding up the drywall for the rooms on the other side. I had no idea where this passage went. For all I knew, Volkov was waiting to ambush me somewhere around a corner. But I was not going to let him get away.

54

raced down the corridor, looking for exits, but didn't see any as it turned right, then left and came to a dead end. "What the hell?"

Had I missed something? I felt along the walls, looking for a hidden panel or release. Nothing. "Where the hell'd you go?"

The pain in my left arm grew more intense. I jammed the pistol I stole from Richardson in my waistband and looked at my arm. The flesh was torn. Blood dripped down the length of my arm onto the floor. But the wound appeared superficial. I looked around for something to put over the wound, but there was nothing.

My right hand pressed on the wound as my gaze drifted to a spattering of blood on the floor. I noticed an odd seam near my foot. A trapdoor. "Son of a bitch."

I found a hinged handle and pulled it up. A metal ladder disappeared into inky darkness. "In for a penny …" I kneeled down, trying not to put too much weight on my left arm. Not easy to do when descending a ladder.

My foot had reached a concrete slab floor when a bullet ricocheted off the metal rung just above my head. I dropped, rolled, and came up with the gun raised. I couldn't see shit. Another shot rang out and impacted the wall behind me. I fired two rounds in the direction of the muzzle flash and was rewarded with screams of pain.

I duckwalked toward Volkov, my eyes slowly adjusting to the dark. The light from the trapdoor above framed objects in the room. I bumped into a wall with my left shoulder and cursed as lightning bolts of pain shot through me, making me see stars.

"We could have been a hell of a team, Ms. Ballou," Volkov said, his voice gravelly and strained. He was wheezing.

Keeping my gun trained on my adversary, I flipped a light switch on the wall. "Happy to disappoint you."

I'd hit him on the left side of his chest. Probably penetrated his lung. Not his heart. I fixed that problem with two more bullets. He stopped wheezing. No use getting chatty with a piece of shit like him.

The numerous insulated pipes running down one side of the room told me I was in some type of mechanical room. A first aid kit mounted on the wall caught my eye. I popped it open, slapped a large nonstick pad on the wound, wrapped it in gauze, then tied it as best as I could with my teeth and one hand. I turned back to the ladder. I needed to get Holly safely out of the building.

I forced myself back up the ladder, grunting and grinding my teeth every time I had to use my left arm. As I raised my head through the floor above, a man in a Polo shirt and with a high-and-tight haircut trained his gun on me. I ducked just in time to avoid two shots that hit the trapdoor behind me. I drew my gun and blindly fired off a couple of shots. I was rewarded with return fire that nearly took off my hand. I pulled the trigger again and realized my gun was empty.

Grabbing Volkov's gun from his dead hand, I dropped to the floor and raced across the room. I killed the lights, trained my gun at the top of the ladder, and slowly approached the opening, peering up at the floor above. The goon appeared in the opening. I put a round right up his nostril, splattering brains on the ceiling upstairs. He fell with a thud.

I hobbled up the ladder, grabbed his pistol, and raced down the passageway, reemerging into Volkov's office. It was empty.

The bathroom door was ajar and riddled with bullet holes. Holly was gone. "Shit!"

A distant scream caught my attention. I hustled out of the office into a large room filled with a labyrinth of cubicles. On the far side of the room, a door was closing. Holly's screams continued until the door shut completely.

I flew across the room, swung open the door, and found myself in a stairwell. Holly's cries echoed from below. I caught a glimpse of the man hustling Holly down the stairs a few floors below me.

When I raced after them, the man turned and fired a couple of rounds that ricocheted off the concrete walls. I kept along the outer wall as much as possible, but doing so slowed my pace. A sign at a landing revealed I was on the fourth floor. I'd never catch him at this rate. Time for something crazy. Or stupid. Whatever.

I launched myself at the center railing and began a controlled fall, bouncing from one rail across to another, screaming as jolts of pain shot through my left arm. The guy holding Holly came into view. He had a confused look on his face as I vaulted over the rail toward him.

Before he could raise his weapon, I drove the heel of my right hand into his nose and used his body to cushion my landing. The back of his head smacked into the concrete wall with a sickening thud, leaving a smear of blood. I caught Holly as she started to tumble down the stairs. My left arm quivered with pain from the effort.

"You okay?" I asked Holly.

She looked at the dead guy beneath me. "He dead?"

I nodded. "Yeah. Are you hurt?"

"I don't think so." Her voice was small and fragile. She looked again like the girl on the telethons but without the big grin. "You going to send me back to jail?"

"Yeah."

She gazed absently at the man whose life force dripped onto the concrete steps. "Figures. Guess it can't be much worse than what I already been through."

"Hopefully my lawyer can help you get the charges dropped. Now let's see if we can find a way out of here."

We descended the stairs and emerged out a fire door marked with a warning that an alarm would sound if the door opened. It didn't. We found ourselves in a small parking lot. The Gray Ghost was parked in a handicapped parking space about twenty feet away. Conor stepped out.

Tempting as it was to rush Holly to jail and leave the carnage behind for someone else to discover, Conor and I opted to do the right thing and call 911 and then Kirsten.

Within fifteen minutes, the surface parking lot was ablaze with flashing red, white, and blue lights. The Fourth of July had come early, though the real fireworks were thankfully over.

When Kirsten arrived, I gave an initial statement to the first officer on the scene, then again to Detective Hardin when he showed up a little while later. Holly was turned over, and I eventually got a body receipt. Kirsten seemed convinced she could get Holly's bail reset in the morning and return her to her aunt's custody.

At Conor's insistence, I agreed to let the EMTs transport me to the hospital to be treated for my gunshot wound and checked for broken ribs.

To my surprise, Conor managed to overcome his hospital phobia and showed up at my bedside shortly after I was wheeled in. He looked agitated, as if he'd start climbing the walls any second.

"Damn, dude, you look as bad as I feel," I whispered, trying to keep my mind off everything that hurt.

"Well, I figured you'd taken on Milo Volkov all by your lonesome. Least I can do is show up at your hospital room."

The X-rays showed no broken bones, only bruised ribs. The gunshot wound would leave a nasty scar but would otherwise heal okay. By the time Conor and I arrived back at my place, it was after two in the morning.

55

At six the next morning, I called Becca and filled her in on everything—catching Holly, killing Volkov, and Conor's dark confession. She had been my confidante since middle school, so I knew she wouldn't tell anyone else about Conor's history. She was as shocked as I was.

"I don't know what to tell you, Jinx. It's a lot to digest."

"Tell me about it. I love him, but I'm still struggling with what he did. All those people."

"I hear ya. But as long as we've known him, he's been an upstanding guy. And he loves you with all his heart. That's not nothing."

"True, though I never thought I'd be dating a former terrorist wanted by British intelligence."

"It's a tough call. If it were me, I'd keep him. But you have to decide what you can live with."

"Thanks, Becks. I have a lot of thinking to do."

Conor and I didn't talk much after he got up. Just a polite but minimal greeting, swimming in a cesspool of awkwardness. I figured he was giving me time to process, for which I was grateful.

At nine, Conor and I showed up at Assurity Bail Bonds. When we walked in Sadie's office, she didn't look happy to see us. Not even when I held up the body receipt time-stamped for the previous night at 11:50 p.m.

"I suppose you expect to get paid, even after I expressly forbid you from involving this no-good son of a bitch." She didn't so much as glance at Conor.

"Okay, flag on the play!" I leaned over Sadie's desk. "First of all, I would never have been able to apprehend Holly Schwartz had it not been for Conor."

"Oh, is that a fact?"

"Yes, it is. Secondly, I know about his involvement in the Omagh bombing."

Conor stared at his shoes.

"And you're okay with him murdering innocent civilians?"

"Hell no, I'm not okay with it. Just as I'm not okay with your father giving kickbacks to attorneys back when he ran your company."

Sadie fidgeted in her chair but said nothing.

I took a deep breath. "I'm trying to live in the present, let the past be the past, and give everybody a fresh start. And considering he helped me save you half a million dollars, maybe you can too."

Sadie sighed, straightened her blouse, and looked at Conor. "Very well, Ms. Ballou. A fresh start. I'm willing to give it a try."

"Thank you," Conor said quietly.

I held up the body receipt for Holly. "Excellent! Time to pay up. Fifty large. Cash, check, or charge."

Sadie pulled out her checkbook and began filling it out. "I must admit I wasn't sure you'd pull it off—apprehending Schwartz."

"It was touch and go for awhile. Especially when Volkov got involved."

Sadie's pen froze in midstroke. "Milo Volkov? The Russian gangster?"

"Chechen, technically, but he's not a problem. He's dead."

"Do I want to know the details?"

"You really don't." I took the check and slipped it into my pocket. "So what else have you got for us?"

"Us?" Sadie looked at Conor.

"Hey! Fresh start, remember?" I said.

"Very well." She opened a drawer and pulled out a few files. "These three have missed their court dates in the past week."

56

We left Assurity and dropped by the bank to deposit the check. I then did a bank transfer to Conor and to Becca for their cut of the bounty. Shortly afterward, I got a text from Becca thanking me and telling me she'd see me soon. But despite it being the middle of the week, I needed a day of some serious downtime.

Conor and I spent the next few hours at my place, catching up on some badly needed sleep and some serious couple time. After our second round of sex, I got up and made some margaritas, and we sat at my kitchen table.

"You still attracted to her?"

"Who? Sadie?" Conor scoffed. "Don't be daft!"

I couldn't help feeling insecure. It was always the comparison thing. "But she's cisgender, right? All original equipment?"

"Jesus, Mary, and Joseph, cisgender, transgender. It doesn't bloody mean a damn thing to me. I fell in love with you. I don't care what parts you used to have. I've only known you as Jinx. You're all girl as far as I'm concerned. As far as Sadie, she's part of my past. She doesn't hold a candle to ya. Ya got nothing to worry about."

"You think she's sexier than I am?"

"Are ya bloody kidding me? Even if she were, which she's not, it wouldn't make a damn bit of difference. You're my girl, Jinxie. There's no one I love more than you."

"Fair enough."

I spent the rest of the day reading up on the three cases Sadie had assigned me. None of them were the big money that Holly Schwartz was, and they weren't anywhere close to going into default. The charges were for minor offenses like possession and passing bad checks.

When dinnertime approached, Conor suggested getting dressed up to go out someplace to celebrate.

"Where we going?"

"It's a surprise."

"A surprise?" I cocked an eyebrow. "Not really a big fan of surprises."

"You'll like this one, I swear on the bloody Virgin Mary."

"This have anything to do with the reasons why you've been disappearing a lot the past week or so?"

His face opened into a mischievous grin. "Maybe."

"All right, mister, out with it." I started to act as though I was going to tickle him. He hated that. And he was extremely ticklish. I, on the other hand, wasn't, one of the few areas in which I had a distinct advantage over him.

"Oh for fuck's sake, Jinxie. It's just a celebration. Okay?"

"Celebrating what?"

"Catching Holly Schwartz, for one."

"And ...? What aren't you telling me, Conor Doyle?"

"You'll see soon enough, I swear." I considered tickling him some more, but I figured I'd let him enjoy his surprise.

We piled into his car, and I spent the ride trying to guess where we were going, but he refused to confirm or deny any of my guesses. We were headed into the East Valley, and that was all I knew.

My phone rang as we passed the Loop 202 interchange. Caller ID said it was Kirsten.

"Good news," she said. "No charges pertaining to your showdown with Volkov and his men last night."

"That's good to hear."

"Also the FBI has dropped all charges against you from the warehouse incident."

I breathed a sigh of relief. "Glad to hear it. Federal prison would really interfere with my lifestyle. How's Holly?"

"She's had her bail reset, and her aunt has agreed to let her stay with her biological father."

"George Peavey."

"How'd you know?"

"Let's just say he's a fan."

"I see. Well, I'll send you my invoice."

"Great." More of my bounty money gone. "Hey, what about the Delgados?"

"They're facing charges of kidnapping, obstruction, and aggravated assault unless you choose to drop the charges."

I thought about it. "What if we agreed to drop the charges in exchange for them paying for my legal and medical expenses associated with this case? Is that possible?"

"I'll talk to their attorney and get back with you."

I hung up and noticed Conor exiting onto Broadway Road. "We're going to my parents'? Are they in on this?"

He whistled along with the radio.

When we reached my parents' street, I noticed a string of cars parked along the road. Conor pulled into my folks' driveway and led me up to the house.

My father opened the door and gave me a big hug. "So happy to see you, honey."

"What's going on, Dad?"

He gave me his cheesiest of grins. "You'll see."

The two of them led me outside into the backyard, where a crowd of friends and family from all areas of my life greeted me with cheers. Jake and Rodeo were there getting awfully chummy. Becca, who looked great in a flowing blue dress, waved from across the yard. Members of my cosplay group and the Phoenix Gender Alliance mingled with neighbors and family friends. Somewhere in the crowd, I could hear Juanita's raucous laugh as she "terrorized the straights." This collision of different aspects of my life felt surreal.

Conor and Jake had installed a misting system overhead to keep things cool. Tables stretched across the yard, decorated with pink tablecloths and covered with a spread of dishes that smelled spicy and wonderful. Finally my mother appeared from the kitchen, holding a large rectangular cake.

I kissed her on the cheek before examining the cake. Drawn in icing was a stick-figure girl in a pink dress and the words "It's a Girl!" I blushed and had the strong urge to disappear.

I looked at my mother. "Mom, what is this?"

"The anniversary of you getting your surgery. My baby girl was reborn eleven years ago today."

"Oh my God! I am so embarrassed. Now everyone knows."

"Oh, baby girl," my father said, "don't blame your mother. This was my idea."

"Dad! Why?"

"Because after what that reporter did, everyone knows, anyway. You needed to know that none of your friends care. We all love you and are here to celebrate you and your journey."

I turned to Conor. "And this is why you kept disappearing?"

"I was helping to arrange things. Ordering the cake and such." He leaned in close. "I wanted them to decorate it with a picture of a big furry—"

"Stop! Don't even say that."

"Fortunately, your father vetoed that idea."

"Thank the gods for that." I looked around the crowd and got some waves from my friends around the yard. "You had to invite everybody?"

"Here ya go, sis. Maybe this will help." Jake handed me a Corona with a squeezed lime already in the bottle. It tasted good.

"Thanks." I noticed his arm was around Rodeo's shoulders. "I see the two of you have met."

Rodeo blushed. "I wasn't even sure I should come since things got awkward."

"It's good to see ya, mate." Conor raised a glass of whiskey.

I gave Rodeo a hug. "I'm glad you came. I missed you."

"Missed you too. Did you hear about Fiddler?"

I grimaced. "Yeah, unfortunate."

"The offer still open to rejoin your team?"

"What's wrong?" Conor chuckled. "Trouble with Big Bobby?"

"Bennies were great, but Big Bobby and Sara Jean have become insufferable now that you're gone."

"Then Conor and I'd love to have you," I said.

"Thanks!" Rodeo raised his beer bottle. "And happy vagina-versary, by the way!"

"Ugh!" I recoiled and punched him in the shoulder. "You're so gross."

"My bad," Jake said. "I bet him ten bucks he wouldn't say that to you."

"Geez! Men! Can't live with him, but you bet your ass I can shoot 'em when the situation calls for it."

"Hey, serves you right for returning my truck stinking of puke!"

Someone in the crowd started shouting, "Speech! Speech!" Everyone joined in the chorus until they formed a mob around me.

There were a lot of things worse than being loved and accepted just as I was. Still, I felt naked. My gender stuff had always been a private thing. And now I was as out as a trans girl could be. But I decided to embrace it. Happy vagina- versary to me!

Books by Dharma Kelleher

Jinx Ballou Bounty Hunter Series

Chaser
Extreme Prejudice
A Broken Woman

Shea Stevens Outlaw Biker Series

Iron Goddess
Snitch
Blood Sisters

Download a free ebook short story
by joining the Dharma Kelleher Readers Club
at https://dharmakelleher.com

About the Author

As one of the few openly transgender authors in crime fiction, Dharma Kelleher writes gritty thrillers with a feminist kick.

She is the author of the groundbreaking Jinx Ballou bounty hunter series and the Shea Stevens outlaw biker series. Her work has also appeared in anthologies and on Shotgun Honey.

She is a member of Sisters in Crime, the International Thriller Writers, and the Alliance of Independent Authors.

When she's not writing, she can often be found riding her motorcycle in Arizona where she lives with her wife and three feline overlords.

dharmakelleher.com

Acknowledgments

I have so many people I want to thank for helping me bring Chaser to fruition.

First and foremost, I want to thank my fellow members of the FF7 critique group: Denise Ganley, Tina Wahl, David Waid, Rissa Watkins, and Carl Wilson. You each bring a unique and brilliant perspective to help me polish the turd that is my rough draft.

Thanks also to my editors—Angie, Susie, and Lynn—at Red Adept Editing. You really helped this story shine.

The Alliance of Independent Authors also deserves so much credit, especially Orna Ross and Joanna Penn. I've been listening to Joanna Penn's The Creative Penn podcast for a couple of years now and she finally convinced me to go indie. And with the Alliance's immense resources of information, I have done just that.

The Desert Sleuths chapter of Sisters in Crime has also been instrumental in helping me bring this story to light. Special thanks to the ever-inspiring Isabella Maldonado, a badass in blue and a brilliant storyteller in her own right.

I want to thank real life bounty hunters Reata Holt, Bounty Hunter D, and Patty Mayo for sharing your knowledge and expertise of the bounty hunter business. If I were twenty years younger, I would love to do what you do. Y'all are so badass and do such an important and often overlooked job in our justice system.

My musical muse for this book was the wonderfully talented Gin Wigmore. When I heard her song "Black Sheep" on that Nissan commercial, I was hooked. Then I discovered her other music and found a kindred spirit. Badass women rule! Keep up the amazing work, Gin!

And where would I be without all of my devoted fans. Your support of my work and of the transgender community turns this badass biker chick into a puddle of grateful goo. Okay, that's a weird metaphor, but you get the idea. I am so grateful to you all.

Last, but certainly first in my life, is my wife, Eileen. I couldn't do any of this without your support, love. You truly taught me the meaning of love. You encourage me to take chances. I am so grateful to have spent twenty amazing years with you and look forward to so many more. Every day with you is a precious gift.